Ruth McEnery Stuart

Carlotta's Intended

Ruth McEnery Stuart

Carlotta's Intended

ISBN/EAN: 9783337023560

Printed in Europe, USA, Canada, Australia, Japan

Cover: Foto ©Andreas Hilbeck / pixelio.de

More available books at **www.hansebooks.com**

"'SHAKE HAN'S WITH ME, WON'T YOU?'"

CARLOTTA'S INTENDED

AND OTHER TALES

BY

RUTH McENERY STUART

AUTHOR OF
"A GOLDEN WEDDING, AND OTHER TALES" ETC.

ILLUSTRATED

NEW YORK

HARPER & BROTHERS PUBLISHERS

TO

MY DEAR SISTER

AND BEST-LOVED FRIEND

SARAH STIRLING McENERY

CONTENTS

ILLUSTRATIONS

CARLOTTA'S INTENDED

CARLOTTA'S INTENDED

I

A SHORT, swarthy, gray‑haired old man who swung his little legs on both sides of the barrel upon which he sat, who smoked a stumpy old pipe, whose one heavy eyebrow ran clear across his forehead, who wore tiny gold ear‑rings and seldom cut his hair, who spoke in monosyllables—such was Carlo Di Carlo, " the dago."

A tall, fat, blooming brown creature, loud‑talking and voluble, full of fun and temper, luxuriant to coarseness, whose bust‑measure and age were both somewhere in the early forties, who seemed fashioned for laughter and unlimited maternity, who sat every evening on the front door‑step of the shop opposite her husband—this was the signora Di Carlo.

A dainty 'bit of a girl, radiant as *petite*, dark as her father, symmetrical as her mother of twenty years ago, whose lithe figure was just throwing out hints of future perfections, whose long black hair was straight as an Indian's, but fine as the down upon the head of the babe who lay crowing upon the mother's lap, who was reticent like her father, but whose mother's fire flashed from her eye on occasion, a girl to love, to hate, to do and dare—behold the sweet daughter, Carlotta Di Carlo! The discerning eye beheld in her promise of romance, possibilities of tragedy, and he who looked upon her once paused to look again.

A row of little black-eyed dagoes of various ages and sexes, of various degrees of beauty, but all handsome, a healthy, picturesque, noisy lot, quarrelsome without pugnacity—these were the little Di Carlos.

A small square front room, with a low shed around its two sides over the *banquette*, an oyster-counter along its partition - wall, a fruit - stand spread beneath its sheds opening on two streets, a red lantern hung out at the corner for a sign— see the mercantile house of Di Carlo.

Within a front corner of the shop in winter, and out on the *banquette* in summer, his chair placed so as to command a view of the fruit-shelves on both sides, sat a one-legged cobbler, surrounded by his professional litter of old shoes, strings, and scraps of leather.

Fourteen years ago Patrick Rooney took this chair, engaging to pay for the rent and privileges of the same by doing the family cobbling—a fair enough arrangement with a circle of three when Carlotta was wearing her first shoes, but, to quote from Pat, "There's been niver a time since but the madam's been aither afther raisin' the rint on me or threatenin' to do that same, an' sure I'd

"SEE THE MERCANTILE HOUSE OF DI CARLO"

've deserrted long since if she'd iver sint me a no-
tification be an ugly messenger; but whin she
sheeps out, 'erself bloominer 'n iver, wud anither
wan o' thim black-eyed beauties forninst her buz-
zom, I do put by a fresh batch o' little scraps for
patches an' trate mesilf to a dozen on the half-
shell, on the strength o' the new-customer to the
thrade."

The Di Carlos doubtless knew a good bargain
when they had it, and so Pat had been encour-
aged to remain by perquisites in the way of oysters and fruit.

This, however, was a scant offset to an increase
from one to nine healthy shoe-wearing boys and
girls.

If Pat had begun to think seriously of the matter
some years ago, the christening of a new-comer—
when Pat had hobbled all the way up the aisle at St.
Alphonse's one morning and recorded a sponsor's
vows for a diminutive little beauty by the name
of Patrick Rooney Di Carlo—held him firm to his
chair for some time, and then—well, the signora
counted on this, and became reckless, and there
were twins, and in a year another. There's no
telling what discontent might have begun to fer-
ment in Pat's breast had it not been that Carlotta
began to grow so startlingly beautiful, and young
men and old men and boys began hanging about
the shop when there was nothing to buy, or buy-
ing things they evidently did not want, and all
the time looking at Carlotta.

Pat had petted the child, called her his "swate-heart," trotted her on his one knee and sung her to sleep to "Lanigan's Ball," from the time he came to the Di Carlo shop.

Only within the last year, however, since the halo of radiant womanhood had been hovering about her, had a tender solicitude for the girl entered his heart; and, although the signora, fortunately, did not suspect it, no added duty would have driven him from his post now.

And yet the Di Carlos had not been entirely unreasonable. Later concessions had been made. A room, the entire garret over the shop, had been placed at Pat's disposal, and here he had finally moved his few belongings—a cot, a chair or two, a huge green box which held his surplus clothing in a fraction of its space (such a wooden bin as the poor Irish emigrant usually dignifies by the name of trunk, and which one need not be English to call a box), a gaudy picture of the Virgin Mother with her heart aflame, a much-framed photograph of Carlotta in her first-communion dress, a rosary and a crucifix, and—hanging across the rafters—the moth-eaten remains of a bright uniform and a broken torch-lamp. For before his accident Pat had been an Irishman, a Fenian, an American ward-politician, and a festive leader in torch-light processions, pat-riot-ism, and the like.

Nobody ever knew just how or by whom the shot was fired that made him a cripple and a cobbler (and, he always added, "a Dutchman and a dago, *to boot*," laughing alone at his final pun). But it was a fearful row. Three men were shot, and all came near dying but didn't die, and, as all the wounded carried weapons more or less spent, they considered discretion the better part of valor, and instigated no investigations.

All this was before the days of telephones and hospital ambulances, and Pat was carried into the shop of a German shoemaker, next door to the saloon where the shooting was done. He would probably have been sent to the Charity Hospital next day, however, excepting that his host, Hans Schmidt, had happened to be in the saloon at the time of the disturbance, and, his recollection of the matter being somewhat hazy, he had feared possible implications, and insisted on nursing the wounded man through his trouble.

The neatness of this arrangement lay in the fact that as soon as the convalescent was able to hold up his head, here was a trade for him, right under his eyes and hands. The ward-politician became an artisan, and, as he characteristically expressed it, "his first tool was his *last*."

" An' ye niver seen an Irishman a-mindin' shoes afore ?" he was wont to say on occasion. "Mebbe not ; an' yet divil a wan ud turrn 'is back ou a *cobbler !* 'Tis thrue enough, in the ould counthry, 'tis the prastes that do be savin' our sowls for us, an' I'm worrkin' at the same thrade, savin' *soles* to feed me *body*. But the edge of the joke is, 'twas losin' me fut that set me to shoemakin'."

Thus by light and witty speech did he cover what he firmly believed to be a broken spirit.

A tedious convalescence, with enforced abstemiousness, had given him ample time for reflection, and by the time he had been nourished back to strength on apple-pie, cinnamon cake, *nudels,* and *smierkäse,* and found himself practically apprenticed to a shoemaker, he felt that he was no longer, even at heart, "one of the boys."

As soon as his period of invalidism was safely over, however, when his cautious and worthy host was assured that his life was no longer in jeopardy, things were rearranged on a business basis, and the terms were not satisfactory to the 'prentice, who, with a true Celtic alacrity, had mastered the trade to a degree that surprised himself.

Before the occupation of the corner shop by the Di Carlos, a cobbler had carried on a business here, by which he and a small barefoot family had managed to live ; and when Pat discovered the change of tenants, the bright idea of slipping into this trade had occurred to him : hence the proposition, conveyed by an interpreter, to occupy a cobbler's chair in the new fruit-shop.

The arrangement had much to recommend it. On wash-days, when the father and the boys were out peddling over-ripe stock, Pat often represented the entire business, calling " Shop !" on occasion, or even effecting a trade when there were no complications.

"Picayune o' lemons, is it ?" he would say, for

instance, to the small-boy customer. "Fetch yer silver heer, till I feel the heft av ut. That's solid—rings like the bells o' heaven! Drop it beyant on the counter—so. Now, pick two big lemons or three little wans. That's a man; takes three middlin' sizes. He's got a business fist on 'im—'ll be a Vanderbilt yet—nades a shoe-string for *lagniappe*." And to himself, as the embryonic Vanderbilt departed, he would continue after this fashion :

" Faith, an' be the time I do worrk up me Dutch, thrade wud a dago's business, an' throw in a Creole *lagniappe*, I do have to run me hand forninst me flabby pockut-book to know mesilf for a Paddy." And his soliloquy held as much truth as humor ; for, notwithstanding the fact that he soon commanded a neat little custom, Pat's heart and hand were those of a true son of the Emerald Isle.

From the day she first put up her pretty red lips for the shaggy old fellow to kiss, his whole heart and purse had belonged to the baby Carlotta. As his mind had begun to run on shoe-leather, his first spare dollar had gone for a pair of little red shoes for her when she was barely able to toddle.

This was the beginning ; and then there were other things—trinkets, a pair of gold ear-rings set with turquoises (and he had locked himself in the coal-house and stopped his ears while they were put into her little ears), and then, later, a thimble, then a prayer-book and mother-of-pearl rosary ; and so it went.

As he petted the little thing and the other

babies as they came, he accused himself of an old man's fondness ; though when this story begins he was in fact but forty years old.

"Little Lottie" came to stand in his life in place of all he had lost, and he took comfort in her, calling himself "an ould grandmother" while he buttoned her tiny gowns or washed her pretty little hands and face for her.

"Say, Carlo," said the signora, one day—this was when Carlotta was about six years old—" wad you say eef we geev-a C'lotta to Meester Pad fo' wife wan day, eh ?"

"Indade, me respicted mother-in-law," Pat had replied, laughing, "sure ye're too late shpakin' ! Lottie an' me's engaged six months, come Moddy Graw."

And so it gradually came about that he called the pretty dark-eyed child "me swateheart," "me intinded," "me future," and the like, while she would always leave her father or mother to go to "Woona" (her best baby effort at his name in the early days when he was "Mr. Rooney" in the Di Carlo household).

Within the last year, however, while as unfailingly attentive and gentle, he called her only Lottie, and any allusion to the old jests was wittily turned aside.

In the evenings, after dark, Pat generally formed one of the family circle on the *banquette* about the doors, flavoring the conversation with his invariable humor and mirth.

Usually at about eight o'clock the little father would jump down from his barrel, and, rubbing the leg that had "gone to sleep," hop around limping while he closed in the fruit-shelves, took down the lantern, and prepared to lock up the shop.

At his first movement Pat hobbled in, carrying his chair with him, the signora following, and bending over her sleeping bundle with a maternal "Sh-h-h !" as she passed in.

Finally, just before entering himself, the father called, "Toney ! Pasquale ! Joe ! Anita ! Neek !" and a crowd came rushing noisily in from the congregation of children half-way down the block, one or two of whom generally pursued them to the door for a "last tag" and "good-night," while a voice or two from the foremost Di Carlos answered from within, "Sleep tight."

As they flocked in, passing the little old father standing in the doorway, he looked proudly upon them and grunted his approval. They were a royal lot, and they were his.

The scene reminds one of a familiar barn-yard group—a little game rooster, a fine Brahma hen, and their brood of handsome chicks. The diminutive but pompous father struts around with a most important proprietary air, and, flattering himself, forgets to look at the mother. So it was with little Di Carlo. Men and roosters are so thoughtless.

It was true, Carlotta was a beauty, and every

one said she was the image of her father; and so she was—his image *inspired*. And the mother was the inspiration.

If the little husband reminded one of a rooster, a rooster who never crowed, it was not so much because the wife persisted in doing the family crowing, as well as cackling, as that it pleased him to sit by and smoke while she toyed with his prerogative. One always felt that the crow was in him, and that he had full confidence in the volume of it. Such is the value of reserve.

In deference to Pat, the language of the evening circle was usually English. But though he had never attempted the Italian speech or professed a comprehension of it, fourteen years of such familiarity with it as the shop afforded had opened the doors of his understanding, and nothing less than a subtlety of meaning as far beyond the Di Carlos as himself would have eluded him now.

A sort of delicacy, however, forbade his revealing this to those who sometimes chose to speak in his presence without inviting his participation.

Among the occasional frequenters of the shop had been for some time an old man, Pietro Socola by name, for whom Pat had always felt an instinctive dislike.

During the past few months Socola had become a frequent guest, and while he sat on a box at the father's side in the evenings and spoke in a low tone in Italian, he was observed to cast frequent covert glances towards the daughter, Carlotta.

Now, Socola was rich, according to the Di Carlo standard, and a widower, and so Pat was not super-suspicious in interpreting these glances as ominous of meaning to Carlotta.

The suspicion quickened his hearing, but the most assiduous eavesdropping had as yet disclosed nothing to confirm his fears. Gossip about the men on the luggers or at the Picayune Tier, discussions as to the rise or fall in prices of fruit or oysters, interspersed with long tobacco-flavored silences, seemed to constitute all their social intercourse; and yet—why did the ugly old fellow keep looking at Carlotta?

Socola was of the one essentially homely Italian type. His blue-gray eyes and reddish hair were bereft of any leaning towards beauty by a heavy swarthy skin, while the entire absence of upper front teeth gave a touch of grotesqueness to his ugly visage. Short-necked and square of build, he had nevertheless a stoop, producing an effect as if his face arose from his chest. The edges of his grizzly-red mustache were further colored from the tobacco which he perpetually chewed, and his hairy little hands bore about their blunt finger-tips similar suggestions of the weed.

Socola was plain, as well as distinctly deficient in the subtle charm which we call personal magnetism.

His wife had been dead but three months when

he first came on Sunday afternoon to the Di Carlos'. For three successive Sundays he returned thus, and then he began dropping in in the late evenings, until now almost any night he could be seen propped up on his box at Di Carlo's side, and whether Carlotta sat on the door-step working on her "sampler" or promenaded the *banquette* with one of the twins astride her hip, old Pietro's eyes followed her.

This, which Pat had been observing for some weeks, culminated one day in a tangible occasion for alarm.

He was sitting inside the shop, putting a finishing-stitch to a patch, when he saw Socola pass the door to join the circle about the steps without.

A moment later Carlotta hastily entered the shop, her face black as a storm-cloud.

"Come heer, Lottie," he called, quickly; and, as she approached him, "Whut ails ye?"

He had never seen her so angry. It was a moment before she spoke.

"Shpake out, Lottie, me girrl, an' tell me who done ye onythink."

"I don't like ol' Pietro Socola," she said, finally, her eyes flashing.

"Norr me nayther," he answered, shaking his head. "But tell me whut 'e done ye."

"He mashed my chin."

"Squazed yer chin, did 'e? An' may the divil snatch 'is mother from heaven!"

"Yas, an' try to kiss me. I hate 'im!"

"Thried to kiss ye, did 'e? Bad luck to 'is lonesome mouth! An' who seen um?"

"My paw an' my maw was a-talkin'. I don' know ef my maw seen 'im or not. She laughed. I hate 'im!"

"See heer, Lottie." He was much excited, but spoke low, lest he should be overheard. "There's throuble a-brewin' for ye, me beauty. Don't ye say northin' to nobody, but ef that low-down, dirrty, blue-eyed nagur av a dago lays the heft av 'is finger-tip on ye again, *ye go for um:* d'ye heer?"

She was silent, and he continued: "Wull ye do whut I tell ye, Lottie?"

"Yas."

"Well, take me advice an' kape out av arrm's length av 'im whin ye can; but whin ye can't, an' he so much as blows 'is breath on a hair o' yer head, ye come down on 'im wud a regular thunderin' polthogue—like this!"

He placed his closed fist against his own temple.

"See heer, colleen," he resumed, with some hesitancy, "I c'd lather 'im for ye—a couple o' hefts o' me peg 'd land 'im pantin' in the gutther—but 'twould do ye no good."

"'F 'e turn 'is sassy ol' eyes on me again, I'm goin' slap 'is face good," she said, as she turned to serve a customer.

A suppressed sigh escaped the cobbler, and his fingers moved nervously as he finished his patch.

His worst fears were materializing. Socola,

the rich, the honored guest, was coming for Carlotta.

His cobbling finished for the day, he rose to go to his room. He had not the heart to join the circle about the doors to-night. He hesitated a moment, and glanced without.

The signora had crossed from her seat on the step, and drawn a stool opposite the men—her husband and Socola.

The guest was speaking very earnestly in a low voice in Italian, and his audience listened with evident deference.

Pat heard distinctly Carlotta's name. Who can blame him for lingering, just a moment, to be doubly sure he was not mistaken?

But no, he heard it again, and then something about money — "a thousand dollars" — and the mother and father of the girl smiled, and, while they exchanged glances, nodded assent.

For the first time since he had been a teetotaler Pat staggered as he walked to the staircase, and when he reached his attic room he sank into his chair, trembling as if an ague possessed him.

He was bewildered as much at his own sensations as at that which had produced them. What did it mean? It was bad enough, but why were cold chills running all over him? Why did he think of the night he heard of his mother's death? Why was he sobbing before he could control himself?

Oh, Patrick Rooney, is it possible that you are in love?

It was even so; and the sudden revelation of the truth to himself seemed to seize and shake him to the foundations of his being.

The exquisite agony of the first discovery soon spent itself in emotion, but all night long he sat as one dazed, lost in wonder, bewildered.

II

When at last the day broke, when the explaining sun's rays lifted the veil that the moonlight imposes, and instead of shadows Pat began to see things clearly, he cast his eyes about him, as if to reassure himself and get his bearings. Everything in his meagre apartment seemed to hold some association with the child, Carlotta. Hanging upon the wall were the little worn red shoes, his first gift to her, bearing yet the impress of her baby feet. Within the lid of his big trunk, open before him, swung the tiny brass hook he had placed there so that she might safely fasten herself within, and, hiding here until the storm was over, she had escaped many a whipping from her mother. A row of auger-holes along the back, ruining the trunk, had further fitted it for her safe retreat. And she had never told. She had always been a rare child.

Every picture summoned by the associations was charmingly pretty, and when finally he cast his eyes down upon himself—upon his toil-stained

garments, his rough hands, his one untidy shoe—
he felt as if he were blushing at a sense of his utter
unfitness for her.

Seizing his mirror, a triangular fragment, he
closely scrutinized his unshaven face and unkempt
hair, and as he laid the glass down he turned his
vision inward and backward upon the years of his
life at the Di Carlos' and before. He thought of
Carlotta when first he saw her, and of the years
since. She had sweetened and cheered his life
ever since he had known her.

She and this sacred love that had come to him
were holy things, but what should he do with
them—he, a poor, miserable, penniless, clumsy
old cripple? It was a terrible, terrible folly, this
love; and yet, despite the hopelessness of it, despite the vivid ludicrous view of it which his Irish
perception afforded, he felt transported by it into
a state of painful ecstasy. What should he·do
with himself—where go?

For one thing, he must bathe and shave and cast
off these ugly, dusty garments. The sacred thing
that had come to him required this much of him.

It was late in the morning before his toilet was
complete. His ordinary hurried ablutions "for
dacency's sake" were performed with reference
to the world. To-day his own consciousness demanded that he should be clean. Even his old
wooden leg received its first baptism, the rite being applied with soft soap and a scrubbing-brush.
The hard old oak, polished from long use, shone

like the Di Carlo biscuit-board—and it must be understood that the signora was of the clean sort, unfortunately in the minority among her class.

Pat had just readjusted his peg with new leather straps, when two little black eyes appeared above the stairway.

"Mr. Pat, dey got a colored lady down-stairs what want her shoes mend." It was the boy Pasquale, and he was all the way up now.

"Tell 'er I'm not worrkin' to-day, Pasquale, me b'y. I'm very sick."

"Oh, Mr. Pat, you scared me awful! I thought you was a man up here."

"An' did ye r'a'ly? Sure an' ye made a terrible mishtake, for there's northin' up heer but three-quarrters av an ould divil av a fool."

"Oh, you look awful white, Mr. Pat! You sick fo' true? Mus' I call my maw? Is dey got anybody dead, Mr. Pat?"

Pat's only previous rigorous toilets had been made to attend an occasional funeral of some former comrade.

"Plaze God, there's a fraction of a loafer dead, sonny, an' I'm dthressed for the buryin'. Call nobody, but go now, don't be delayin', and tell the lady below I'm tuck suddintly ill an' I'm not worrkin'."

It was with manifest reluctance that the little fellow at last withdrew his eyes from the gentleman in the attic to deliver his message.

In a moment the signora's voice was heard at the foot of the stairs:

"Oh, Meester Pad! Pasquale say god-a sometheen the matther weeth-a you. 'F you feel-a sig,
mus-a shore call-a some*body*."

"Much obliged, ma'am, but sure I'm takin' a
day off, jist, an' I'm in nade o' northin' but a
broom, if ye'll lind me the loan av one."

Pat was not an artist, and his hands were
clumsy, yet the result of a single effort in the direction of respectability wrought a transformation
in his apartment. After he had swept, dusted,
and rearranged his shabby belongings, he took
from his box a little old-fashioned daguerreotype
of his mother and gazed upon it in silence for
some minutes. When finally he spoke, his voice
was tremulous and tender:

"Indade an' yer b'y's in great throuble, mammy dear. Ye always said I was the biggest fool
o' the dozen, an' sure I want to take back me
sassy conthradiction."

He drew his sleeve clumsily over it, wiping a
tear from the face of the picture, and, hobbling
across the room, placed it open upon the shelf that
served for a mantel.

He did not go down-stairs that day. Though
cleansed and clothed, he was not assured of being in
his right mind. He dreaded to meet Carlotta, lest
she should detect the insanity that possessed him,
and despise him as he despised himself for it. Of
course this nonsense would die out in time, and he
would always be just the same old "Woona" to her
as of yore, and when the time and the right man

should come he would do his best to have her suitably married. It was absurd that right here at the outset he should be having trouble with himself.

For three days he felt constrained to put off "till to-morrow" his going down-stairs. While he could not treat with this exquisite, delicate thing without purifications of himself and surroundings, it was yet only a something to be surely overcome. A few days' banishment and fasting would restore him to himself. The fasting, it is true, he practised only because he *could not eat*, and the banishment on a similar principle, yet he counted on this discipline, with time and resolution, to quell a passion which could bring him only ignominy, and to the girl, should she suspect it, but embarrassment and estrangement from her best friend. But she should never know it.

In a few weeks, at furthest, Socola would press his suit; for was there not every reason to expect haste? He was old (old men are always in a hurry), a widower (who ever knew a widower to dally with a proposal?), and he came from Sicily, from Palermo, that warm clime of impatient love and ardent adorers.

In a few weeks Carlotta might have need of a friend. Socola was rich. The Di Carlos' one weakness, in Pat's eyes, was love of money. The signora had laughed when the old man tried to kiss Carlotta. It was a bad omen. She would favor his suit.

It was on the morning of the fourth day that little Pasquale reappeared at the head of the stairs, bearing this time in his hands a half-worn shoe.

"Back wud ye, now!" exclaimed Pat, anticipating the application. "Sure an' I'm on the retired lisht for a couple o' days. Fetch me no more ordhers."

"Who's a-talkin' 'bout orders?" drawled the pert boy. "Give a fellow time to talk, won't you? My maw sez, she sez C'lotta's feet's on de groun', and somebody haf to sew 'er shoe."

The old shoe, torn and muddy, which the boy laid in Pat's hand, bearing the unmistakable impress of the physical vigor and undiscriminating step of a growing girl, was neither small nor shapely, but Pat's hand trembled visibly as he touched it, and he felt so queer that he was frightened. He seemed to see Carlotta standing in the flesh before him.

"An' my maw sez, she sez if you'll sew it righd away, 'cause C'lotta ain't got no more shoes, an'—"

"All right. Tell 'er she'll have a new shoe built around the patch I'll putt on it, an'—off wud ye, now."

As the boy disappeared, Pat turned the shoe about in his hands slowly, and, perceiving the trembling of his fingers, exclaimed :

"The divil's grandmother! Sure an' I wouldn't know mesilf from a shakin' Quaker or a quakin' Shaker, I'm that rattled! But I'll kiss the fut av 'er, onyhow!" And he laid the old shoe against his lips with a caressing movement.

It needed many stitches, and Pat was still at work upon it an hour later when he heard the signora trudging up the stairs.

"Hello, Meester Pad; 'm-a come talk weeth-a you," she began, while still invisible. "God-a so much-a troub', haf to spik weeth-a you." And as she finally reached the landing she exclaimed, looking about her, "Name o' God! Well, I swea'! Pasquale ces-a tell me you was-a pud on-a plenny style up here." Crossing, she dropped into a seat at Pat's side, putting the baby which she carried upon the floor before her.

"Fo' God sague! Never was-a seel you so fine-a biffo'. B'lief you goin' a ged-a marry, Meester Pad."

"Arrah, thin, I may's well confess; Carlotta an' me's plannin' to shtep over to S'int Alphonse's some fine mornin', an' run across to Algiers for a weddin'-tower an' back again be the Magazine Marrket f'r a bridal breakfasht. Sure an' we're only tarryin' for me mother-in-law's perrmission."

This bravado helped him immensely. He had said the same thing substantially a hundred times before, but not for a long time. Instead of laughing as of yore, however, the signora grew serious.

"Dthaz-a just-a fo' wad I'm-a goin'-a talk weeth-a you, Meester Pad. Of-a coze I know you god-a nobody an-a northeen, you haf to mague a lill-a fun some time, but know sometheen? Young gal ligue-a C'lotta ces-a god-a no senz. C'lotta *b'lief thad.* She thing you ees-a lov' weeth-a her."

“An’ who sez she does?”

“I am-a sho’, *sho’* she b’lief thad.”

“An’ who sez she does?” he repeated, with keen vehemence.

“Nobody, only ’erselve ees-a say it.”

“An’ who did she say ut to? She niver said it, ma’am!”

“My God, you thing me I’m a liar? C’lotta sez to me, sez I don’-a lov-a no man bud-a just-a Woona. Wad you call-a thad?”

“Begorra, an’ I suppose she loves her father betther yet. Who the divil shud she like betther nor me—she that’s afther cutt’n’ ’er eye-teeth on me thumb-nail?”

“Of-a coze; dthaz-a thrue; bud-a you don’ un’erstan’, Meester Pad. God-a so much-a troub’ weeth-a thad chil’.. Now ees-a raise ’er so big, an’ she sassy me to my face. God knows, I weesh me I was-a dead! God-a so much-a troub’. Fo’ two days, can’d do northeen weeth-a C’lotta. God-a fine chanz, C’lotta, an’ she don’ care northeen ’boud.”

“A fine chance, has she? An’ whut is it?” His heart stood still.

“Pietro Socola ees-a wan reech-a man, Meester Pad. *Wan’-a marry weeth-a C’lotta!*”

“The divil’s pitchfork! An’ whut does—whut does she say?”

“Say she *won’-a* marry weeth-a heem. Can’d do northeen weeth-a C’lotta. Her pa ees-a w’ip ’er, me, I ees-a w’ip ’er, an’ the mo’ we ees-a beat ’er the mo’ she ees-a sassy me to my face.”

Pat was speechless with surging emotion, and the mother continued :

"Pietro Socola ces-a prormis me an' Carlo a t'ousan' dollah, an'-a tague 'eem een-a pardners, 'f 'e can-a ged C'lotta. Oh, 'ees-a crazy fo' C'lotta—lov' er so hard."

"An' did 'e shpake love to 'er ?"

"One time 'ees-a try speak weeth-a C'lotta, an' C'lotta ees-a slap 'is face."

"An' whut did he say ?"

"He ees-a just laugh. Lov-a C'lotta so hard 'e don' care. Want 'er all-a same. Theng God fo' thad. Tell you, Meester Pad, plenny troub' een theze-a worl'. Come-a talk weeth you 'boud C'lotta. 'M goin-a call 'er talk weeth-a you. You muz-a please talk-a senz weeth 'er. Tell 'er she haf to marry Socola. C'lotta do anytheen-a fo' you."

Pat was diplomat enough to see the worse than futility of opposition. He let her call Carlotta.

Paler than he had ever seen her, her pallor exaggerating a dark bruise upon her cheek, but with her head erect, she appeared before them.

"Whut ails yer face, Lottie ?" said the man, gently, as, drawing a stool to his side, he motioned to her to be seated.

She remained standing, however, and the mother answered :

"When some*body* slap-a company in-a face, muz-a show 'er how it feel to have-a face slap."

"An' who done ut ?"

"Me myselve done it. Slap 'er face good fo'
her! Muz-a teach-a my chil' some manners. Lill-
a mo' would-a pud C'lotta's eye oud. Hit 'er good
weeth a tin cup. Take plenny pains, yas, teach-a
C'lotta manners an-a raise 'er nice."

The tension of the situation here was happily
relieved by the signor Di Carlo, who called loud-
ly in Italian for his wife to come and light up the
shop. She would have hesitated, but an imperative "*Non posso sestare! Spicciatevi!*" warned
her that her lord was impatient.

She rose hastily, slipping her feet deftly from
under the child who had crept up against her and
fallen asleep, and, bidding Carlotta "min'-a the
baby," hurriedly descended the stairs.

The child, disturbed, began to fret. Seating
herself, Carlotta raised the little one upon her
lap, where in a moment it slept again.

She sat opposite Pat, in the seat her mother
had vacated. Sitting thus, with the beautiful
babe in her arms, in the tender twilight which
was further sensitized by the subtle insinuation
of light from a new moon which hung just without, she looked not unlike the statues in the
churches of the Virgin Mother and Child.

Even Pat saw it, and felt like crossing himself
as he looked upon her.

He had never seen her look like this before.
The habitual spirit of joyous childishness had
passed out of her face, which seemed clothed
with modesty and sadness.

She had not spoken since she entered the garret. She had not even looked at Pat.

Though silent also for a time, he was first to speak :

"Well, mavourneen, me poor child o' sorrow, the throuble's come quicker nor I thought for. Betune the two av us, ye've got a black eye, for yer mother only paid ye for takin' me advice. Forgive me me share o' the blame while I talk to ye plain, Lottie."

Raising his eyes, he muttered to himself, "The Lord o' light give me courage this night !" Then he turned to her :

"An' ye must answer me plain, Lottie. Ye must shpake to-night plainer nor ye iver shpoke since yer firrst confession. Answer me questions like the Holy Virgin, whose image ye are, answered the angel o' the Lord, kapin' northin' hid. Wull ye do ut, Lottie ?"

She turned and looked at him.

"Wull ye answer me questions an' kape northin' back, mavourneen ?"

She gave assent by an inclination of her head, keeping her eyes upon his face.

"'R ye goin' to marry Peter Socola, Lottie ?"

She shook her head.

"No ? An' why not ? D'ye know he has riches an' jew'ls an 'll make a fine lady av ye ? I'm kapin' northin' back from ye, an' ye must answer me thrue. D'ye know all that, Lottie ?"

"Yas."

"An' ye don't want 'im, nohow?"

"No."

"Not if 'e was tarred wud melted gold an' feathered wud diamonds till 'e'd shine like a government light-house! Ye don't want 'im noway, sick norr well, alive norr dead, raw norr cooked, mummied norr shtuffed, divilled norr on the half-shell! If I'm not mishtaken, I know yer sintimints on the Chinese question, an' that's about the size av ut! Ye don't want Peter, not if he does come wud the golden keys o' the kingdom o' this airth! Ain't that so?"

"Yas."

"Yis whut?"

"I don't want."

"That's it; ye don't want an' *sha'n't have* the antiquated ould pill coated for a sugar-plum! Ye sha'n't have um, an' nayther shall he have you. That much is settled, an' the hows an' the whins an' the wheres come aftherr. An' now for the next question: Is there onybody else ye like?— that ye'd like to marrý, I mane?"

She looked straight into his eyes and answered not a word.

How his heart thumped!

"Shpake, Lottie. Out wud ut! Is there onybody else ye like betther nor all the worrld?"

But still she, looking into his eyes, answered not.

He flinched visibly as he put the next question:

"Is it Joe Limongi, Lottie?"

His heart was dancing a highland fling now.

With an almost imperceptible, but steady movement, she shook her head.

It was not Limongi — Limongi who sold cantaloupes for her father and liked to talk to Carlotta. Maybe it was—

"Is it Antonino? Shpake out an' answer me thrue. Is it Toney?"

Another head-shake.

"Norr yer cousin Nicolo? Sure I niver seen 'im shpakin' wud ye."

The Madonna head shook again.

"Arrah, musha, an' sure an' it can't be Pat Murphy, the bit av a grocery-b'y at Keenan's beyant — a freckled, red-headed, blue-eyed Paddy, wud a brogue on 'im as thick as a mush poultice. Sure ye wudn't care for the likes av a blazin' divil av an Irishman, wud ye?"

He waited, but she answered nothing nor moved her head.

He was frightened. His voice was lower when he spoke again :

"In the name o' God, Lottie, answer me, me child. Ye're not demanin' yerself wud love for Pat Murphy, are ye?"

No, it was not Pat Murphy. The head shook now with solemn decision.

"Thin who, in the name o' the Poydras Marrket? I don't know no more a-comin' round heer. Sure it can't be the cross-eyed baker's man wud a crooked—"

It was not the baker's boy, nor yet the young American who lived at the corner.

Pat could think of no other.

"An' fo' the love o' Heaven, is it onybody, Lottie?"

She did not answer. It was surely some one.

"An' does he love ye, me child? An' are ye engaged to um?"

"I don't know." This slowly, after a pause.

"Don't know if ye're engaged? Is it afther makin' a fool av me ye are, Lottie?"

He was wounded. The girl saw it, and was suddenly roused.

"You don't *like* me no more!" she exclaimed, her eyes flashing. "Since two years you never call me no more 'intend'—never say you want me—never, never say *nothing!* I don't care, me. If you want, I'll marry ol' Pietro Socola. Anyhow, he loves me — speak with me kind, an' talk with my maw an' my paw fo' me. An' you—you say nothing! Anybody can come, say love-words an' get me—you don't care! It's all right. Me, I don't care neither, only fo' what you took me when I was little an' know no better, an' speak love-words with me—say I am for you—fool me like that—an' now, now when I am mo' bigger an' know better, now when I know to love, you turn your back! like to see me marry some strange man! My God, if I thought some bad man do like that to my lill sister here, me, I'd throw 'er *right now* out the window! Better so than like me—me to love always one, to think only fo' one, since I am like this baby, an' you pet me, make like you love me, buy me every pretty thing—an' then when I am mo' older, say I am fo' you—call me always your 'intend'—*before my maw an' my paw an' everybody call me so*—an' never in all my life speak no cross word with me—an' now, when I am only for you, an' you know it, *you hate me!*"

"Whist! Sh-h-h!" Pat fairly hissed, raising his arm wildly. "Hush, mavourneen! Ye're shpakin' blasphemy. Hush-h-h! Fo' the love o' God say no more!"

For a moment he was silent. Then, raising hands and face heavenward, he said, reverently:

"Holy Mary, Mother av God, an' all the saints an' angels, pass out in a full-dthress parade this day, an' wutness this mericle in the little shanty on S'int Andthrew Street!"

A sob stopped his throat for a moment, but presently, in a voice pitifully weak and low, he said:

"An' did ye think yer ould 'Woona' turned ag'in' ye, me purrty—he that was kissin' the sole av yer dirrty shoe this minute! Sure I love ye betther nor I love me mother that's in heaven, an' God knows I'm not takin' 'er down a peg from 'er high station in me recollection whin I do be sayin' ut—all honor to 'er name, though she's left me a couple o' shpankin's shorrt in me ginteel education! Sure 'twas the love in me heart that sint me on a retrate from ye, colleen bawn. For two yeers yer name thrimbled on me lips, an' yet I feered to own the truth, an' since I knowed ut for a fact sure I was afeered to show me face, lest the whole story'd lake out through the pores o' me skin if I kept me lips shut, an' ye'd hate me for a dizzy ould fool. An' now I fale—I fale—my God, I do fale like a pig in a puddle, when somebody t'rown 'im a bookay—sure he ate it up! Fo' the love o' God, gi' me the baby to howld, Lottie, afore I do take ye for a bookay!"

Reaching forward, he actually took the sleeping child from her arms.

"Sure I'll howld 'er for ballast, to kape me from risin' into the air, till I do talk wud ye sinsible! I'm that delerious I'm like a dthrunken man wud the William o' Thrimities! An' did ye think I loved ye since ye were like this to fool ye? Oh, but I must talk wud ye like a major to-night, Lottie." He hesitated, and when he spoke again his voice was touchingly tender:

"Ye're but a child, darlint. I niver thrifled wud ye in me life, an' I won't thrifle wud ye now. Sure an' if I tuck all ye're sayin' to me to-night, an' held ye to ut, all I'd nade 'ud be a pitchfork an' a tail for me rigimintals; but I'm not lookin' fo' that line o' promotion! If I was half or a quarrter fit for ye, I'd thry to qualify the remainder, but wud three-quarrters o' unfitness an' the ither quarrter beyant redimption in a jar o' alcohol, sure I'd be a dog to thry for ye."

"You don't want—"

Her eyes flashed again.

"Sh-h-h! My God, I *do want*, I tell ye, an' from this night for'ard, till he comes that ye like betther nor me, *ye're mine*—promised an' pledged over the head o' this slapin' image o' yerself when firrst ye thricked me ould heart! I'm bound to ye, remimber, Lottie mavourneen, *be me own will, to love ye, to help ye, to fight for ye—to die for ye, the day me grave 'll be a safe bridge over yer throubles!* But ye must be free yet, me purrty little innocent—free till ye've listened to love at its best. The old man Socola can't give ye a sample o' the gen*uine* arrticle, through his empty gums. Sure it's stale an' warrmed over in a cracked oven an' all out o' shape afore ye do get it from him. Let purrty young lips tell the story an' purrty young eyes thry to hide ut from ye in vain. Let one sing ut in rhyme an' anither clinch 'is fists an' swear ut to ye, an' then come an' tell yer ould Woona all about ut. Ye see, ye can't fully undtherstand till ye've had the best lessons in the language, no more nor I c'd polly fronsay wud a Frinchman. Take yer own time, me darlint, an' remimber, whativer comes, *I'm yer intinded!* (I'll say ut, if me ears grow six inches to the minute, to designate ass-ification!) Wull ye thrust me now, an' do what I say, an' kape northin' from me?"

"Yas; but I don't want no French lessons."

"Aha, but sure I insist upon ut!" he replied, laughing heartily at the unconscious humor of her naïve reply.

"Sure an' I've waked the baby wud me thrumpet's voice. Take 'er, darlint, an' go, afore yer mother calls ye, an' if she asks ye, tell 'er I urrged ye to marry ould gum-drops, but ye'll die firrst. If I do show me hand I b'lave she'd put me out; an' I think ye may nade me manœuvrin' more norr a skirrmish. Ye just come down like a thousand o' brick on him an' the whole lot, an' say *ye won't an' nobody can make ye!* An' I'll see ye through ut. Good-night, an' God bless ye. Sh-h-h-h!"

This last was to the baby, who fretted again in the transfer to Carlotta's arms. Placing one of her hands over the other about the shoulders of the sleeping child, Pat laid his lips against them reverently.

"God bless ye—an' God bless ye," he said, and again as she went down the stairs, "God bless ye," and he hobbled back to the open window, sank upon a chair, and in a moment was sobbing —and sobbing.

He felt so old, so dilapidated, so lonely and forlorn, so rough and uncouth, so far removed from his ideal of the man who should dare aspire to the love of Carlotta—Carlotta, whose exquisite youth and vestal beauty stood her in stead of all the graces and refinements of life; and yet he was so madly in love, so deliriously jubilant over her loyalty, which, no matter what should come, was now wholly his, that he wept from a full surrender of himself to his conflicting emotions.

He had sat here an hour, perhaps, when the sound of excited talking below drew him to the head of the stairs. It was the mother's voice. "Ogly!" she was screaming. "Ogly! Fo' God sague, Carlo, list'n ad C'lotta! Sayee Signor Pietro Socola ees-a wan ogly ol' man! Ogly ees-a northeen! Ogly ees-a good fo' wan man, pritty ees-a for a woma'. 'F a man ees-a pritty, ees-a no coun'. 'Z god-a too strong eye fo' pritty, haf to look all-a day een-a glass. Talk aboud-a ogly! My God, loog ad yo' pa! You thing me I ees-a marry heem fo' pritty?"

The voice passed out into the other room. This was only an argument by the way. Pat turned, and, going to his shelf, lit his candle, and, raising his glass, moved it from one angle to another, studying his own face:

"An' I do wondher, fo' the love o' God, does the little darlint think me purrty? Faith an' mebbe I am, but me style is peculiar—a rustic landscape forninst a turrkey-egg background, a mammoth cave, a natural bridge surrounded by a dinse perrarie on fire, wud chips o' snow in among the blazes—throuble on the borrders, but refuge in the middle! An' mebbe that's what the poor child sees in ut!"

The interpretation was touching in its mingling of humor and modesty. The face, while perhaps a stranger to recognized elements of beauty, was yet more than attractive to the observer who cared to read its meanings. Generosity, tender-heartedness, intelligence, wit—can the face on which these are written be called ugly ?

The little blue eyes twinkled anew as he dropped the glass and, fastening a last thread in Carlotta's shoe, hurried down-stairs. There was no longer occasion for retreat, as there was nothing to hide, naught to reveal.

A general murmur of welcome from the family greeted him when he appeared in the shop. Even Socola, who had just come in, grunted a pleasant inquiry as to his health.

"Sure an' I'm convalescent, Misther Socola," he said, his eyes dancing as he turned to the old man with a friendliness entirely new to him. "An' how's yersilf this day o' the wake ?"

"Oh, me, I am-a all-a-way kip well. Feel-a mo' young efera day."

"Droth an' they're all alike," said Pat to himself, as he passed out. "There's northin' like a wife's grave for makin' over ould min. Sure if I'd had the foresight to marry lame Biddy O'Shea afore ould Brindle hooked 'er into purrgatory, I'd be as much too young as I am too ould for love. It takes an ould codger like Socola to shtand sich a h'avin' set-back an' land out av the cradle."

Instead of joining the group at the door this evening, Pat preferred to walk abroad, to get the fresh open air and to find a quiet retreat to think over things.

Hailing a passing car at Jackson street, he rode out to its terminus at the river, and, passing beyond the ferry-landing into a shadowy corner behind high piles of freight, he sat down.

In the new retrospect, Socola and his little affair dwindled into utter insignificance as a trivial incident by the way.

He sat here until past midnight, absorbed in his own thoughts, which, no matter which way he turned, seemed punctuated with interrogation-points. "Would Carlotta always love him? Was it fair to her to hope for this? Was it human not to hope? What should he do now?"

The last question was that which remained with him. "What should he do?"

He knew that these revived energies and ambitions that filled him to his finger-tips were not transitory thrills—unless the whole were a dream; and, even so, he would dream out an honorable solution.

If he were really a man worthy a true girl's passing fancy even—to put it safely—and not the "ould granny" as which he had posed to himself for all these years, surely there must be standing-room for him somewhere in the world; not in the rollicking, frolicking world he had left, perhaps, where two feet on which to stand often fail to keep its inhabitants erect, but in the industrial world of workers on the edge of which he had dozed so long.

During the week following, while he worked at his bench in the Di Carlo shop, he was so engrossed with his own schemes that, but dimly conscious of his surroundings, he saw the old suitor, Socola, come and go, and the young men congregate about the shop and disperse, with but a passing smile. It was only the diverting by-play in his own drama — and Carlotta's — the drama for whose leading part he must equip himself.

Strange to say, the signora had never interrogated him in regard to his interview with Carlotta, presumably in behalf of Socola. The girl's sustained attitude of resistance was evidence enough of its result. So far as Pat observed, the affair was drifting without special incident.

The little father Di Carlo still opened his best old wine for Pietro on Sundays, and the signora made up in attention for whatever was lacking in Carlotta.

So a week passed, during which Pat had had scarcely a private word with the girl.

"Pst! Come heer, Lottie," he called, as she was passing through the shop on Saturday afternoon.

"Sit down an' putt up yer fut till I take yer measure."

She obeyed, coloring as she did so, for she knew the request was only a ruse. Did he not have hanging behind his door a row of lasts made for her feet at every stage of growth from her infancy till now?

"Now," said he, "while I do thrick the inquisitive wud me tape-line, Lottie, I want to talk wud ye. Don't say northin' to nobody norr let on ye know ut, but I'm goin' off for a thrip for a wake or so. I'll say I'm goin' for me health, but sure it's wealth I'm afther. (Faith an' if I do lie about the firrst letter o' the worrd, I do spind the remainder in repintance.) I'm lookin' out for a betther job norr the exterrnal tratement av corrns an' bunions—poulticin' over wan man's worrk in the corrner av anither man's shop."

"I'm glad," she said, and the rosy color in her face turned to scarlet.

"I knowed ye'd be glad, mavourneen."

"Where you goin'?" she added, quickly.

"I'm goin' up the Jackson railroad to visit me frind the Dutchman, jist. They tell me he has a boomin' thrade at Chattawa in the shoe business, an' he's only a yeer there, an' sure an' begorra where Hans Schmidt 'll go I'm safe to vinture, for he an' 'is ould frau are but two solid lumps o' prudence."

"When you goin'?"

"I'm off airly o' Monda' morrnin', plaze God, an' look for me back whin ye do heer me peg on the *banquette*. I'm goin' a-scrimmagin' an' a-skirrmishin' till I find what I want—a barefutted town a-wailin' for a wan-legged shoemaker; an'"—lowering his voice—"Lottie mavourneen, be a good girrl till Woona comes back, d'ye heer? An' let no one bully ye into listenin' to the ould man's complaint. Remimber, *nobody can make ye, if ye won't.* If they helt ye up afore the praste, sure ye cud shtiffen out into a dead faint an' they'd be compelled to carry ye out, *Miss Di Carlo* — an' don't ye forget that."

"I'm not 'fraid. My maw an' my paw knows me. They won't try nothin' like that on me."

"Ye're solid on that, colleen. An' now I'll l'ave me adthress on a shlip o' paper, an' in case ye do nade a friend, sind me a line. *An' now*," —in a louder tone, raising his tape-line—" nine inches an' a quarrter across the inshtep—the same from heel to toe." And lower again, "I seen the madam a-peepin' twice-t ; mebbe ye betther run off now—me purrty little intinded."

The last, in a whisper, just reached her ear, spreading a fresh blush over her face as she arose.

III

Pat's business tour extended itself from one to two weeks. The idea of establishing himself in some suburban town was not new to him, but it had never before seemed quite worth while. His really worthy but conservative friends, the Schmidts, though evidently quietly prosperous, were non-committal, and would give no advice. His impressions were favorable, however, and he returned to New Orleans buoyant with promising schemes.

It was after dark when he reached the city, and

as he approached the Di Carlo's a row of carriage-lights before the door startled him so that he felt in danger of falling. Something unusual was happening. If any one had died he would have heard: besides, who ever heard of a night funeral, except under extraordinary circumstances? *Could it be a wedding?* He had had a strange foreboding of ill. Why had he left Carlotta?

Reaching the house, he hesitated without, in the shadow of an open shutter. He must have a moment to still the mad beating of his heart.

The window was up, and through the venetian blinds the scene which greeted him was of the utmost confusion.

Socola, attired in his dress suit and white kid gloves, bloodless as yellow wax and blue of lip, was excitedly walking up and down the room. About him, standing in squads or sitting in groups, whispering, was a gathering of people, among whom Pat recognized some of the Di Carlo kindred, while others were strangers. All were intensely excited.

Just as Socola reached a point near the window, a young woman crossing from the other side of the room stopped him.

Pat recognized her immediately as a cousin of Carlotta, and, by a coincidence, one who bore her full name.

"I'm-a shore I woun'-a grief myself 'boud-a Carlotta, signor," she said, as she excitedly fanned her dark fat face with a light-blue feather fan.

And so Carlotta was dead! Pat leaned against the house for support.

But wait. The old man was answering in Italian:

"Grief! I grieve not for her. She may go to the devil. I care not for her, but for myself! It is the disgrace! I have come here to marry her, and if I wait all night I will have her! Money is nothing to me. I can pay the police—order the detective force out—scour the city."

The girl shrugged her shoulders. "Oh, well, 'z-god-a just-a so good fish in the riv' 'z-a come oud."

"But I am not to be mocked!" The old man was hoarse with passion. There was a majesty in his wrath which might even have won respect from Carlotta could she have seen him.

"She shall not mock me!" he continued. "Every laborer down at the Picayune Tier—every man on the luggers—all my business comrades—*everybody* knows the name of Carlotta Di Carlo, and that I come to marry her to-night. I have her mother's promise. She must be found!"

"Carlotta Di Carlo ees-a no gread-a name," she replied, still in English, toying with her fan. "Z-a my name just-a the same ligue-a my cous'n. Neva ees-a bring me sudge-a so gread-a good-luck." Just here the door opened at Pat's side, and a man stepped out. Fearing discovery, he immediately entered the house, where a chorus of exclamations greeted him:

"Carlotta ees-a run away!"

"Z-a jump oud-a window!"

"—— run off!"

"Cand fine-a no place."

In the back room the mother was noisily bemoaning her misfortune, sometimes in Italian and then in English.

"Come in, fo' God sague, Meester Pad!" she cried, when she saw him. "Come-a see wad-a troub' we god-a theeze day. Come, loog!" Drawing him into the back room, she pointed to the bed, upon which was spread an array of finery.

"Loog—loog here! All-a fine silg dress, silg pock-a-hankcher—silg stockin'—silg hat—keed-a glove—keed-a shoe—gol' watch-a chain—gol' ring —loog! Everytheen-a so fine Signor Socola ees-a bring Carlotta fo' marry weeth-a heem to-nighd —an' C'lotta ees-a *run away!* Sez to me, 'Mus-a lock-a door fo' wash-a myselve'—just a ligue thad—an' ees-a climb oud-a window an' gone! Oh, my God, me I'm-a crezzy!"

"An' had she given her consint, ma'am?" Pat managed to ask, at last. He had only listened yet.

"Consen'! Geev-a consen'! No! Geev-a northeen! C'lotta ees-a god on'y six-a-teen year. Wad-a chil' ligue that knowee aboud-a man? Don' know northeen boud-a consen'!"

"That's whut I say, ma'am!" It was all he could do to hold himself, but he remembered her he loved, and in her interest was silent.

His only fear, and this was slight, was that they should find her.

A half-hour passed slowly. At any unusual sound in the front room every one looked anxiously towards the door, as in a church when the bridal party is due.

Presently a distinct and sudden movement and a renewed hum of voices indicated that something had happened.

It was true. Something was happening.

The old man Socola, leading by the hand the other Carlotta, the cousin, entered the room and approached the bed. With a dignified inclination of his head to the company, and pointing to the display of gifts, he said (he spoke always in Italian):

"I present to Carlotta Di Carlo those presents which are marked in the name of Carlotta Di . Carlo, and when she is dressed as my bride we will drive to the church. The announcement in to-morrow's papers shall prove that Pietro Socola has not been disappointed."

Hesitating here, and gathering emphasis by a lowered voice, as he glanced with menacing brow about him, he continued :

"What happens here to-night is in the bosom of Mafia society!" They could have heard a pin drop now. "Mafia's children can keep her secrets." He paused again and looked from one to another. "But if there is a Judas here—*if one word passes that door—the knives of a hundred of Mafia's sons are ready to avenge it!* And I am Pietro Adolpho Socola who speaks!"

Pat was the first to break the death-like silence which followed.

"An' accept me warrmest congratulations, Misther Socola," he said, stepping forward and grasping the old man's white-gloved hand.

Others followed closely. Congratulations were now in order, the new bride-elect receiving her accidental honors with ill-concealed pride.

A fresh wedding-stir arose, but beneath it all was a suppressed moan, like the irresistible under-tow of a playful sea. The missing girl, the lost wealth, the mystery, the humiliation, Mafia's authoritative command of secrecy, with its death-penalty—all these, as elements of possible tragedy, were felt, even by the satellites of the new bride, and showed themselves in the subdued air and blanched faces of the family of the supplanted.

Pat was the happiest person present, excepting perhaps the fat little creature who in the next room was holding her breath and panting while one squeezed, another fanned her, and a third burst off hooks and eyes in the determined effort to prove that the bridal gown designed for Carlotta Di Carlo had not proved a misfit.

It was a relief to all when finally the wedding-party started off.

Those who came in the back carriages rode now in front, the family of Carlo Di Carlo bringing up the rear as relations of the bride—" like

the asses which always follow on the tail of the
Rex procession on Mardi Gras," Pat heard the
little father say in Italian to the signora, adding,
as he and his' sons got into the last carriage, "You
have made us a pretty pack of fools !"

There was that in the husband's tone that made
the wife keep silent, but when they had gone she
turned to Pat and burst into violent weeping.

For once a woman's tears were powerless to
move him. Turning abruptly, he left her without a word, and mounted the stairs to his own
room.

In a moment, however, he heard her following.
She was not to be so easily eluded. She must
have an audience. Her habit of finding relief by
pouring her complaint into Pat's ears was too
firmly fixed to be given up at this crisis, when her
ignominious failure seemed more than she could
bear. Her cup had been spared no possible dreg
of bitterness, even to the summoning of the hated
family of her brother-in-law Di Carlo to witness
and reap a triumph in her defeat. This was the
refinement of cruelty ; and then, as a finishing-
touch, came Mafia's command. They dare never
explain. Those stuck-up Toney Di Carlos might
give the world any story they chose *but the true
one*—the one they would love to keep.

When she appeared before him, panting from
her hasty ascent, Pat thought she resembled nothing so much as a hyena at bay.

"*Haf to lis'n ad me, Meester Pad,*" she began,

dropping into a chair. "God Almighty ees-a turn 'is back on me to-nighd—pud-a me down ligue wan dog biffore all-a doze nasty Toney Di Carlos!"

"God Almighty done ut, d'ye say? Ye're payin' yersilf a purrty round complimint for a wake-day, Misthress Di Carlo! I'd kape that for a Sunday, till we cud buy ye a tin halo an' putt on our Sunday clothes an' say our beads to yer Holiness."

His wrath oiled his tongue. Of course she did not understand.

"'Z-a no time fo' play, Meester Pad. Fo' God sague, you god-a no heart? See wan-a poor woma' in-a so gread-a troub'!"

"I have, 'ma'am, a palpitator in the vicinity o' me left lung, but it's engaged at prisent in behalf o' the slip av a child that's turrned out av 'er father's house on a darrk night to escape worrse nor a livin' death at the hand av 'er mother. 'Tis a black night, ma'am, an' where is the child?"

"My God!" her whisper was heavy with passion, "you tague-a side weeth-a C'lotta? Me, I don' care where ees! Hofe-a the dev's got 'er!"

"An' I'll warrant ye, ma'am, he has an orrganized detective forree out in searrch o' the likes av her to-night, ye may be sure o' that! An' plinty illuminated transums above hell's sky-parrlors 'll open their thrap-doors to welcome 'er in, wud music borrowed from heaven to entrap an angel!" His voice trembled with wrath. "Sure they'll give 'er 'er pick av bridal dresses, an' a sate at a faste where the bread she'll ate 'll be as honest as that ye offered 'er—raised from the same leaven an' at the same price !"

"Wad you talk, Meester Pad ? 'Brida' dress' an'-a same price !' Thing yo' head ees-a gone wrong ! 'Z no mo' rich-a man's wan'-a C'lotta. Wad-a you say ?"

"I say the divil has a shtandin' ordther out for brides, ma'am, an' the city strates av a darrk night are his harvest-field, an' whin an angel is thrapped unbeknowinst to his bed, he does mock heaven wud fresh fireworrks an' ring the bells o' hell for a holiday ! 'Tis tin o'clock, mother Di Carlo, an' rainin' cats' an' dogs this minute. Ye have a child, a fair bit av a daughter, out hidin' from ye. She knows no people. 'Tis the firrst time nine o'clock iver missed 'er from her little thrundle-bed. Can ye tell me in whose back alley I'll find 'er skulkin', like an odd cat, an' bring 'er home to the mother that's grievin' after 'er ?"

His passion calmed the woman. She looked dazed, but answered him nothing.

"If yer Divinity 'll parrdon me shirrt-slaves till I do putt on me rain-coat, I'll shtep out mesilf an' see if bechance her ould granny can thrace 'er."

Crossing the room, he proceeded to raise the lid of his trunk, but it resisted. It was fastened —*on the inside!*

For a second only voice and wit failed him.

"Ye'll excuse me manners, ma'am, fer lavin' me saloon-parrlor whin I've company, but I've a call to enlist on the opposition to the divil's forrce," he said, and, with a bow, "Wull ye walk firrst, Misthress Di Carlo?"

Sniffling, but silent, the woman arose and preceded him down the stairs.

Following, he hurried into the street, but returned in a moment.

"Betther go back for me rubber boot an' me bumberel," said he. "Sure the strates are flowin' wud wather." And hastily he reascended the stairs.

"Whst!" he called, tapping gently upon the trunk, and "sh-h-h!" as the girl's head pushed up the lid.

"Glory be to God Almighty!" he whispered, as he carefully aided her to rise from her cramped position, though she remained sitting in the trunk.

"An' did me ould box harber ye again, me little wan? An' why didn't ye write me the letther?"

"I never knowed I haf to get married till tonight. My maw sez to me I mus' marry Socola, on 'coun' o' my po' lill brothers an' sisters an'—"

"Sh-h! Spake aisy, mavourneen."

"Then I seen my only chance was to run away. It was dark outside. I was afraid. So then I thought about the trunk, an' I climbed up over the back shed—"

"Niver mind now, darlint. I musht go; the

madam 'll be afther missin' me. But you stay heer.
Make yersilf at home to-night in me ould din. I'll
shlape below in the shop, an' tell thim I'm on the
watch for ye, which 'll be God's truth. Ye're not
to make yer appecrance till she's wapin' an wailin'
for a sight av ye. Shtrike no light, an' off wud
yer shoes. I'll manœuvre below-stairs, an' ye
kape silence above."

"You think the old man 'll come back for me to-
morrow again?" she asked, anxiously.

"Heavens above! An' didn't ye know he's married to yer cousin Carlotta?"

The tension had been so great that, at this sudden relief, the girl, trembling, bent her head upon
her arm over the edge of the trunk, and fell to
sobbing hysterically.

Pat was frightened lest she should be overheard,
for he dreaded the mother's unspent rage. He
laid his hand tenderly upon her head.

"Sh-h! The throuble's over now, darlint, an'
Woona's heer to thrash onybody but yer mother,
an' it's she that mustn't heer ye!"

A sound of loud talking below reassured him,
however. The father and brothers had returned
from the wedding.

Carlotta heard it, and the distraction soon quiet-
ed her. With Pat's aid she presently arose, and
together they cautiously approached the opening.

In the tumult the father's voice prevailed. He
spoke in Italian:

"What am I, that my wife *lies* to me? You

said the child consented. You lied, *lied!* I told
you you should not compel her. You are paid.
I am glad. But I want my daughter. Where is
the child? What can I do? Where I go to seek
her I spread an ugly tale — Carlotta, the pretty
daughter of Di Carlo, is not in her father's house
at night. A sweet story, that! Oh, my wife is a
fine schemer — got a rich husband for Toney's
ugly girl with the pimply face. Ha! she is
kind, yes—I am glad, but, only, I want my little girl."

In the midst of this, but not heeding it, the
woman was contesting her position in broken English — an appeal for sympathy to the English-
speaking boys, her sons.

"Fo' who ees I lie?" she screamed, between
sobs. "Wad ees-a money fo' me? Rich or po'
ces-a all-a same to me. God-a rock-a cradle fo'
you—dthaz all! 'F I lie, 'z fo' you, an' fo' C'lotta
selve. An' now everybody ees-a blame me!
Weesh, me, I was dead. You ces-a curse me,
Meester Pad ees-a sassy me to my face, an' all on
'coun' o' C'lotta!"

"Shp!" hissed the old man. "No more! Show
me my child, and we speak never of this again.
I am not blameless. I consented, but not to force
her. You were tempted, and she saved you. It
is well. We have not sold our first babe to feed
the last. But I want her here. I want my little
girl."

"I'm goin', Woona," said Carlotta, starting suddenly. She would have descended the stairs, but Pat held her arm.

"Not from heer, darlint. Ye've kept the thrunk secret for a dozen years—"

She understood, and, agile as a cat, had dashed by him in the other direction, and was out the window on the roof before he realized her intention. She would return as she had come.

Pat hobbled after her to the window. She had just reached the corner of the low shed (where an' overhanging fig-tree afforded safe and private transit to the ground), when she suddenly returned and laid her hand on the Irishman's arm.

"Don't be mad. You are good. I like you, Woona, but I never knowed—"

She began to cry.

"I never knowed my paw liked me before; haf to go to him."

Pat was choked with emotion, and before he could answer her the slim shadow of the girl had flitted down, and was merged into the broad shadow of the tree.

Though the rain was over, the night was dark.

Pat's heart was thumping so when he returned to his vantage-ground at the head of the stairs that he had to sit down.

Soon he heard a timid knock at the street door — Carlotta was a cute one — then a rush of boys' heavy feet, a clank of iron as the hook was raised, and now, through the open door, loud crying, like

the heart-sobs of a little child. So Carlotta met
her father.

By ducking his head very low, Pat saw, for a
second only, the little reticent old man with out-
stretched arms going to meet her ; and he, sitting
alone on the top step, blubbered like a school-boy,
but no one heard him.

Pat could scarcely realize that he had been home
hardly three hours when, a few minutes later, he
looked at his watch to find it but eleven o'clock.

So far as he could discover, the affair was never
alluded to in the household afterwards ; but for a
long time between himself and the signora a distinct coldness was felt which made him uncom-
fortable.

His anger towards her had soon melted, but he
wanted it forgotten. She was no worse than many
rich mothers. Her methods were only a little
more crude.

He had easily forgiven her, since she had failed.
Though she had had no conception of the force of
his words, she realized that he had blamed and
silenced her—had " sassied her to her face "—and
it was hard to forget it. And then, too, her relations were somewhat embarrassed with all who
knew of the affair.

"I wonder," said he one evening a few weeks
later, as he sat near her at the door—"I wonder
wud the madam wear a pair o' shoes o' my makin'?
I'll guarantee I cud make ye a bully pair 'll do ye

through the next christenin', an' ye'll be dthrag-
gin' 'em slip-shod till the wan afther that ag'in."

"Oh, you ees-a so bad, Meester Pad!" she exclaimed, with a hearty laugh delightfully like the
familiar ring of old times. "How much-a price
you goin'-a charge me?"

"Charrge ye! Well, I'll be dog-goned if ye're
not complimintary! I'll charrge ye enough, sure,
whin ye do bring me yer ordher for a pair, but
whin I do make ye a presint I'll ask ye a returrn
o' what I do putt into the job—a free confession
o' frindly feelin', jist. Whut do ye say, ma'am?"

Laughing, she stuck out her heavy foot. "'Z big
'nough speak fo' heemselve!"

And so the old relations were restored.

Pat had been especially desirous of this reconciliation because of his contemplated change of
residence, which of course the signora did not suspect.

Exactly what arrangement would result from
his reconnoitring tour he did not yet know, but
the matter was unexpectedly decided one day by
the receipt of a formal business proposal of part-
nership with his German friend, Hans Schmidt.

The old fellow was growing decrepit, and wished
to rest. The offer was framed with characteristic
caution, and its terms were hard, but in his present mood Pat was all the better pleased, and so
the matter was settled.

He would still call the Di Carlo garret "home,"
and would come on Sunday mornings and stay

until Monday. Chattawa was but a few hours' run from the city.

All the signora's sentiments towards him were sensitized and perfumed with the generous odor of fresh shoe-leather when Pat told her of his plans, and she said so many touching things about breaking up the family, and the like, that he added forgetfulness to his forgiveness of her sin, and they almost wept upon each other's bosoms when he went away.

IV

Time dragged rather heavily at the Di Carlos' after Pat's departure. There was no one now always ready to give a humorous turn to commonplace things—to raise a playful breeze over the dull monotony of every-day life. Whether the baby bumped her head or a customer quarrelled over his bill, the occurrence, served up with Pat's piquant wit, had always become a delightful joke.

It is possible that not even Carlotta missed him more than did the signora. And the little family toes missed him! Dainty·pink buttons that had not been allowed to see the light came all the way out, as if to inquire for the absent Pat, and grew familiar with the floor and the *banquette*, like other little dago children's toes. And yet the signora vowed that she had done nothing but pay out money for shoe-patching ever since Mr. Pat went away.

In the evenings the young men and boys still came and laughed and talked with Carlotta.

At first there had been occasional expressions of surprise, with inquisitive glances, at Socola's marriage to the other, but the mother's flat and surprised denial of her Carlotta's ever having been thought of in so absurd a connection soon silenced all concern about the matter.

Pat came usually on Saturday night or Sunday, and was always an honored guest. "The madam" never tired of rehearsing to him the events of the week or exhibiting the baby's last tooth or promising gums, nor did she ever fail to hold out for his inspection "the mos'-a easy-walkin' pai' shoe ees-a ever was-a wear."

And so weeks lapped over weeks until months had passed and folded likewise one upon the other.

Carlotta was still to her fond old lover a dainty little saint within a high niche, and when he said his "Hail Mary" at night, as he had tried to do ever since he had confessed himself in love, he kept seeing *her* picture sitting in the garret window in the moonlight, and wondering how far his piety was at fault. Even irreligious men say prayers when they are honestly and purely in love. Pat was only unreligious.

He still told himself, as he told her, that she was free, and must listen untrammelled to any story of love that should please her; and yet, when he laid by small sums of money, he thought, "How purrty it'll shtuff out 'er little pockutbook!" or, "I wondher wull she lave ut in a dhrygoods shop or hide ut in an ould shtockun'!—but, savin' or shpindin', sure she'll be handlin' 'er own, God bless her."

He expected to find young men sitting around the shop in the evenings when he came home, and the sound of an accordion or flute or tambourine or familiar laughter reaching him, as he approached the house, served but to identify the crowd.

It was only when the accordion became his invariable greeting, when, even descending upon the family in the middle of the week, he found it still there, that he began to consider that Carlotta had never told him about this young musician, except to give his name in answer to a question.

It seemed absurd to think seriously of so trivial a matter; and yet, when a long time passed and the accordion, long-winded or short of breath according to the player's mood, sent its voice out panting or trilling to meet him, he began to hate the sound of it, and to wish that Carlotta would sometimes talk upon the subject.

She had told him how young Alessandro Soconneti, who won a prize in the lottery, had wanted her, and how Joe Zucca, the peanut-vender, had vainly insisted on her love, and even of her cousin Angelo, who had tried to coax her to forget his kinship. Why had she forgotten to mention this strange boy who played the accordion?

Pat seldom saw her alone now excepting when occasionally on Sunday afternoons he would take her with the children for a ride up to the park, as had been his habit for years. While the little ones played under the oaks or braided clover wreaths near, he would sit at her feet on the gnarled roots of the old trees and tell her about his life at "the Dutchman's," and sometimes, though not often, he would speak of how he had missed her out of his daily life.

He avoided this as much as possible, however. It was so hard to be a little tender when in his Irish heart was smouldering a fire that at the lightest breath would flare into a flame.

He had promised himself and her to wait until she should pass her eighteenth year before allowing her to bind herself by solemn promise.

She knew that he loved her—that he was working early and late, living with people who were in touch with him only in their determination to make money—and that it was all for her.

Sometimes, growing weary of his silence, she would invite a declaration by some naïve question put in monosyllables, as when she said, one Sunday, as they rose to start home:

"You like me yet, Woona?"

"Like ye yet! Arrah, musha, an' whut 're ye sayin', darlint? *Like* ye? Sure I *love* ye, from the crown av yer purrty little black head to the sole av yer two feet, an' all the way back, wud a lap over! An' why d'ye ask me that?"

But instead of answering him, she only colored like a rose, and said :

"I'm glad."

And Pat, lifting the children into the car, felt like kicking his wooden leg to the winds and flying; but he only said, as he sat beside her:

"Begad, an' I'm glad ye're glad, mavourneen. Sure sorrow 'll dim my day whin ye're sorry." And as he raised his eyes he saw, sitting opposite, a young man who smiled and tipped his hat to Carlotta—and under his arm he carried an accordion.

As he looked upon him, Pat felt a shiver pass over him, for he thought he had never seen a youth so beautiful as he.

"That's Giuseppe Rubino," said Carlotta, looking into his eyes with the directness of a child.

"Is it, indade? Sure I tuck 'im for a vision of S'int Joseph or wan av the angels. An' isn't he a beauty?"

"He sings pritty," replied the girl, as she might have said, "It is growing cold," or, "The river is rising."

Pat regarded her with covert scrutiny for a moment. Could it be possible that she did not see that this tall brown boy, with his soft red lips and white teeth, his lofty movement and languid grace, was a creature of rare and poetic beauty?

Had she too not seen the red deepen beneath the olive of his cheek when his eye met hers? Had she not learned in all the summer evenings what Pat had caught in a twinkling — that the youth loved her with all the fresh ardor of a nature fashioned for romance?

It seemed not; for she remarked, in the same even tone :

"He comes ev'ry evenin' pass the time away. He plays nice."

If she had been saying she hated the boy, it would not have kept Pat's heart from thumping against his waistcoat while his eyes rested on the beautiful youth who was helping the girl he loved to "pass the time away" during his absence.

"An' whut does he do for a livin'? Sure there's little money in the machine he carries, wud all its puffin' an' blowun'. "

"He's pore. He works fo' ol' Socola. He hates him, too. He's savin' up. Bimeby he's goin' to start for 'isself."

"An' who told ye all that, Lottie?"

"He tol' me."

"An' where did ye meet um?"

"He come to fetch my paw a note from ol' Socola. He say he seen me first in his sleep one night. He talks funny. I don' pay no 'tention."

It was time to stop the car; but before Pat could do so the young man had pulled the strap and was going out.

"Please to make you 'quainted wid Mister Rubino, Mister Rooney," said Carlotta, as Giuseppe, smiling, joined them, and the three, Carlotta in the middle, followed the children home.

"AND THE THREE FOLLOWED THE CHILDREN HOME"

If Pat appeared at a disadvantage, no one was half so conscious of it as himself as he hobbled beside the youthful pair on his wooden peg.

Ever since he had loved the girl, he had been keenly sensitive in regard to his lameness. Indeed, he had even once gone so far as to try to repair it by wearing an artificial leg, but, as Carlotta had shrunk away from it as something uncanny, declaring that it "made her think about dead people," he had discarded it after a single experiment.

It seemed but natural that Pat should sit with "the old folks" while Carlotta and the youth joined the young group at the other door to-night ; it was quite natural that Giuseppe should presently be playing the accordion for the crowd—the same thing had happened before, many a time; and yet to-night Pat felt it all as he had never done before.

"A fine-lookin' chap is this young man Rubino," he said, presently, to the signora.

She shrugged her shoulders.

" And who is 'e ?" he pursued.

" Carlo sayee ees-a wan good steady young man; bud me, I know northeen 'boud who ees-a keep-a comp'ny weeth-a C'lotta." And the shoulders shrugged again, a movement so distinctly reminiscent of the previous affair that Pat thought it discreet to change the subject.

As the evening wore on, he grew restless.

" Well, I b'lave I'll thry a promenade for me

complexion," said he, rising finally. "Sure me left fut is itchin' for a walk." And, with this characteristic allusion to the missing member, he started down the street. He had not gone far, however, when he came upon a crowd of young men, Italians most of them, sitting upon the steps outside the closed doors of a shop — a common Sunday-evening congregation—and, as a familiar voice accosted him, he had soon seated himself with them.

Several of the *habitués* of the Di Carlo shop were present, and were bantering one another in Italian about Carlotta. Pat was not supposed to understand.

All went smoothly for a time, until young Tramonetti, an ugly, heavily-set fellow who had been the target of several sallies on the score of his well-known unsuccessful suit, suddenly turned in anger.

"I could marry her to-morrow if I had money!" he exclaimed, with a sneer.

"Psh-h-h! You'd have to get a new face on you first!" came a quick retort.

"I think my face is just as pretty as old Pietro Socola's; and she tried hard enough to get him, all the same!"

"You better say he tried for her, yes," was the reply.

Pat, although talking quietly aside, caught and understood every word.

"Tried nothing!" continued Tramonetti. "He

never wanted her. Married her rich cousin, yes ! But Carlotta tried pretty hard to get him. Myself saw her every minute pass before him in the shop and make sheep's-eyes !"

Pat could stand no more.

" An' I say ye're a liur!" he exclaimed, rising and facing the speaker.

The effect of his words was magical. A stillness fell upon the assembly. After an interval, an old man, Tramonetti's uncle, broke the silence.

" Wath-a you knowce 'bouth ?" he asked, turning languidly to the Irishman with that apathetic manner beneath which anything may lurk.

" Sure an' I do jist happen accidintally to know that that young man is a liur !"

The object of his accusation quietly lit a cigarette.

" How ees-a you knowce ? Socola selve ees-a tell evera-body neva ees-a lov'-a tall. Wath-a you knowce ?"

And now another spoke—a cousin of Tramonetti.

" Socola ees-a tell all-a mans on Picayune Tier she ees-a try for 'eem all-a same."

Grunts of assent in several directions testified that the story was familiar.

" An' he's another liur, an' I'd tell ut to 'is gums, the toothless ould macaroni-sucker ! Sure an' I've had me two eers pricked for this same lie this twelvemonth, an', bedad, I've laid low an' kep' shtill for ut ! An' did 'e say she thried to catch 'im—the contimptible little river shrimp—he that had 'is two eyes set out like yung telescopes afther 'er!"

"Fo' God sague, don'-a mague-a no troub'! Blief Socola ees-a just talk fo' play!" suggested another.

"Thin I'm playin' when I tell ye that he thried wud all the iloquent perrsuasion av his money-bags to buy 'er!—offered the ould man a thousand dollars down for 'er, an' pitched 'imself in at the end o' the thrade, like a punkin-colored chromo for *lagniappe;* but the girrl—sure I do raise me hat whin I do sphake 'er name"—every hat followed as he lifted his own—"but the girrl wudn't look ut um! An' the night he married 'er pug-nosed cousin, sure he kem in the kerridge wud all 'is crowd for 'erself, an' she shkipped out the window an' hid. So whin he cudn't get corrn 'e took shucks, as mony o' ye 'll do afther 'im! Now, putt that in yer pipe an' shmoke ut!"

He turned now again to Tramonetti.

"An' this yung gas-chandelier heer, who sez 'e seen 'er wink at 'im, is a dirrty black—"

"Ah-h-h-h! Ged oud! 'M just a mague a lill-a fun!" drawled the boy.

"An' ye take ut back, wul ye?"

The men were all laughing now at the new version of the Socola marriage.

"So the ol' man got fooled, eh?" said one.

"But I say, d'ye take ut back?" persisted Pat.

"Ain't I sayee was-a play'n'? Fo' God sague,

how much-a mo' you wan'?" And he rose
to go.

The storm was past, and by twos and threes
the men dispersed, laughing and talking as they
went.

As Pat moved away, an old man who had sat
apart in the shadow stood up, and the light from
the gas at the corner fell upon a visage sinister,
one-eyed, and lowering.

Pat instantly recognized it as the face of a man
who had been present at the Di Carlos' on the
night of the Socola wedding. Indeed, it was he
who had been sent to Pat as interpreter, on this
occasion, of the Mafia anathema. Pat thought of
this, but he did not care.

As he turned his back, another man arose out
of the shadow at the other end of the shed. He
too had been a guest at the wedding.

The two Sicilians, who were presently left alone,
regarded each other in silence for a moment, when
the last to rise made the sign of the Mafia. The
answering motion was given, and the two, still
silent, sat down together again in the shadow.

They were bound by oath to report this disclosure to Socola, and they knew what the inevitable
result would be: the Irishman's words would
prove his death-sentence.

Under the vow of perfect obedience, either or
both of them might become the executors of an
old man's personal vengeance.

It was an ugly business, and neither of the men

5

welcomed it. Both knew Pat's cordial relations with many of their countrymen, among whom, indeed, he had not a single enemy. Even the old man Socola liked him. But they understood too well the imperious pride of the vindictive old Sicilian to hope that a personal friendship, or even a tie of blood, would protect any man who dared betray his dignity. Certainly the casual feeling of negative good-will which he felt towards Pat would melt like snow beneath the hot breath of his wrath when he should learn that the Irishman had given his secret to the common herd of his countrymen. The indomitable pride which had led him to marry an ugly, unattractive woman the first time he met her, rather than brook the odium of a disclosure of his rejection, would not spare him who, although forewarned, had dared divulge it.

It was some moments before either of the men spoke, and then one said, in Italian :

" Well—"

" Well—" was the answer. And, after a pause:

" I wish I had gone home to-night."

" And me too. I wish I had stayed at the coffee-house."

" He's a good friend to all the Carlo Di Carlos, that old Irishman."

" Yes, I know. Last year, when all the babies took the small-pox and the shop was shut up, he signed for the rent ; and he paid every cent since—three months' rent."

"Yes, and old Di Carlo says Carlotta's schooling never cost him a dollar. This cripple paid it all."

"And when the old man was stung with a tarantula hidden in a bunch of bananas, while everybody cried and ran every way, they say the shoemaker threw his hat on the spider and sat on it quick, while he took little Di Carlo across his knee like a baby and sucked the poison from the back of his neck. Di Carlo was carrying the bananas on his shoulder when the little devil stung him."

"Yes, I heard that. And all the people laughed while they cried, because when he was sucking the poison he said, 'Let me kiss you for your mother.'"

They were silent again for a time.

"If Tramonetti had only kept his big mouth shut—"

"Yes, I wish he had choked before he spoke to-night. He made all the trouble."

Another silence.

"Well—"

"Well—"

"It's a bad world, this. One minute we play an organ at the corner for any beggar to dance, the next minute maybe we get orders to file our stilettos and put on a black mask."

"Me, I am tired. I wish I was out of it."

"And me too. Tell the truth, I've never been the same since that job you and I did at the old

Basin. I see, a thousand times a day, that young man's face the way it looked in the moonlight. Sometimes I am playing my organ laughing, and he comes and stands before me with his neck *so.* And, I swear before God, I believe the monkey sees him. Many times when he is dancing he looks up and runs and crawls behind me, crying, and I look around, and I see the young man with his neck cut. I kiss the cross, but it's true. Four times last week Jocko did that, and I trembled so I missed the time in my music. You don't believe it's true?"

"Yes, I believe you. I've seen them again, too. But now they are too many. They don't frighten me. I laugh in their faces, and they dance and run one through another, like clouds of smoke. I am an old man, and I have struck many a blow, but not one for hate, thank God— only obedience."

"Nor me either. Only twice I have been on duty. Once my partner did the work, and the other time—you know. And now, my God! if I have to listen all my life to that Irishman's wooden leg, '*tap, tap, tap,*' in my ears, I'll go crazy ; I'll drown myself."

The other man laughed.

"Oh, don't hurt yourself. Maybe old Socola 'll put somebody else on this job. And the next time that young fellow we finished at the Basin comes fooling around you, showing you the cut in his neck, you send him to me. I believe I gave him his send-off, anyway. 'Twas good enough for him. His tongue was too long."

"No, no! They know whom to follow—and *I know*. I am left-handed, and the hole in his neck was *here;* and sometimes my left hand burns like hell. You can laugh," he continued, rising, "but it is no fun to me. But I am not a teething baby. Easy or hard, I am good for my duty."

"Well," said the other, "*dimani*" (to-morrow).

"*Dimani*," was the answer.

And so they parted.

As the younger man walked away, the older sighed. ·

"Poor boy!" (he spoke still in Italian), "I was like him too, once. The first drop of blood on a man's hand burns like a coal of fire, and a ghost stands beside it always, blowing upon it to keep it burning. The only relief is more blood. When once he is bathed in blood he burns the same all over, and he knows himself for a devil, and the air of hell feels good to him. All around him are ghosts blowing upon him, and he likes their breath and laughs because he is solid fire and they are like a roaring wind around him. If they would go and leave him to cool he would go all to gray ashes and fall to pieces. He would go crazy and kill himself. Anyhow, I am sorry for this business."

He rose, and, as he started home, curiosity led him somewhat out of his way to pass the Di

Carlo shop. He walked on the other side of the street. He looked over.

Pat stood among the children on the *banquette*, throwing a little one into the air and catching her, while the others stood waiting and begging:

"Take me, Mr. Pat!"

"Teresa had four turns."

"Little Pat always gets the most."

It was a pretty picture.

"Well, I'm sorry," the man repeated to himself as he passed on. "In the name of God, why can't men keep their tongues? But, anyhow, I am sorry."

The picture of the amiable man in the bosom of the family of his countryman playing with his children, unconscious of impending evil, remained with the Sicilian as he walked home. Indeed, Pat's offence seemed to him more than half a virtue; for was it not provoked by his stanch championship of the young Italian girl, Carlotta?

If only Socola would be made to see it in this light!

Before reporting the case, even, this man of the sinister face, who had never before troubled himself with a personal concern for his victims, summoned his best English and wrote a word of warning to the Irishman.

It ran about like this:

"Mr. Rooney at Carlo Di Carlo,—This warn you to run for your life. Leaf New Orleans rite

way. It is not in power off man to safe you neither God if you remane before the eye of Mafia.

"One man's spite it is whitch mare you to die.
If you remaine a nife go throught your heart. It
is true. I swear before God."

When he passed through the shop early Mou-
day morning on his way home, Pat found this
note with another slipped in beneath the edge of
the front door.

The other was shorter, but, as if to add weight
and solemnity to its almost affectionate warning,
across the top of the sheet were written the words
"Jesus,.Mary, Joseph."

Both notes were unsigned. Pat read them hastily; and, chuckling, as he slipped them into his
pocket, started out.

He had proceeded but a few steps, however,
when he suddenly hesitated, took off his hat,
scratched his head for a moment, and, turning,
went back into the house.

Five minutes' reflection had sufficed to decide
him as to what he should do.

V

It was two hours later when Pat started out
again, and this time he went directly down to the
fruit-shop of Pietro Socola, where a most unexpected and festive scene greeted him.

The little old man, surrounded by a dozen or more of his countrymen (and others were coming and going), was opening bottles of wine and drinking freely.

As Pat entered, Socola bowed delightedly, and, filling a glass, presented it to him.

Everybody was laughing and drinking, and the host, although it was yet scarce ten o'clock in the morning, showed the effect of many glasses in his flushed face and hilarious spirits.

Not understanding in the least, but unable to resist so social a spirit, Pat, at the signal, raised the glass to his lips. It was only when some one pronounced the name "Pietro Socola Junio" that the situation flashed upon his comprehension.

Unto the house of Socola a son had been born.

The last time Pat had met the old man, a year ago, on the night of his wedding, he had grasped his hand in congratulation, and he did so again now.

"Accept me congratulations, Misther Socola," he exclaimed; and, with a twinkle in his eye, raising his glass again, "Heer's luck to the junior partner in the future firrm av Socola an' Son. May he niver cross 'is father an' niver boss 'is mother, an' be a shinin' example to all 'is yunger brothers an' sisters!"

Hearty laughter greeted this toast, and the old man insisted on refilling the glasses all round, saying, in Italian, to the men as he did so, "He has come a great distance to wish me joy. Keep his glass full."

Socola was not a heavy drinker, and his voice was already growing unsteady.

While they stood here, the one-eyed man whom Pat had recognized in the shadow the night before joined the group. He winced visibly, Pat thought, on perceiving him in this crowd, and while he and Socola touched glasses, Pat withdrew, and, joining some of the men whom he knew, walked out upon the levee.

When he returned, an hour later, he glanced into Socola's shop. The hitherto childless old man, translated by his tardy honors into a state of gleeful irresponsibility, had by this time gotten right royally drunk, and now some friends were trying to induce him to go home.

Pat laughed to himself as he saw him stagger up to the carriage door. "Arrah, musha!" he exclaimed, "sure an' it's a holy thing to be a father! Faith an' he waddles like a puddle-dthrake on a hatchin' day! I hope the young duck'll be big enough to crowd murdher out av the ould dthrake's heart, if ut's in ut."

The truth was, Pat had gone down to Socola to propose that they confess themselves mutually aggrieved, and proceed to settle the matter at once by a square hand-to-hand fist-fight.

He had withheld the facts about the wedding until Socola had first lied about it. He was willing to fight for the truth. If Socola wanted to fight for the lie, let him come and "have it out" then and there; or if the old man preferred to have a subordinate member of the Mafia to represent him in the affair, let him send any one of them to him.

It was only as a vague intangibility that Pat objected to deal with the Mafia.

He was sure that as soon as Socola should see that all he demanded was a "fair showing" they could come to a satisfactory understanding: so little did he comprehend the nature of the man with whom he had to deal, or the character of the organization which threatened him.

As Pat surmised, Socola had not yet even heard of his offence. The two men who went to make their reports were, like himself, treated to wine, and saw their host carried home *hors de combat.*

As Pat hesitated at Socola's door, the one-eyed man was coming out, and they met, face to face.

Pat touched his hat. The Sicilian responded by a like salutation, and would have passed on, but Pat detained him:

"Shtop a bit, Misther —— ; sure, I don't know yer name, but whilst no one's by I'd like to thank ye for the bit of a love-letther ye sint me last night."

The man shrugged his shoulders. "Loaf-a-letther?" he asked, with inimitable blandness. "Me, I no write-a northeen."

"Mebbe ye don't call it a love-letther itself. Now I do think again, I belave it's not a heart wud a dart run through ut for a bookay at the top o' the sheet, but a couple o' shin-bones forninst a graveyard photograph wud a company shmile on 'im. But sure what's left out av the crest is indicated in the text. Ye've hinted purty clear at the piercin' o' me palpitator at the end o' the po'm."

Fumbling in his pocket, he now brought out the two letters.

"Pity ye cudn't get ould Socola to set for a Cupid aimin' wud his bow an' arrer at me hearrt. Ye see, Irish litherature is different ag'in from Italian. Sure an' if a bunch o' Paddies wint into the tinder correspondence like this, like as not they'd have me in a picture, peg an' all, shlapin' in the heart av a rose, like they do be in Hoyt's Gerrman Cologne advertizemints, an' mebbe a bumble-bee wud ould Socola's face on 'im threatenin' the unconscious shlaper wud wan av his regular breech-loaders! Ye see, it 'd be a bit cheerful, but aqually to the point. Sure there's no life nor joy in a bare shin-bone, lest ye'd have it raised like a fearless sprig o' shillelah."

By this time he had opened both letters.

"Now," he continued, "droth an' I don't know which o' these two shtate dokimints ye sint me, or whether ye're wan o' thim scriptural chaps that kapes yer right hand in ignorance o' the thricks o' the left, an' yer two hands unbeknowinst to wan anither have sint me a frindly warrnin'; but r'a'ly and truly I'm very much obliged to ye."

Pat had given him no chance to reply, but now

he saw that the Italian's attitude was one of protest.

"Know northeen 'bouth," he was saying, gently.

"Whut! D'ye mane to say ye niver sint me nayther wan o' dthese letthers?"

"Know northeen 'bouth," he repeated, with an apathy of manner that was almost convincing.

Pat scratched his head.

"Mary Ann's mother-in-law!" he exclaimed, and, after a pause:

"Thin who in the name o' Donnybrook Fair done ut? Ye're the only mon who *cud* write ut. Sure none o' thim chaps last night knowed northin' about the throuble at Socola's marriage till I towld ut, an' faith ye're the only mon there that knowed I shpoke the truth."

The old man shrugged his shoulders.

"Me, I no know 'f ees-a thrue."

This was too much.

"Don't know if ut's thrue! The divil ye don't! An' didn't ye come the night o' the marriage an' explain to me, worrd for worrd, the way Socola put the Mafia currse on him that 'd tell?"

The Sicilian smiled. "Me, I know northeen 'bouth-a Signor Socola—northeen 'bouth-a Mafia —northeen 'bouth-a northeen!"

"An' ye weren't at the Di Carlos' this night twelvemonth past?"

"Scuza me, my frien', 'f you please. 'M in-a gread-a hoary. Me, 'm-a allawa fo' business."

He hesitated here, and, looking round cautiously, lowered his voice as he took Pat's hand.

"Tell-a you thrue," he said, with a nearer approach to animation than he had yet shown—"tell-a you thruc, 'f I was-a ged a ledther ligue thad, me, I would-a theng God I haf time run quig hide-a myselve. Well—goo'-by! Hofe-a you good lug." And he turned away.

A sudden light came into the Irishman's face.

"Howld on a bit!" he exclaimed. "Howld—on—a—bit! I've a purrty thick shkull on me, but I do begin to see the dthrift 'f yer iloquence. Plaze to presint me complimints to the gintleman that sint me the letthers, if ye do chance to run aground av 'im on the boulevards, an' tell 'im *I'll not run, nor hide nayther!*"

Gathering emphasis here by a moment's silence, he leaned forward and looked the Sicilian squarely in the eye.

"There's a bit av a song we do sing in the ould counthry. Perchance ye've niver heerd ut, but I'm that interested in the cultivation av yer mind I'll tell ut out to ye partly:

> "'S'int Patthrick was a gintleman,
>   And kem av dacent people;
> He built a church in Dublin town
>   An' on ut put a shteeple.
> His father was a Gallagher,
>   His mother was a Brady,
> His aunt was an O'Shaughnessy,
>   His uncle was O'Grady.

So success attind S'int Patthrick's fist,
For he was a saint so clever—
Oh, he gave the shnakes and toads a twist
That bothered thim forever.'

"Ye see, that's a beautiful po'm, Misther—Misther Know-northin', wud solud Irish sintimints, an' the whole moral law jellied down into shtandin'-shape in the chorus."

He moved backwards a step here, and touched his own breast as he continued:

"The 'umble perrson ye do see before ye is a fractional descindant along 'th bein' a namesake o' the gintleman, S'int Patthrick himself, an', up to the prisent moment, sure *success has always attinded his fist!* We're av a pedigree that has no use for toads norr shnakes, norr onything toadyin' norr shnakin'—beyant givin' thim a twist that'll bother thim forever. Sure I kem down this morrnin with the 'onerable intintion o' latherin' the bit av a varmint, Socola, wud me fist, but the wave o' prosperity—or posterity, whichiver ye like—lifted him beyant me entirely. But I'll be down again, plaze God, in a couple o' days, *wud S'int Patthrick's weapon!*"

He held up his clinched fist. "And now," he added, extending his hand, "I do wish ye good-day!"

The Sicilian stood and looked after him a moment in bewilderment, and then he said something, presumably in Anglo-Italian; at least, it sounded like "Damfool," a word not found in

English print—even in the new Century Diction-
ary.

By a strange coincidence, Pat said the same
word as he turned the corner. He had picked up
a good deal of the colloquial *patois* of these people.

When Socola returned to his shop on the next
day, a little withered grotesque impersonation of
bilious pomposity, his inner consciousness nevertheless corresponded to his own best ideal of a
noble, dignified, and tender father.

Indeed, he felt father to all the world, excepting, of course, the dear woman to whom he was
husband ; and this exception was as distinct and
as tender and sensitive as only this particularly
potent occasion could make it.

He had hitherto known nothing so exquisitely
refined as the almost reverential tenderness with
which his intensely masculine heart went out to
the sallow little mother and the tiny yellow man-
child who lay upon her breast to-day.   The com-
bination was something to live for, to fight for, to
die for—almost.

And Pat's offence was against this embodiment
of sacredness—this woman—this infant.

The accidental wife—the incidental babe! How
the thought would cheapen the sacred possessions
in the vulgar mind!   To Socola himself, when it
all dimly recurred to him, it seemed almost a dream
which he no longer more than half believed.   If
he were choosing again, he could choose no other

woman of all the world ; and surely he would have no other babe than this!

When the two men, the one with the blind eye and the other, came together in the shop on this second day and gave to Socola, separately, as opportunity offered, the sign of the Mafia, it was a signal to withdraw hastily with them into his private office.

A subordinate gives the summons to his chief only when a communication of importance is pending.

When he returned to the shop, an hour later, the old man was still blue about the lips, and his hands trembled as he swore promiscuous oaths indiscriminately at the employés of the shop for imaginary offences.

The two men had gone silently together out of the side door with their heads down.

Although Pat was restless in view of an impending row and eager to have it over, gauging the probable duration of an Italian's spree by the Hibernian standard, he did not think it worth while to return to the city for several days.

The gentleman from Palermo had in the meantime had much time for sober reflection. He had, of course, heard of Pat's projected visit, and was ready for him—with an extended hand.

Indeed, no crafty diplomat ever confounded an adversary with a more gracious and smiling suavity than that with which he greeted and disarmed his ingenuous guest when, on the Thursday following, Pat re-entered his shop.

Socola's English vocabulary, at best a matter of a few hundred words, seemed to-day to have shrunken until it was less only than his comprehension.

He failed utterly to understand that there could be anything disagreeable in his visitor's mission.

The interview, a ludicrous pantomimic affair throughout, ended by a mutual hand-shaking confession of friendly feeling, and Pat went away entirely satisfied that either a mistake had been made, the Sicilian had forgotten his oath, or the coming of the babe had indeed crowded murder out of the father's heart.

He had personally no longer a quarrel with the old man. He had refuted the lie, and was simply willing to stand by the refutation.

If he had glanced backwards as he left the shop and seen the menacing scowl that followed his receding figure, he would perhaps have understood.

From Socola's presence he went up "home," to the Di Carlos'. Here, to his dismay, two more notes of solemn warning awaited him.

Both were unsealed. Indeed, they were written on unfolded scraps of paper, and were found slipped in beneath the door, just as the first had been.

When the signora had called Pat into an inner room, she closed the door and turned gray with pallor as she handed them to him.

Her fear of the law, of death, of purgatory, of hell, was vague and as nothing to her terror of the vengeance of the Mafia. None of her family were members of the dread organization, but she remembered only too vividly how the husband of her first-cousin had years ago received just such a warning as this, and one day he had gone as usual to his work and had never come home again.

Ever since she had had the letters in her possession she had felt as if the angel of death were hovering over the house.

As she stood at Pat's side and saw him read the words of warning she began to cry.

"Fo' God sague, Meester Pad, wad you ees-a been do?" she moaned.

Pat laughed.

"Well, ma'am," said he, "at the present moment I'm jist afther a second visit to yer yung frind, Socola. We're that thick ye'd think we were twins—or thriplets mebbe, an' I was two an' he only wan — the way he does bow an' schrape right an' left to me."

"Socola!"

If Pat had said he had just returned from a visit to his Satanic majesty, she would not have been much more startled. "Socola! You ees-a been see Socola! Fo' God sague, how you ees-a fin' 'im?"

"Find 'im! Faith an' he's as well as cud be expected afther havin' a fine b'y a-Sunda' night. Ye see, it does be very dangerous whin a firrst b'y is borrn to an ould man. It does fly to his head an' set 'im ravin' crazy. I b'lave the docthers do call it puerile faver. Did ye niver heer av ut?"

The woman was too much concerned even to realize that he was jesting.

"Wad 'e sayce to you?" she asked, eagerly.

"Sure an' he sez he wants to name the yungsther afther me; but I'm that proud I won't allow ut. Ye see, the shtyle av beauty in the Rooney family has been preserrved through thick an' thin wud great pains, an' I'd niver consint to take a risk on Socola's f'atures, wud no promise av relafe from her loyal accidency the madam. Ye see, a proud man must protect his name as well as his fame."

This bantering, really only a ruse to gain time to reflect a little on the situation, was becoming very trying to the signora. Pat became suddenly conscious that there were genuine tears in her eyes.

"Niver mind, now, niver mind," he said, with real feeling. "Don't fret yersilf because a couple o' cranks do sind me a valentine. Faith, there's northin' in ut, but mebbe a thrick o' the shoe thrade to dthrive me out o' the competition."

He then briefly reviewed his two visits to the old Sicilian, omitting the occasion of his going, and laying special stress on all the pleasant features of their meetings.

But she was not to be so easily appeased. She

lowered her voice almost to a whisper when she spoke again :

"Tell-a you thrue, Meester Pad, me an' Carlo ees-a been hear sometheen."

"Heerd something, did ye? An' whut was ut?"

"Plenny young mans ees-a tell me an' Carlo you ees-a say sometheen 'boud-a C'lotta an' Signor Socola. All-a peoples ees-a talkin' 'boud."

"They are, are they? An' whut if I did? An' whut did ye say ?"

"Me? Of-a coze I sayee ees-a no true : Socola ees-a neva was-a lova-a C'lotta."

"Ye did, did ye ? An' whut did 'er father say?"

"Carlo sayee you ees-a just a mague-a lill fun ; *'z no true.*"

Pat scratched his head. "An' betune the two av yez ye've made me out a bloomin' liur, now—haven't yez?"

"'F I mague you oud a lie, I mague you just-a pardner fo' myselve. Fo' God sague, lis'n ad me, Meester Pad. 'Z no time fo' talk 'boud lie. 'Z-a time fo' business. You muz-a go just-a so quig as you can-a go an' tell all-a doze young mans you was-a just-a play'n'."

Even the strong friendship evinced by her intense anxiety failed to palliate the affront of her proposition in Pat's eyes. He looked at her, bit his lip, and, without a word, turned on his heel and left her.

As he passed out the door the sound of a sob reached his ear. He was back in a moment.

" Fo' the love o' shad, ma'am, don't—*don't fret.*
Niver mind, now, I tell ye. If ye cry anither dthrop
I'll howl out a high tenor mesilf to match ye. Sure
it 'll be all right now, I'll promise ye. I'll shtep
out by-an'-by till I do find the crowd, an' I'll make
a bit av a spache that 'll silence thim, an' they'll
niver lay a hand on me. I'll promise ye that.
Come on out, now."

" Tell 'm ees-a no true, Meester Pad. Say you
was just-a mague fun. An' anyhow, I b'lief ces-a
bedder you go 'way."

She sobbed again.

" Well, I declare, ma'am, I'm that ashamed av
ye! Ye're frettin' yersilf about northin' — an'
Socola an' me like two peas, a green wan an' a
dthry wan, in wan pod. Come on out, now. Sure
the crowd around the shteps are all half ashlape,
an' they'll have no fun till ye do come an' wake
thim up wud a good laugh. Come, now. The
royal consorrt an' all yer majesty's loyal subjects
'll not dare open parliamint till the queen does
arrive."

With a comical bobbing courtesy he made way
for her to pass out. Sniffling and wiping her eyes,
she escaped to her own room for a moment, but it
was not long before she joined the circle on the
banquette.

It was a sultry summer afternoon, and the scene
about the doors was drowsy enough indeed. The
little father Di Carlo nodded on his barrel. The
baby, a mosquito-netting stretched over her face,

lay sleeping in her willow cradle at his side. Several men lounged on the benches, talking lazily in Italian, and fighting the flies with their red cotton kerchiefs.

Within the shop the boy Pasquale stood languidly opening oysters for a black girl, who, leaning with half her tall length spread over the counter, indolently chewed a cud of gum as she waited with bovine patience while her bucket was slowly filling.   -

Half-way down the block a chattering group of neighborhood children, among whom was a generous sprinkling of Di Carlos, were playing in the doubtful shade of a tallow - tree. Some sat with their laps piled high with china blossoms, which they strung on threads into fragrant purple necklaces. A pair of girls played "jack-stones" on the fronts of their dress - skirts lapped one over the other on the ground, while others, arm in arm, promenaded up and down, shading themselves, after the fashion of Paul and Virginia, with tall green banana leaves, purloined from over a neighboring fence.

Somewhat apart from the other children, and nearer the shop, two taller girls sat crocheting cotton lace, while their toddling charges slept at their sides.

Pat, whose seat commanded a view of them, was not long in discovering that the smaller of these two was Carlotta, and, while he passed idly from one subject to another, challenging conversation at random with his drowsy company, he delighted to watch her as the oblique rays of the sun revealed her each moment more clearly to him.

"Five times thim two childer have dropped their nadles to measure their lace, or fringe, or whativer ye call it," he said, presently, laughing. "Sure I'm goin' to watch thim now, an' the seventh time they do measure ut I'll up an' be off. I've a call to make a spache to some o' me constituents, an' I must hunt thim up. I do fale as lazy as the fly on the banana here at me elbow. See him walk like a bug from wan black ind to take a sup at the ither, too lazy to raise his wings an' fly. There they go again, the childer, God bless thim! measurin' again! Six times in forrty minutes. Sure they've harrdly time to put a tuck in ut betune the two measures."

The signora laughed heartily. "Lis'n ad-a Meester Pad! Pood a tug in-a lace! I swea' you would-a mague a dead dog laugh."

Her laughter did Pat good. "Sure a tuck or a him are all wan to a tailor in leather," he replied, unconsciously coming into the domain of Carlyle's thought.

"But tell me, ma'am," he continued, "how do ye ladies him fringes, onyway? I cudn't forr the life av me him a fringe, nor scallop it nayther."

She screamed with laughter now. "My God! Hem a fringe! Nobody can-a hem a fringe."

"Is that so? An' d' ye fringe the hims? I'm not jokin'. Faith I niver so much as fringed a scallop in me life, let alone a him. Tell me, now, d' yez dthraw threads, orr dthrop stitches, or pucker it on the bias? Och, there now! I must go! the two girrls beyant are measurin' their scallops again. Well, so long, ma'am! I'll be back in the autumn, plaze God, 'whin the l'aves begin to fall.' "

She was laughing so that she could not speak when Pat rose to go.

"Since ye do insist upon ut," he added, as he turned away, "I b'lave I'll change me summer plans an' come back be supper-time. Put an exthra sup av coffee in the dthripper, plaze, an' dthrop the name av Rooney promiscuously in the pots."

" All-a righd! Muz-a be shore, shore come to supper. Prormus you somtheen good."

This was a thing Pat rarely did; and she was delighted. Even had she not known that he would come in laden with paper bags full of good things to add to the supper-table, she would have been just as glad to set his plate in between little Pat's and Carlotta's.

Pat had no trouble in finding the " constituents " whom he wanted to meet. He knew that at this hour certain Italians would be sure to congregate at their favorite rendezvous, a coffee-house near the levee. He was glad to find Tramonetti, and others who were present on the former occasion, already there.

It took but a few moments to repeat his former

account of the Socola wedding, which he colored with new drolleries in the narration, and to add—. and this was the object of his visit — the item carelessly omitted before — viz., Socola's threat that the Mafia would avenge a betrayal of the affair.

This, he carefully explained, was the reason his good friends the Di Carlos had felt constrained to deny it. They were afraid of the Mafia. They couldn't understand how he and Socola understood each other perfectly now, and, after all, it was a small matter whether Socola had been jilted or not: who cared? It was a thing of the past. For himself, he only mentioned it again to prove that he hadn't lied before. The whole business was, he finally declared, "a timpest in a tay-pot," and the sooner forgotten the better. He ended by begging them not to "worry the madam" by saying anything more about it at the Di Carlos'.

"Sure the madam's been wapin' an' wailin' for feer I'll be kilt entirely. She thinks I'm out this minute tellin' ye all I was jokin' an' thryin' to back out av the whole shtatemint. Sure I'd back out in a minute if I knowed a back-shtep; but when I tuck dancin'-lessons in Paris whin I was a yungshter, I niver learrned the craw-fish movement, an' faith it's too late in life now to dthrag me wooden peg into a new figure. There's but three-quarrters av me left, onyhow, but it's three-quarrters av a *man's shape*, praise God, an' I'll not disgrace the fraction, for the likeness it does bear me mother, God rest her."

The crowd were rather still and subdued for some time after Pat left them.

"I'm sorry I ever opened my lips about Socola's business," said one, finally, in Italian; "but, anyhow, I told where I heard it."

"I never said anything to anybody," said another, "and I'm glad. I don't want any of his flock of vampires following me in the dark."

"But I'd hate to be in that Irishman's shoes!"

"In his one shoe, you mean. And me too. So would I."

VI

For several months after this things seemed to drift along as usual.

Pat's prosperity, already assured though plodding, had been unexpectedly accelerated by the sudden death of his partner, whose widow had preferred a settlement in cash to the possible risk of an investment subject to the vicissitudes of trade. This left Pat in sole possession of a promising little business, and he was doing well.

He still went "home" nearly every Sunday; and, as Carlotta had of late been especially kind to him, he began to feel that the materialization of his hopes was not far distant.

The youth Rubino still hung about the shop

with his accordion, and once Pat had found him
and Carlotta out walking together when he came
on Sunday afternoon. He said to himself that it
was all right for her to be happy in her own
youthful way, and he tried to feel glad. Indeed,
if he were not wholly so at the time, her hearty
greeting when she came home in a little while
made him forget it all.

So the winter passed—a second since the Socola
affair. In a month Carlotta would pass her eighteenth birthday. Things were coming very close.

Pat feared no opposition from the Di Carlo
parents. Indeed, the signora, in her relation of
unconscious mother-in-law elect, was a joy to his
Irish heart. She had evidently no suspicion of
the truth, and, in face of Pat's blossoming out
into a successful gentleman, had been unable to
refrain from throwing out occasional hints recall-
ing his early fancy for Carlotta. And Pat, the
while laughing in his sleeve, kept her in continual
suspense by hinting at other possible alliances,
as when he said:

"Sure an' I wush ye cud see the widder
Schmidt, how purrty an' yung she is since the
ould man's gone. Troth an' ye may heer any day
av an elopemint in high life. Sure I tould 'er we
betther wait till the Berrmuda is firrmly rooted
on the ould gintleman's grave—God rist 'im!—
an'—wud ye bel'ave?—she does northin' but
shprinkle it wud a watherin'-pot since."

"Oh-h-h, 'z-a shame fo' you, Meester Pad, talk

"like thad! Can get plenny pritty young-a woma' yed."

"I've not fully made up me mind yet, ma'am, sure, till I do see wull she turrn back all the capital she dthrew out av the thrade an' promise me a day off once a wake from cinnamon-cake till I do fale me pulse an' starrt fresh."

It was no wonder the signora missed Pat out of her daily life. He made so much fun. Was it strange she wanted to secure him?

It was at last Carlotta's birthday. Pat had come to town rather earlier than usual, intending to take her — alone for the first time — out for a ride. They would go up to the Carrollton Garden and sit on one of the little benches together under a tree; and when they came home they would tell "the madam" and ask her blessing.

He knew just the funny things he would say as he would present the little bald spot on his head for her maternal blessing. And then they would have to tell — or rather to ask — the father. He scratched his head a little nervously at this thought, and wished the ordeal were over; yet he would get through somehow, and "carry it off" with whatever inspiration the moment should bring.

He was dressed in his very best, and would have given much to wear his artificial leg for the occasion. He would have liked to appear as a whole man walking at her side to-night.

It was just merging into twilight when he approached the shop, and the family sat, as usual, about the doors.

"An' where's Lottie?" he asked, as he joined the circle.

He had never called for her in this way before, but he was too near the edge of things to-night to care to think.

"C'lotta ces-a just now gone oud-a walk weeth Giuseppe Rubino. Sid down, Meester Pad." And the signora lifted her foot from the rung of a stool and pushed it towards him.

He sat down, but he was uneasy.

After a little while, during which, the signora afterwards said, he had never been more lively or witty, he rose and left them.

For the last three Saturday evenings Carlotta had been out with Giuseppe when he came, but he had tried not to think seriously of it. But to-night! Had she not remembered? Did she not realize that to-day meant much to him—and to her? He would pass the hour until he should be *sure* to find her at home in his favorite retreat on the river-bank, alone. There would be no demand upon him here, and he could get himself together again; for he was keenly hurt.

As he left the Di Carlos', he could not see that two men — Sicilians they were — who stood together in the shadow of the wall across the way moved slowly after him until he stopped the car, when, quickening their paces, they also jumped aboard, one seating himself within, while the other passed out to the platform with the driver. Neither could he know when he crossed the wharf that these two men watched and by separate routes followed him at a distance as he disappeared among the shadows between the piles of freight along the pier.

The river was high, and when he reached his accustomed seat the floating wharf which was chained to the heavy timbers attracted him. He had never been down here, but a pair of hanging steps invited the folly of his descent to-night, and he had soon hobbled down and seated himself on the inner edge of the raft, and thus within the shadow of the pier above. It pleased his mood to get thus near the turbulent, restless waters for a while.

To sit in a little black shadow while he waited for Carlotta to come home with Giuseppe suited him to-night; while the booming, swelling, resistless river that lifted him upon its bosom and seemed threatening to submerge everything was typical of his love.

His thoughts had hardly begun to cool and shape themselves when, first vaguely, as at a distance, and now nearer, clearer, came the sound of an accordion.

On summer evenings, almost anywhere along the river-bank one may expect to find a sprinkling of accordion-players—usually German kitchen-courtships out for an airing—and there should have been nothing very startling in the sound ;

yet its first note made the Irishman's heart stand still. He knew the most distant reach of Giuseppe's accordion. It had come out to meet him too often in the evenings for him to mistake it now. It was coming very near, and soon he began to hear voices—Carlotta's and the youth's. They were sitting down on the wharf just above his head. Broken snatches of tunes proved that Giuseppe was toying thoughtlessly with his instrument, and while he played he was earnestly talking. Soon the music stopped altogether, the voice fell lower, more serious, more indistinct. It seemed to Pat that the boy talked for an age; but he could distinguish nothing.

But presently Carlotta spoke, clearly:

"No, no, Giuseppe. Hush! I can't lis'n at you!"

Then again Giuseppe muttered in a tone indistinct as to words, but full of pleading.

And now Carlotta again:

"Hush, I say, Giuseppe! I *mus'n't* lis'n at you! I wish I was dead! I hate you!—I hate myself! —I hate your music!—I hate everything! Before you came, I was satisfied. Everything was promise good, an' I never knowed no better. Now, when I put my finger in my ears, I hear you sing —I hear that music. Oh, I hate it all! To-night I ought to be home, and I am here with you—always with you."

He spoke more clearly now in Italian: "But why do you speak so, Carlotta? It is not true that you hate me. You love me—I know it, I feel it. Since first I saw you, I knew we were for each other."

"But no, Giuseppe. Hush, I say! I can't be for you. Since two years I am promised. My word is passed."

"And who is it that holds a child by her word when she loves him not?"

"Oh, hush, Giuseppe! He don't hold me. I hold myself. He is the best man in all the world. He loves me more than even my maw. Since I was *so* big he loved me and I loved him good; but since you came I am not the same. I am not fit. I run away with you, and then when I see him I am sorry, and speak kind with him, but all the time I see you. He trusts me, Giuseppe, same like I trust the blessed Mother—he even put my name by her name once—and you have all broken me hearted, Giuseppe, an' made me turn away from him. I wish I was dead!—and you !—and him !"

There were tears in her voice.

"But listen, Carlotta. You don't understand. Nothing is true but love. Everything else comes after—promises, mistakes, all—everything ! Love is from God Almighty. He never sends love like mine but he sends the answer too. For two months I have read my answer in your eyes, and was satisfied ; but it was sweet to wait, to sing, to play, to laugh all around it, making believe I was not sure. But *I am sure. You are mine !*"

“Oh, but no, no, no, Guiseppe! I am not for you. If I was that mean, God would never bless me nor you. It would be a curse. You cannot understand.”

“Who is this coward who holds you?”

“But hush! He is no coward, Giuseppe. Me, I am a coward—but not him. It was me what made him speak love. You talk about God! For what does God let us make mistakes! How can we be *sure?* I was crazy for him, and in my heart I felt sure—*sure* it was love, and I told him, Giuseppe. I made him to love me. And now— if only you go away, Giuseppe! If you love me true, go, and let me have peace and not trouble. Go far, and let me forget the sound of your music—let me forget your eyes—let me not see your shape in the air which way I turn. Then it will all pass away, and I will be like before. I love him good, Giuseppe. I am not a liar. Only now I am like in a dream, and in my dream I see only you. Now I see, I know, what you meant, Giuseppe, when you said in your sleep I stood before you. But soon I will wake. I will see his kind eyes, and it will pass. He will never know.”

“And who is this man for whom you put me away?”

“It is time enough, Giuseppe; but better if you never know him. Go far away.”

“I go not away without you, Carlotta. Every day I will come till I get you. I will walk by your side before this man, and when he looks at us he will see he is a fool.”

“I walk with you no more, Giuseppe. To-night finishes. Come, let us go. I heard a noise, and just now over there a shadow moved. I am afraid. Come.”

As they rose to go, the accordion, which Giuseppe grasped hastily in rising, opening by its own weight, sent out an attenuated discordant wail. And to Pat, sitting alone in the shadow beneath, it sounded like a weird Banshee’s shriek coming from far over the seas.

The tender tremor in Carlotta’s voice when first she spoke Giuseppe’s name had struck his heart like a death-knell, and the words which followed were but as clods falling upon a coffin. The girl’s loyalty through it all seemed to mock him like a hymn at a grave. It was as the silver sheen upon the silken fabric of a shroud—the smile upon the face of death.

For a long time after they had gone the heavy timbers about him were not more still than he.

Once he thought he heard soft steps above him. If he had risen, he might have seen two dark figures peering stealthily about as if looking for some one. They might have been assassins in ambush.

But Pat did not even glance upward.

Can any one, by simply imagining, be sure he half understands how this man felt? or must he have passed through the shades of a like sorrow

"THE HEAVY TIMBERS ABOUT HIM WERE NOT MORE STILL THAN HE"

to know its black, bleak depths and the hopelessness of it?   It is hard to say.

His first movement was to cast his eyes about him upon the water.   It was all around him—so near—so inviting.   It seemed almost to call him. It would have been so easy, from where he sat, just to lean over and over, like Maupassant's little blue-and-red soldier, as if he were trying to drink. There would be only a few bubbles—fit emblems of his life and its story—and so it would end.

Had he not promised her his grave whenever it would be a safe bridge over her troubles?   The time had come.   Or had it come?   Would the plunge be for her sake or his own?   Was he, after all, a coward—he who had never run from a foe in his life—who had even fought and vanquished his *potheen* with a flask in his pocket?

Distinct rapid footsteps above startled him, and he raised his eyes.   As he did so, a bundle fell at his side into the water, and the steps retreated.

He seemed to see a struggle as the dark object twisted for a second within the rings of the eddy that swallowed it down; but he could not be sure. In a moment, however, he heard, quite near, the thin, wiry cry of a young kitten.   He looked about him and above, but could see nothing of it, though the sound came again and again.   Finally, however, a desperate wail located the sufferer.

On the outside of the heavy timbers, caught in its fall by a protruding splinter or spike, the wretched little creature hung suspended, its own weight and struggles imprisoning it more securely each moment within the notch.

The struggling contents of the whirling bundle were explained. This little unfortunate had slipped out of the open bag in its fall, to perish high and dry in the night wind, or to be scorched by the sun should it survive the night.

Pat regarded the writhing little form a moment only.

"Sure we're in the same boat, kitty, you an' me," he said, aloud; "we're wan too many in a crowded worrld. But, plaze God, I'll give ye the same chance I'll take meself—in the name o' Him that shaped the two av us."

With this, seizing the fragment of a broken oar, he swung himself outside the timbers.

At the sound of his voice two black shadows rushed noiselessly across the wharf, and, quickly reaching the edge, peered over.

What they saw was only a whining young kitten crawling feebly along the raft.

The upward reach with the oar which liberated the little beast and sent him back to life had thrown his deliverer accidentally backward. The grip of his one leg about the post had served only to let him down, down, gently, noiselessly, into the eddying current, which sucked him under the raft without even a twirl or a twist. There was not so much as a gurgle of the waters as he sank.

The black figures waited a long time, lying on their faces and listening, and two stilettos were drawn and ready. When the voice should speak again, they would do their work quickly; for the emissaries of the Mafia are wont to use despatch.

It was past midnight, and the moon was rising, when at last, despairing and mystified, they separated reluctantly, and by different routes went to report another failure to old Pietro Socola, their chief.

The Di Carlos wondered with great anxiety why Pat did not come home, and all during the night the signora started at every sound, fancying she heard his wooden peg ascending the stairs.

It was on the second day afterwards when a boy in the shop read from the daily paper that the body of a one-legged man had been washed up against a coal-barge floating in the river near Canal Street.

The father Di Carlo went immediately to investigate the matter, and when he came home an hour later, and the family gathered about him, anxious to hear the news, he only shook his head sadly, and, taking from his handkerchief an old red baby shoe, he said, "It was in his inside pocket."

Customers who came in at the time, and people passing by, thought from their distress that a member of the family was dead.

Carlotta, trembling and white as marble, went away alone.

An investigation of Pat's affairs and effects disclosed a will, made some years before, bequeathing to Carlotta all his worldly goods.

A large proportion of this—which proved quite a neat competence—she expended, despite her mother's frugal protest that it could do him no good, in a handsome marble shaft to his memory. In its unique inscription, which was of her own dictation, she sought to make some sort of reparation for the sin of which she accused herself.

The monument still stands in the corner of St. Patrick's Cemetery, and reads:

IN MEMORY

OF

Patrick Rooney,

INTEND OF CARLOTTA DI CARLO,

AGE, 42 YEARS.

And on any All-Saints' Day, Carlotta and Giuseppe, with their flock of beautiful children, may be seen to stop there for a while, leaving a bouquet of plush-topped coxcombs and a cross of white chrysanthemums.

BUD ZUNTS'S MAIL

BUD ZUNTS'S MAIL

A Romance of the Simpkinsville Post=office

"'Nothin' for you, Bud Zunts!' Seem like I ought to've heerd that often enough to know it by this time—but I don't. I don't even to say half b'lieve it when I do hear it—no, I don't."

Bud Zunts had just come out of the Simpkinsville post-office, and, mounting the seat of his wagon, he turned his oxen's heavy heads slowly homeward.

"Th'ain't been a night sence she's been a-sayin' it," he continued, as the ponderous beasts made a lunge out of the deep ruts—"th'ain't been a night in three year sence she's been a-sayin' it but I've mo'n half expected to see her han' out a letter, an' I c'n see the purty blue veins in 'er han's when she'd be handin' it out — " He chuckled. "'N' I c'n see 'er smile like 's ef she was tickled to see me paid at last for stoppin' every night in all these year t' inquire. 'Tis purty tiresome — some nights — but of co'se when a man's a-co'tin' he can't expec'—he can't expec'— Tell the truth, I reck'n I dun'no' nothin' 'bout co'tin'. I wush 't I did know. Seem like ma tried to teach me a little bit of every kind o’ learnin’ she knew about, but don’t seem like she could ’ve knew much about co’tin’, nohow.

“Th’ain’t never been a time, turn my min’ free ez I can, thet I c’n understan’ how in creation pa ever co’ted ma—th’ain’t, for a fac’. I’ve ’magined it every way I c’n twis’ things, an’ I’ve made ’er young *an’* purty, ’n’ I’ve plumped ’er out—pore ma was awful thin and rawboned, jest like me, ever sence I c’n ricollec’—but I’ve plumped ’er out in my min’, ’n’ I’ve frizzled ’er hair, ’n’ smoothed down ’er cowlick, but even then I ’ain’t been able to see ’er bein’ co’ted ’thout fussin’—noways. Pore ma. She cert’n’y was the best an’ the most worrisome woman thet God ever made.

“I won’t say she had was *the* best neither, for I been a-co’tin’ Miss C’delia now three year ’n’ six mont’s an’ three nights to-night, ’n’ watchin’ ’er constant, an’ I *b’lieve* she’s ez good a woman ez ma was — ever’ bit — ’thout ’er worrisome ways, too—pore ma.”

Bud Zunts mused here a few moments, but presently he chuckled again :

“Here I set a-talkin’ ’bout co’tin’, ’s ef everybody knowed it, ’n’ I dun’no’ ez *any*body do but *me*. Wonder ef Miss C’delia think I’d stop every night for fo’ year—goin’ on—’n’ ast for letters ’n’ never git a one, ’n’ wait tell the las’ person goes out every night, ’n’ stop ’n’ lock the gate ’n’ climb over the pickets (she thinks I lock the gate on the outside 'n' fling the key back—she mus' think I take a mighty good aim to hit the aidge o' the do'-sill every time). Wonder ef she do think I do that-a-way ever' night, th' way I do, jest to be a-doin'? 'N' I wonder ef she ever heerd me a-tryin' the winder-shetters to make shore nobody 'd bother 'er du'in' the night?"

He laughed softly.

"Move on, Bute! Bute 'n' Fairy 's about ez down-hearted a pair o' oxen to-night ez ever I see."

The roads were heavy and wet, and man, beasts, and wagon were old, so the equipage moved slowly, bogging and sputtering occasionally in soft spots —like the soliloquy.

"Yas," he resumed, presently, " I been a,co'tin Miss C'delia for fo' year — goin' on—'n' I 'ain't never spoke yet—many nights ez I've laid off to. Ef she didn't keep the pos'-office, so's I c'n see 'er every evenin' an' a Sund'y mornin's thoo the little winder, 'n' get my daily *in*cour'gements 'n' *dis*-cour'gements, I'd 've spoke long ago—'n' maybe 'stid o' me an' Bute 'n' Fairy trudgin' 'long so slow in the mud to-night, not keerin' much whether or when we git home, I might be—we might be—she might—

"I do declare, the way I do set up here 'n' giggle is *re*dic'lous!

" W'o, Bute! These here slushy ruts is awful —mud clean up to the hub!"

So Bud Zunts proceeded on his lonely way,

until he finally reached his own gate—the humble
entrance to the two-roomed cabin that dignified
his meagre little farm, lying on the edge of Simpkinsville.

After the front door was closed to-night, Miss
Cordelia Cummins, the post-mistress, stood for a
long time behind her pigeon-hole barrier, looking
over the remaining mail.

"Here's mo' letters 'n enough for Kate Clark
—'n' papers, too," she said, audibly. "Some o'
the papers got 'er po'try printed in 'em, an' some
'ain't. Here's one o' hers now— 'A Midnight
Monody'; wonder what that means? It's hers,
I'm shore, 'cause it's signed by her pen-nondy-
plume, 'Silver Sheen.'

"I s'pose that *is* mo' suited for a po'try-writer's
name 'n 'Kate Clark' 'd be; but seem to me I
wouldn't deny my name, noways — po'try or no
po'try!

"These paper-wrappers stick mighty tight. I
'mos' split this 'n gettin' it back on.

"I see she's got two letters from the telegraph
station. Funny how thin an' fine that young man
does write—like he craved to whisper. He writes
precizely like a lady. Ef ever I did get a letter
from a male person, I'd choose for 'im to have a
mannish handwrite—'clare I would.

"Two *f'om* 'im to-day an' one *to* 'im. Well,
I'm proud to see Kate's a-keepin' 'm where he
b'longs. I dun'no', either; come to feel 'em, I

b'lieve her one letter's heavier'n both o' hisn; 'n' it's writ on pink paper, too; 'n' it's got smellin' stuff in it—shore's I've got a nose!

"I do wonder ef Kate writes love-verses to 'im! I hardly b'lieve it of 'er—though I dun'no'.

"Here's at least fo' love-letters in a row, 'n' I don't doubt the las' one of 'em is so sweet inside thet ef they was lef' open in the sun the honey-bees 'd light on 'em.

"Sometimes I do wush 't I'd get a letter myself —jest a reel out-'n'-out love-letter, same ez ef I wasn't pos'-mist'ess—not thet I'd b'lieve any writ-ten-out foolishness, of co'se—but jest for the fun of it. Maybe ef I didn't handle so many I wouldn't think about it.

"I do hones' b'lieve thet th' ain't another per-son a-livin' in the county—that is, no grown-up person—black nor white, but's got a letter some time 'r other—less'n, of co'se, Bud Zunts.

"But I'm jest a *leetle* bit ahead o' you, Bud, on that. I *know* you 'ain't never got none, 'n' you don't know how many I get.

"Sometimes I do hate to tell 'im th' ain't nothin' for 'im, pore boy! Lis'n at me a-callin' 'im boy, 'n' he a month 'n' three days older'n me, an' I'm— jest to think, I'm purty nigh ez ole ez Bud Zunts, an' he gray ez a rat! But I reck'n his ma wor-reted 'im all but gray.

"Pore Mis' Zunts! She was a good woman, Mis' Zunts was, but I've seen some worse ones I'd a heap ruther live with.

"She cert'n'y was worrysome—but I don't doubt Bud is the best-trained young man in the county to-day. He turned out 'is toes, 'n' said 'ma'am' an' 'sir,' when he warn't no mo'n knee-high to a toad-frog. An' he knew the whole Shorter Catechism 'fore he could pernounce a half o' the words; . but as for understandin' it—well, I often think maybe that's reserved for Heaven, anyway.

"I do wonder what pore Bud does when he goes home of nights? It mus' be awful lonesome for 'im when the lamp's lit—ef he lights a lamp. You never can tell jest how low down a man lef' to hisself will get. Pore Bud! They's jest one thing his ma didn't teach him—an' that's cour'ge. Sometimes the most c'rageous person agoin' 'll seem to squench all the cour'ge out of another person, 'n' not mean to do it, neither.

"Now I know Bud's a-yearnin' to speak to me —ef I know anything—'n' sometimes I'm a'mos' tempted to help 'im out, but I'd never half respect 'im ef I did—nor myself neither.

"I did start one night to say, '*I'm sorry* th' ain't nothin' fo' you to-night, Bud Zunts,' 'n' then I wouldn't—*an' I won't!* I won't have it said I give 'im *that* much encour'gement.

"'Ef he's a womanish man, I won't match 'im by bein' a mannish woman. But I do wush 't I knew ef he was wearin' woollen next to 'is skin or not." She sighed. "Ef—ef Bud was to take the pneumony to-morrer—well, I dun'no' what I'd do, but I reck'n, knowin' what's on his min' an' what's on mine, it 'd be my abounding duty to go, 'thout sayin' a word, an' nurse 'im thoo it—to sort o' finish out the pantomime he's done started. But it 'd pleg me awful—'deed it would. I've laid awake mo'n one col' spell jest a-prayin' the Lord not to make it my clair duty to go an' nurse Bud thoo a spell o' sickness befo' he's foun' cour'ge to speak 'is min' to me. I *would* o' prayed the Lord to *give* 'im cour'ge—but *I won't do it!* Ef it's come to sech a pass thet a man has to ask me to marry 'im with the cour'ge *I* prayed for—then I'll keep pos'-office all my days, 'n' jest live along with Polly like I do." As she spoke she glanced up at a parrot, who sat half asleep on his perch near.

"I won't give Bud no encour'gement; no I won't, Poll—*nor myself neither.* I won't even make a extry yard o' tattin' tell he's spoke—'deed I won't. But I do wush 't I knew 'bout his wearin' good flannen next to 'is skin. These red-headed 'n' red-whiskered folks is mighty thin an' delicate-skinned, 'n' Bud's been so watched over 'n' preserved by 'is ma, he ain't never took none of his diseases in proper season, not even the whuppin'-cough, 'n' the first heavy col' he gets 'll go purty hard on 'im. I do b'lieve Mis' Zunts wouldn't o' let 'im cut 'is teeth ef she could o' helped it—jest so she could o' had the excitement o' chewin' for 'im.

"I declare! Ef Sally Ann Brooks ain't a-sendin' a postal-card to New York to order a ready-made night-gownd! I do vow some folks 'ain't got a bit o' modesty—'n' her own name mentioned, 'n' her measure too; 'n' everybody 'twixt here 'n' New York liable to read it—'n' most o' the postal clerks young men at that!

"They's a good many postals thet I disapprove of lef' this office, but this is *the worst*.

"I've got a good notion to put it in a envelope n' 'dress it over again—not for Sally Ann's sake, ef she wants to discuss her night-gownds with the readin' public gen'ally, but for the sake o' Simpkinsville's reputation in New York city. I'm a-goin' to do it!"

Seizing an envelope, she proceeded forthwith to clothe and readdress the offensive card, and then clapping a stamp upon it, she exclaimed, with satisfaction:

"Now, you're decent!"

Then she took up a letter.

"I see Miss Sophia Falena Simpkins is gett'n' letters right along f'om Washin'ton city. Like ez not some ef not every one o' them all-devourin' Yankees 're sett'n' up to 'er for 'er fortune—but I do hope she won't give in!

"I see she's taken to puffin' 'er hair lately, but maybe that's on account o' its gettin' skimpy. A holler puff makes a little hair go a long ways. 'Twouldn't do mine any harm to puff it a little— 'n' I'd *do* it ef 'twasn't for Bud Zunts. I said I wouldn't turn a hair to encour'ge him — *an' I wont!*

"He's jest about gettin' home now—I see it's

eight o'clock — 'n' like ez not he's a-sneezin' 'is head off this minute—pore Bud!"

During this prolonged monologue, much of which was scarcely audible, Miss Cordelia had assorted all the outgoing mail, stopping only once to set her coffee-pot on the fire.

Turning now, she seated herself before the single plate upon the table, and had dropped her head for a silent grace, when there came a rap at the door. This narrow portal opening on a side-street answered for "front" of her humble domicile, whose former front was on government duty, as we have seen.

"I'm a-comin' right now," she responded, somewhat flurriedly, as she opened the door.

"Why, howdy, Mis' Brooks! Come in, Sally Ann!"

"I do declare, Miss Cordelia, you an' Polly 're as cozy as two bugs in a rug," said Mrs. Brooks, unwinding a rose-colored "fascinator" from her head as she sat down. "I thought I'd run in 'n' set awhile. The children 're so fussy, I jest slipped out to let their pa get a tas'e o' the picnic I have every day. I left 'im a-playin' horsy, crawlin' on all-fo's on the flo', with the baby on 'is back, chas-in' little Sally Ann, with the twins a-whippin' 'im up behin' with a towel, 'n' I thought it was a good time for me to take a vacation. I did have a let-ter to pos', but of co'se I could o' slipped that in the box f'om the outside 'n' run right back. Fo' goodness' sake, look! There's somebody a-slip-

pin' in a letter now.   I heard it, 'n' saw it too.
Wonder, for gracious' sakes, who it was ?   Don't
it make you feel sort o' creepy, Miss Cordelia,
settin' here by yoreself some nights, jest you an'
Polly, to see a letter come a-droppin' in ?"

Miss Cordelia had set a second cup on the table,
and was pouring out the coffee.

"It did seem sort o' funny at first, Sally Ann,
'n' I ricollec' I used to push up the winder 'n'
try to see who dropped it, but I foun' they was
mo' neuraligy than satisfaction to be got out o'
that, 'n' I c'n gen'ally tell who drops mail now
'thout lookin.'   Draw up yo' chair, Sally Ann, 'n'
take some coffee, 'n' I'll go see what letter that is."

She rose and stepped to the box.   She was
thinking of Sally Ann's postal, and a sense of guilt
in the matter made her somewhat nervous.

"Law sakes!" she exclaimed, bringing forward
the letter.   "This here's a ole nigger's mail.   Jest
s'posin' I'd o' bumped my head an' maybe broke
a winder-pane (both o' which I've did a-many a
time) jest to see the tail of old Solon's mule ez he
ambles down the road—wouldn't I feel cheap ?
You know Solon's wife, Hannah, is cookin' down
to the telegraph station, an' they write to one another jest the same ez white folks."

" You don't say !"

" Why, yas; th' ain't a week but one letter goes
each way; an' I don't reck'n they's one but's got
po'try in it.   Every time *I* write for 'im he makes
me put it in, I *know*."

"For the land sakes! I wouldn't think he knew any."

"He *don't* know but two pieces—'Rose 's red,' and,

> "'Ez shore's the vine grows roun' the stump,
> You is my darlin' sugar lump.'

Seem like he don't keer much which one I put in, an' sometimes he jest leaves it to me, an' I write either 'How firm a foundation,' or 'When I can read my title clair,' an' he seems jest as much tickled; 'n' I'm shore she's likely to get more good out of 'em. Didn't you say you had a letter to mail?"

"Yas, 'm; here 'tis; an' I want to ast you, Miss C'delia, ef I couldn't get back a postal I sent this mornin'—that is, of co'se, less'n it's already gone."

Miss Cordelia caught her breath. "Why, no, Sally Ann, 'tain't to say gone, but—but—"

"But you've done put it in the bag—an' it fastened?"

"Well, yas, Sally Ann; tell the truth, the bag it's in is fastened up secure."

"I thought maybe 'twould be, 'n' I'm half glad. I spent all yesterday tryin' to decide whether to order a night-gownd with lace let in or a solid Hamburg yoke, 'n' ever sence I ordered the lace one I've had the fidgets for the other. So now I've wrote 'em to sen' both, 'n' ef they get the postal too, I reckon I'll have three; an', Lordy, won't I be fine?"

Now was Miss Cordelia's chance for her moral lecture, but so had conscience conscripted her into its legion of cowards that she sat with thumping heart, silent, until it was given her to remark, by way of escape, "I see you an' Lucy Jones 're correspondin' agin."

"Not *again*, but *yet*. We're jest as thick as ever. We've jest been changin' wrapper patterns again. She sent me this'n last summer. Look how purty it sets."

Mrs. Brooks rose and turned around. "It does set lovely, Sally Ann—Mother Hubbard front, an' sort o' bas' back—ain't it?—with a—what's this?"

"Why, that's a Watter pleat. They're all the go."

"Mh-hm. It's *mighty* purty. Funny how they get names, ain't it? Now I s'pose they call that a water pleat on 'count of its a-fallin' all the way down like a water-fall."

"I don't reely know. 'Tain't spelled that a-way. It's W-a-t-t-e-a-u, printed on the pattern, but maybe that's French. Come to think, e-a-u is French for water, *that* much I *know*.

"But guess what's a-comin' in nex', Miss Cordelia. Ole Mis' Bradley 'll lead the style at last."

"You don't mean hoops!"

"Guessed it the first pop! Yas, I do mean hoops, too. They're jest a-sailin' in, big as life."

"But tell me, does Mis' Bradley know it?"

"I don't know 's she does. I'd go an' tell 'er, but she's so deef I can't talk to her. Don't she look too funny when she comes in church a-Sundays with 'er same old hoops, an' that silk mantilla an' shoulder-pins, 'n' that curtain on the back of her bonnet? She shorely is a sight. 'N' yet seem like Simpkinsville wouldn't be like Simpkinsville 'thout Mis' Bradley."

" Mis' Bradley is a mighty nice lady, Sally Ann, an' a good Christian."

" An' don't I know it? Th' ain't anybody thinks mo' of 'er 'n I do, but that don't make me borry 'er cape patterns. But she's a Christian, shore. Do you know, she's taught my children nearly every prayer in the prayer-book — not to mention hymns. She gets 'em over there Sunday evenin's, an' has a reg'lar Sunday-school for 'em. She makes 'em come up, one by one, an' say their verses right in 'er ear-trumpet, 'n' the young ones 're tickled to death over it. She *ast Bud Zunts* to come an' help her, an' sort o' be super'ntendent. But I reck'n she was jest a-tryin' to get Bud interested. They say he don't show interes' in nothin' much but writin' letters sence 'is ma's gone, 'n' they *do* say he's *a-co'tin' somebody* by mail, 'n' thet he never goes to sleep 'thout comin' in town for 'is letters. Is that so, Miss Cordelia ?"

" Well, Sally Ann, sence you ask me, Bud does call for 'is mail purty reg'lar."

" You don't say thet he gets a letter every day ?"

" Oh, I don't say he does, an' I don't say he

don't. Even ef I kep' a 'count o' Bud's mail in a book, which I don't, 'twouldn't be right for me to tell mo'n he choose to tell 'isself."

"Well, I've begged Teddy to watch an' see what he gets of evenin's, an', tell the truth, I've come myself; but seem like Bud waits till purty near the last one, an' I've got jest enough manner's mixed up with my curiosity to make me go out with the crowd."

"Well, you see, Sally Ann, when folks wait their turn, I give 'em their mail where they b'long in the A B C's, 'n' Zunts, you know — that comes purty far down in the alphabet, 'n' Bud never pushes 'isself. 'F anybody was to stay a Z out, it 'd look like they wasn't no mo'n a sort o' *so fo'th*—no 'count on earth excep'n' *to* foller behin' somethin' thet does count. You'd get yore mail purty soon, anyway, bein' a B."

Miss Cordelia could be severe on occasion.

"An' so ole Bud's a-co'tin'! I do declare! I s'pose it's all right fo' ole folks to co't, but it does seem to strike my funnybone, somehow."

Mrs. Brooks laughed merrily. Miss Cordelia cleared her throat.

"Mind you, Sally Ann, I never said Bud Zunts *was* a-co'tin'. Ef he is, he 'ain't never tol' me."

At this point both women were startled by a shrill scream quite near. In a high falsetto voice came the exclamation "Nothin' for you, Bud Zunts!" Whether Poll the parrot had been studying over this oft-repeated sentence, keeping it on deposit for timely utterance, or, as seems more probable, the only connection in which he had ever heard the name was to him a complete form, which he instinctively recalled on hearing a part of it, would be hard to say; but there was something distinctly uncanny in the opportune delivery, an effect decidedly heightened by the dark corner from which the voice came, as well as by the peal of ringing bird-laughter which followed.

Mrs. Brooks drew her shawl over her head, and, falling upon her knees, put her face in Miss Cordelia's lap.

"Lord have mercy!" she exclaimed. "I b'lieve that bird is the ole boy 'isself; 'deed I do. Good gracious, Miss Cordelia! An' did you hear that? Another letter in the box! I heard it fall—'n' the clock's a-tickin' like thunder—'n' I hear footsteps; I declare I do!"

"Cert'n'y, Sally Ann! How'd the letter come in the box 'thout footsteps?" Miss Cordelia managed to say, finally; but it was with much effort, as she was far the more seriously startled of the two.

The sentence she had been saying daily for years—that had become, indeed, a sort of refrain in her own life—had burned deeper into her sensibilities than she knew, and to hear it from other lips even would have startled her, but coming from this weird bird, just at the critical moment when she was struggling between veracity and loyalty to Bud Zunts, filled her with something akin to terror. It seemed an imperative challenge to her for the whole truth. If she would not tell it, Poll would.

There is no telling where it might have led had Sally Ann kept silent; but she had soon taken the floor figuratively as well as literally, and was presently laughing and crying in so hysterical a fashion that Miss Cordelia felt it necessary to chafe her hands and temples, and finally to accompany her across the field, where she cringed at every shadow until she reached her gate.

When Miss Cordelia returned to her own door she touched its latch for the first time in her life with trembling fingers. She felt almost afraid to enter her room. The secret she had scarcely turned over in.her own breast had been glibly spoken by a senseless bird, and in the confusion of the first shock she had half believed the prating creature a thing of evil, as Sally Ann had said.

Mrs. Brooks had turned white and "gone to pieces" simply to hear the bird supply a sentence fitting exactly into the theme of conversation. He knew they were talking of Bud Zunts's mail. To Miss Cordelia he knew all—the years of waiting, the silent courtship, her resolution to stand firm at her end of the line, her present dilemma.

She stood some moments irresolute, her hand upon the latch; but finally, with a determined movement, she walked in. The room was nearly dark, the candle burning low in its socket, and flaring up occasionally, only to throw out hints of grotesque shadows.

Miss Cordelia locked the door, and, seizing a match, lit first the two candles standing on either end of the mantel, and then the lamp, which she turned up to its highest point; and now she threw an armful of pine knots upon the fire. For one thing, she would have plenty of light. Then walking directly up to Poll's perch, and regarding him sternly, she said, in a voice almost as metallic as his own:

"Well, Polly Cummins, you an' I might ez well have it out first ez last. I wouldn't talk to no sech unearthly figgur ez you in the dark, but I've done struck a good light, 'n' I'm bigger 'n you are, 'n' I reckon I'm older. It's already come to words between us, 'n' maybe it'll come to worse; but whatever it is, I'm ready for it."

She approached a step nearer, and folding her hands · behind her and looking keenly into the bird's eyes, said: "Now I want to know, *how much do you know ?*"

Poll, curious at the novel proceeding, craned his neck, turning upon her first one eye and then the other. The sudden glare no doubt made him blink.

"No, you needn't to wink at me, Polly, 'n' you needn't put out yore paw to shake hands, 'n' you needn't to make out like you don't understand. You've done committed yoreself, 'n' you can't back out of it. Speak out this minute when I tell you. *How much do you know, I say ?*"

The silence that followed was broken finally by Miss Cordelia. Her voice had lost somewhat of its severity when she spoke again.

" I've mistrusted you befo' to-night, Polly Cummins. Many a night when you've said 'Goodnight, Cordelia,' an' ' Pleasant dreams,' an' ' God bless you !' I've felt mighty quare about you, ef I did teach it to you myself. It's made me feel mighty shivery an' quare, I tell you, an' many's the night I've gone to sleep with a pretty creepy feelin' with yore human words a-ringin' in my ears. But with it all I've been mighty fond of you, an' proud of you too, an' th' ain't a livin' soul ez knows thet you say ' Good-night, Cordelia,' to me 'thout the ' Miss ' to it, 'n' thet I call you Polly Cummins. That's jest a little sociability 'twixt you an' me, an' I've allowed it an' encour'ged it jest because I *was* fond of you, 'n' I've reckoned you to be the most consolin' bird for a lonely person thet ever I see, not to say the smartest. *That* much I *knew* by what I could teach you to do an' to say. But ez to what you've held back from me — though I've had my suspicions, I've never reelly b'lieved it tell to-night. But you've had yore chance to play smarty, an' you've done it ! You know thet of all the people in town th' ain't nobody thet 'd make more o' what you said 'n Sally Ann Brooks will. She'll put on one o' them catarac' wrappers o' hers 'n' run over to the 'xchange quick ez she's swallered her breakfast, 'n' she'll tell that tale to everybody thet comes in —'n' what she don't add to it they will, *'n' you know it.*

"Ef you know ez much ez you've showed you know, why didn't you talk it over with me by ourselves, an' not make me an' him both cheap befo' the whole o' this gapin' town? Answer me, Polly Cummins, *how much do you know about me an' Bud Zunts?*"

At mention of this name, Poll raised his head and exclaimed, as before, "Nothin' for you, Bud Zunts!"

Standing thus near, Miss Cordelia caught, as she had not done before, a something in the repetition that made her start and turn suddenly white. It was the exact reproduction of her own intonation. In it she discerned all the pent-up tragedy of the long waiting, the tenderness, the resolve to be unyielding, which she had felt safely concealed by the oft-repeated form.

Turning suddenly, she staggered to a chair, and dropping her face into her hands over the table, she sat a long time, thinking. When finally she raised herself, her whole manner was changed.

"He don't know nothin'," she said, sadly. "He don't know a thing but what I've learned him. He's only a bird, after all—pore Poll! But ef my voice has been that encouragin', it's a wonder Bud ain't spoke long ago. Pore ole Polly!" she repeated. "He's jest said what I've been a-

learnin' 'im for goin' on fo' years. But *he's got to
be unlearned*—that's what he's got to be! 'N' it's
got to be did *right away*, 'n' I might ez well begin now. Ef Poll has got to talk about Bud, I'll
see to it thet he says somethin' to 'is credit, that
I will, 'n' the Simpkinsville folks can make what
they choose out of it. They've done give 'im
credit for gettin' love-letters, an' I'll see thet he
keeps it."

Rising, she went back to the perch, and said,
slowly and distinctly, "They's a love-letter for
you, Bud Zunts."

"Nothin' for you, Bud Zunts!" answered
Polly.

"A love-letter for you, Bud Zunts!" repeated
Miss Cordelia, calmly.

"Nothin' for you, Bud Zunts," insists Poll
again; and while he laughs, Miss Cordelia, raising her voice, reiterates:

"A love-letter for you, Bud Zunts!"

"Nothin' for you—"

"A love-letter—"

"Nothin' for you—"

"A love-letter—"

"Nothin'—"

"A love-letter—"

Miss Cordelia, in her growing excitement, raised
her voice higher and higher, until it was a shrill
scream, while Poll, not to be outdone, screeched
his loudest. It was a fierce argument dramati-
cally sustained on both sides, and there in the

blazing light woman and bird appeared at their best.

Poll, safely perched somewhat above his opponent's head, had perhaps the best of it. He did not grow red in the face nor lose his poise, and his back hair of course could not come down, as did poor Miss Cordelia's, from the insistent shaking of her head.

There is no telling just how long the contest might have continued or how it would have resulted had not a sudden swishing sound just behind her told Miss Cordelia that somebody was dropping a letter in the box. There was some one, of course, just outside the door. Would he notice the blazing light? Had he heard? Starting suddenly, she quickly turned down the lamp and blew out both candles. Then she hurriedly got into bed. She did not so much as say her prayers. She did not even look at the letter in the box. She was too much frightened.

Poll, awe-stricken into silence by the sudden darkness, made no sound for some minutes, and then, in a somewhat querulous voice, he ventured, "Nothin' for you, Bud Zunts!" And Miss Cordelia did not contradict him.

But when after a prolonged silence Poll said, "Good-night, Cordelia!" she answered, feebly, "Good-night, Polly!"

"Happy dreams!" continued Poll.

"Happy dreams!" responded a weak voice from under the covers.

"God bless you !" said the bird. But Miss Cordelia could not answer. She was crying.

When Bud Zunts got home that night he sat for a long time looking into the fire. He did not light a candle. He rarely did, in truth; but wiser men than he have eschewed candles when they could sit and weave gold and silver life webs before a fire of friendly logs.

Bud's evening reveries took much of their mood and color from the temper of the fire upon his hearth, but he did not know it. He never got far enough from himself to get a perspective on things belonging naturally to the only home life he knew, as do the dear wise ones who enrich the world with charming and poetic studies of logs and fireside reveries. But Bud did feel sensibly to-night that the logs were wet and burned badly, and that little narrow blue flames curled over their mossy barks. These blue jetting blazes he always felt unpleasantly, as if their meaning were bad— perhaps because of their likeness to the ignition of brimstone matches. Bud faithfully believed in the old-fashioned hell.

His clock had stopped. There had been times when he had felt rested to have the old clock stop. Such a lapse had never occurred during the' nearly forty years of his life with his mother. It had been as incessant as her voice, as faithful and unswerving, but just a little wearing. But to-night, when the wood sputtered and the wind rustled around the corners of the house, it made him feel lonely.

"Somehow, I miss ma to-night," he said, wearily, at last. "But I know she'd scold ef she was to come in sudden an' see the way things are. Seem like I can't ricollec' to wind up that clock reg'lar, noways. 'N' ef she was to see ole Dominicker a-sett'n over yonder on the flour-bar'l—well, I dun'no' what she *would* say. How ma has wrastled with that hen! Lay an' set on that flour-bar'l top she would, spite o' the devil—'n' pore ma jest ez set on breakin' 'er !

"How I have begged 'er to let me nail a little strip aroun' the top to keep the eggs f'om rollin' off ! But she wouldn't, an' jest ez reg'lar ez her back was turned seem like Dominicker 'd up an' lay a egg, an' it 'd roll off an' smash, 'n' ma'd whup 'er—but of co'se she whupped 'er so easy it didn't hurt—an' nex' day, maybe jest a hour sooner or later, jest quick ez ma'd get both han's in the dough, or maybe be tiltin' the wash-kittle, she'd up an' perform, 'n' they'd have the same picnic over agin. Lordy ! but it was tur'ble. I've begged 'er to kill Dominicker a-many a time when the preachers 'd come out to dinner, but 'twasn't no use. She 'lowed thet she'd kill 'er after she'd conquered 'er, an' not befo'—'n' then she'd make me go an' kill some easy-goin', Christian-sperited hen, an' she'd *continue* to wrastle with Dominicker. I do b'lieve ma's read passages o' Scriptur' an' prayed over breakin' up Dominicker f'om sett'n on that flour-bar'l. An' it would shorely pleg her mightily to know I'd fixed 'er nes' there, jest the way she wanted it. But I 'lowed thet maybe ma wouldn't know it, an' when she was here she had her way, 'n' now th' ain't no *contrairy* person roun' *but* Dominicker, an' I 'low to let 'er have her turn at hers.

"Wonder ef Miss Cordelia 'd mind 'er sett'n' on the flour-bar'l? She mightn't like it—right here in the house—but I b'lieve ef she saw me a-favorin' it she'd let 'er 'lone — though she mightn't. Th' ain't no flour in the bar'l—they wasn't when ma was here. It's jest filled up with pa's ole saddle an' things yet, the way she packed it ten year ago.

"Reck'n Miss Cordelia 'd— I declare, lis'n at me a-talkin', 's ef I'd clair forgot what she's jest said to me; but I ain't, nor the way she said it, neither. 'Nothin' fo' you, Bud Zunts.' It's a ringin' in my ears yet. Seem like, when I look back, it's been said in my ear all my life, 'n' I didn't seem to hear it. 'Nothin' fo' you, Bud Zunts.' Ricollec' when I wanted to go off to school—'n' *was* goin'—'n' then pa died, 'n' I couldn't leave ma. 'N' then when I went a-soldierin', 'n' expected to come back on a white horse, holdin' a Confedrit flag in one han' an' knockin' at the Cummins gate with the other—'n' 'stid o' that I come in a ambulance, 'th a s'oe leg, 'n' I was puny an' ragged, 'n' they wasn't no Confedricy—'n'—'n' ma met me at the cross-roads, 'n' took me home roun' the

"'SEEM LIKE I CAN'T RICOLLEC' TO WIND UP THAT CLOCK'"

other way. 'N' then Miss Cordelia she was teach-in' school, 'n' ma needed me constant — 'n' — 'n' then *she* got the pos'-office, 'n'—'n' ma died—'n' I started out to co't Miss Cordelia, 'n'—'n' then she started sayin' it to me, 'n' she's said it to me ev'ry day sence—'Nothin' fo' you, Bud Zunts.' That's jest the way she says it.

"I do wush 't the clock 'd tick! I'd wind it up an' set it, ef I knowed the time. I'd do it any-how ef I could forgit what ma used to say : 'Any-body that 'd set a clock wrong, 'd tell any other lie.' Now I wouldn't lie—not ef I know myself —but I'd set that clock agoin', 'n' *resk* gittin' it right in a *minute*, ef I didn't know thet the first tick it 'd give, seem like I'd hear ma start to scol' me fur it.

"I didn't half try them shetters o' Miss Corde-lia's to-night. Sence the boys 've started to pleg me about gittin' letters, seem like I think some-body's a-watchin' me all the time. But I don't reck'n anybody 'd trouble 'er. Ef—ef I could jest say the *first word* to 'er, seem like the rest 'd come easy. I've made up my min' a hund'ed times, 'n' — 'n' then when she comes out with 'Nothin' fo' you—' I jest can't do a thing but turn roun' an' walk out, to save my life—seem like."

Miss Cordelia rested very little during that night, waking often from short snatches of sleep haunted by vivid and harrowing dreams. Once she seemed to see Bud with Poll's face, standing in his accustomed place and saying in the bird's hard voice, " Won't you marry me, Cordelia ?" And then when she started up, and turning over, slept again, it was only to see Poll a woman grown, dressed in one of Polly Ann Brooks's wrappers, sitting in the exchange talking so loud and fast that no one could stop him — and so the night passed.

The bed had yielded her so little rest that she rose at the first gleam of day, and as she moved about her room she seemed to see things more clearly. The more she thought upon it, the more important it seemed that Poll should forget the fateful sentence. She felt heartily ashamed of her excitement of last night.

" 'Tis awful pervokin', though, to have anybody, even a human person, conterdic' you to yore face, but I ought to had better sense 'n to get riled at pore Poll the way I did. He cert'n'y is a mighty smart bird, Poll is, 'n' I'm shore, ef I half try, I can teach 'im the way I want to."

Feeling the room chilly, she bared a bed of coals and threw fresh kindling upon them, and when Poll stirred on his perch she said, slowly, not moving from her chair, " They's a love-letter for you, Bud Zunts."

" Nothin' for you — " responded the bird, promptly.

Miss Cordelia allowed him to finish the sentence, and then again, calmly, she repeated the new form. Over and over again, as fast as Poll reiterated the old sentence, Miss Cordelia submitted her amendment.

She bore it well, and, excepting that two crimson disks soon appeared upon her pallid cheeks, she gave no sign of agitation. She had never in her life undertaken anything with a firmer resolution, and never had she felt so hurried by the exigences of circumstance. She was afraid for the day's routine to begin, lest Poll should air his new accomplishment for the entertainment of the first-comer into her door.

When finally the day was fully come she set about her duties with an abstracted air, reciting his new lesson to Poll every few moments. So all during the day, whenever she felt sure no one was hanging about the open door, she said, or sometimes even sang, the simple sentence; and once, when a prolonged hum of voices without forbade this, she went close to her pupil and whispered it; but Poll did not whisper his retort, and so she did not try this again. The day was long, but it was at last safely passed. Only one ordeal more, when Bud should come in and wait, and then, that over, she would close her door and go early to bed.

There was a heavy mail to-night, and she was kept pretty busy. When finally the crowd dispersed, and ere she in the least realized it, Bud alone stood without, backing with his usual diffidence against the opposite wall, she opened her lips to say the familiar words, when Poll, close at her elbow, happened to duck his head and look through the window at Bud Zunts. A sudden panic seized poor Miss Cordelia. The bird had seemed to challenge her, and before she knew it she had said, defiantly, "They's a love-letter for you, Bud Zunts!"

Bud jumped as if he had been shot, while Poll, as if realizing the mistake, shrieked at the top of his voice, "Nothin' for you, Bud Zunts!"

There followed now a critical moment for all three, and Poll's last words seemed to proclaim him master of the situation. If Miss Cordelia had not had a healthy heart, she would certainly have dropped dead then and there.

Poor Bud's face was as red as his hair as he staggered forward, grinning nervously. Seeing his eager countenance approach the window, Miss Cordelia stammered, "Th' ain't a thing for you, Bud. I don'no' how on earth I come to say that. My min'—my min' 's been considerable worreted to-day, an' I did't sleep very good las' night, an' Poll fretted me consider'ble, an'—an' I—I—tell the truth, I dun'no' what in the world put sech a word ez that into my mouth—"

Bud was as awkward as she, but he had gained confidence during her apology, and his voice was firm, though a little husky, when he said, leaning in the window upon his folded arms:

"Ef you want to know my thoughts about it, Miss C'delia, I reck'n God A'mighty put it there.

He knowed thet it was about time I was gitt'n' a love-letter—ef ever I'm goin' to git one—an' He knowed there wasn't but one person I'd keer *to* git it from, an' He knowed thet you was that special partic'lar person, an' He knowed mo'n thet—He knowed thet I was such a chicken-hearted ejiot thet less'n *some* sign come fo' me to speak, I'd 've come an' gone out o' this Simpkinsville pos'-office eternal 'thout openin' my head to you—I'm jest that big of a dummy."

He hesitated only a second, as if to gain breath.

" 'Th' ain't no love-letter waitin' fo' me to-night, I reck'n. Even Poll knowed that much—didn't you, Poll? But maybe they's a leetle bit mo' to it thet Poll *don't know.* He don't know thet I been a-comin' here ev'ry night fo' three years an' six mont's an' fo' nights *to-night,* jest a-hopin' to fix things so's they *would* be a love-letter a-comin' to me. You didn't know that, did you, Poll?"

During all this time Miss Cordelia had stood as if petrified before Bud, her face rigid and white.

"And you didn't know it neither, Miss Cordelia," he continued, lowering his tone. "You didn't know it neither—did you, honey?"

At this, Miss Cordelia, covering her face with her hands, protested desperately.

"Oh, don't, Bud! Don't, I beg you! I'm disgraced enough already, 'thout—"

Bud misunderstood, and was wounded.

"Of co'se I'll hursh ef you say so," he said, sadly. "I wouldn't o' started ef I'd knew it 'd pleg you that a-way. I reck'n it do seem a sort o' disgrace for a nice ejercated lady to be co'ted by a outlandish ole tacky like me—I reck'n 'tis."

There were great tears rolling down between Miss Cordelia's thin fingers now.

"'Tain't that, Bud," she sobbed. "'Tain't that, 'n' you know it — 'n' you know thet what I've done to-night is jest ez much ez askin' you to speak love to me—'n' you know thet ef I'd o' had any manner o' shame, I'd 've died befo' I'd 've said it—but it all come o' me tryin' to teach Poll to tell a story—an' now I'm paid—I've done disgusted you fo'ever, 'n' I know it."

"Disgusted who, honey?"

"Why of co'se I've disgusted you the way I've acted. After me standin' up here an' encour'gin' you to speak, night after night for fo' years, goin' on, an' you've not done it—fo' me to out an' out *say* love-letter to you. Oh, Bud, what *to* say I *don't* know—*but it's awful!*"

She sobbed again. Bud seemed somewhat dazed.

"What's awful, honey?" he asked, vaguely. "Th' ain't nothin' awful been did thet I can see but the way I've done acted, like a plumb ejiot, time out of min'—but ez to yo' *encour'gin* me—I don't want to conterdic' nothin' you say, but reely, less'n you'd o' put me out, I don't jest see how you could o' give me less encour'gement—*'deed* I don't."

"'Tain't what—what I've said, Bud. I know I ain't said much, but it's—*it's the way I've said it.*"

Bud shifted his position.

"An' did you 'low thet you was a-sayin' it sweet, honey? Jiminy crackers! But I wush 't I'd 've knew it. Seemed to me jest the other way —'n' all the way home every night yore words 'd be a-ringin' in my ears—'n'—'n'—"

He chuckled softly.

"—'n' ef they hadn't o' been sweetened by yore mouth, they'd o' been the mos' *dis*cour'gin' words I ever hear."

Miss Cordelia wiped her eyes slowly.

"Well, Bud," she replied, evidently somewhat mollified, "I'm mighty glad you can say so—but it did seem to me some nights thet my voice 'd get so persuadin', *in spite of all I could do*, thet ef they *was* anything on yore min' you'd 've spoke it out, then an' there. But, tell the truth, Bud, it was mo'n half worrymint over yore takin' them long rides in the col' win' an' not knowin' ef you wore flannen under—under-garments nex' to yore —yore skin."

She blushed crimson.

"Th' idee o' you a-frettin' 'bout my ole skin! I do declare I've growed a inch in the las' minute— I know I have."

He chuckled again.

"An' you do wear 'em, do you, Bud — good warm ones?"

He drew his flowered kerchief from his deep pocket and wiped his eyes, as betwixt laughter and tears he answered her.

"Th' idee o' her a-keerin'!" he began. "Yas, honey, co'se I wear 'em—good thick ones, all ma-knit; 'n' I've got a pile o' new ones tall ez this winder thet she's stacked away for me—some knit narrer and some wide, so's ef I growed ole like either side o' the fambly, fat or slim, I'd never go col'—nor tight nor bulgy neither. Pore ma! She never forgot nothin' in her life, I don't reck'n. 'N' I've got perserves enough to do us too, honey," he resumed, after a pause. "I ain't never opened no perserves sence she's went. I've been a-savin' 'em for whenever you'd — but never min', I see you're gitt'n' plegged agin, 'n' I ain't a-goin' to say another word to-night—not a one; 'n' I'm a-goin' out 'n' see ef yore winder's bolted good, 'n' then I'm a-goin' to lock the gate 'n' go home, 'n' when I get there I'm a-goin' to write you the neares' to a love-letter thet I can write, 'n' I'm a-goin' to mail it in the mornin', an' I'm a-comin' for my answer to-morrer 'bout this time—you hear?"

Miss Cordelia colored afresh.

"But," continued Bud, "they's jest one thing I do ast you to do to-night befo' I go. Shake han's with me, won't you, thoo the winder, jest ez lovin' ez you know how?"

If Miss Cordelia's usually pale face was already aglow, it flamed a brilliant scarlet now as she timorously presented her thin hand. Bud took it in both his and held it tight for one brief moment; then, without a word, he turned and walked out.

IIe found it necessary to wipe his eyes before he mounted his wagon seat, and at intervals all along the road a tear rolled down his cheek, though it usually found him chuckling.

"I do declare," he was saying when he passed the first mile-stake, "seem like I c'n see 'er han' yet, the way she put it out to me so modes' an' shy, 'th all the purty blue veins in it jest like the rivers on a geogerphy map. IIow I have studied 'em these fo' years! I could see 'er han's, 'n' she couldn't see me. 'N' I know every vein on 'em, 'n' jest where the two little moles set like little towns on the aidge o' the rivers. 'N' to think o' me a-holdin' 'em! Th' ain't a bit o' use in putt'n' it off, 'n' I'm a-goin' to say so in the letter. She won't need mo' clo'es 'n she's got. She *might* want to sew a little trimmin' roun'—I think a little lace or ruffle 'd look mighty purty. Ma never had no trimmin' on none o' her inside things, 'n' I ricollec' I use ter wush 't she would. She could sew on lace afterwards jest as well, *an' better*. That pos'-office mus' hinder 'er consider'ble.

"I'm glad I saved all the perserves, 'n' never opened none. That's one thing I do believe ma'd praise me for. 'Cept'n' thet I've jest put off speakin' f'om day to day, though I don't reck'n I could o' held out—'n' they all put up in thick syrup, too, 'n' ef they's one thing I do love—

"I vow I don't see how I'm a-goin' to stan' it 'n' not tell nobody all day to-morrer—I don't reely. B'lieve I'll git out an' walk 'longside o'

Bute 'n' Fairy. Seem like I ought to 'umble my-self some way, God's been so good to me."

Bud actually descended from his seat and trudged along beside the oxen, talking to them as he went :

"Nemmine, Bute 'n' Fairy, we ain't a-goin' to keep up these night trips much longer—no, we ain't; 'n' Mis' Brooks 'll have to hunt up some new joke in place o' me an' my fiery untamed steeds a-passin' her house every night—yas, she will. I have knew tongues in my day thet was purty fiery 'n' untamed thet 'd do well to take a lesson f'om a stiddy-goin' ox thet min's 'is own business; but 'twouldn't do to say so, I reck'n, bein' ez they was ladies' tongues, mos'ly. But we ain't a-goin' to take a-many mo' o' these trips, I say, 'cause we goin' to fetch the "—he giggled —"we goin' to fetch the pos'-office out home— that's what we goin' to do—so's we won't have to go to it; 't least, we'll fetch all of it thet's any good; the letter part can stay where 'tis."

No one will ever know what was written in the letter that Bud spent that entire night in shaping, and over the difficulties of which he by turns groaned, chuckled, bit his lip, and walked the floor; but when it was finally written, it was a living, breathing love-letter, which, if innocent of protestation or impassioned avowal, was redolent of the timid heart-blossoms of a long life of un-spoken devotion.

Bud knew about capital I's, and he knew that honey was a common noun to be spelled with a small h, but how can one remember all these trifles when one is in love? Such substitution of values is not infrequent, we are told, in Cupid's repository of authentic MSS.

No one will ever know what was written in the perfumed pink-papered answer that Bud received on the second day afterwards. Yes, it is true, Miss Cordelia did her part with all the dainty accompaniments she had learned through years of close observation. Only of the *inside* of love-letters was she ignorant; and so, guided simply by the promptings of her maiden heart, she wrote the womanly and brief epistle which, Bud declared to her afterwards, "knocked off twenty years of his age at a single pop."

The Cummins-Zunts courtship, albeit it was a brief one, must have been carried on with exceptional discretion, as, though Bud had given abundant evidence of his approaching nuptials in sundry improvements about his home, no one suspected the future bride in Miss Cordelia, until she actually went over and asked Miss Sophia Falena Simpkins to "stand up" with her. Mrs. Brooks never did recover from her consternation over the affair, nor did she ever feel entirely sure that Miss Cordelia quite forgave her remark about "ole folks a-co'tin'."

The Zunts cottage sits like a smiling expression

of domestic bliss by the road-side. The cedars that stand about its front yard, and which had grown riotous and disorderly in the interregnum, hold up shapely tapering heads that defer in the soft breeze to their new mistress — like well-ordered ladies-in-waiting — while the pair guarding the front gate have fallen upon one another's shoulders for the shaping of a triumphal arch through which in her comings and goings she may pass.

There are flowering plants in season standing in tins and earthen pots about the little porch, where two rocking-chairs are generally to be seen swaying, very close together.

In the late evenings, while his wife sets her bread to rise, or, rocking softly, plies her crochet needle, Bud sits with his pipe musing in the chair opposite, but he seldom speaks, having said all he had to say. But his eyes beam with a peaceful light as he chuckles to himself; and when she asks, "What you so tickled at, Bud?" he replies, "I was jest a-thinkin'"; or sometimes he adds, "I was jest a-thinkin' *this*, thet 'a ole fool is the wors' kind o' fool.'" And then he rises, and, crossing over, kisses her, and quietly goes back to his seat; or perhaps he stops to pull down the lamp-shade a little, so that it may not shine in Dominicker's eyes, for the old hen still pursues her maternal vocation unmolested on the flour-barrel, and is in no wise disquieted because her indulgent mistress has insinuated the braided rim of an old basket scoured to whiteness, around the edges of her nest, while her pedestal is arrayed in a gathered flounce of Turkey-red calico.

It is quite immaterial to her virtuous ladyship that she has come to be regarded, as she sits thus æsthetically enthroned, as an article of *virtu* quite worthy its place on the shining floor of a room grown beautiful through a woman's touch.

Poll drowses blinking on his perch until he falls nearly asleep, and when the clock strikes, he starts up from a nod like a child, and says: "Good-night, Cordelia!". . . "Happy dreams!". . . "God bless you!". . . pausing after each salutation until he is satisfactorily answered, and then he adds, "They's a love-letter for you, Bud Zunts."

And Bud answers, "I know it, Poll, 'n' I've done taken it out o' the pos'-office, too."

And then Poll, satisfied, goes to sleep.

"CHRISTMAS GEESE"

"Ef Lucetty an' Dr. Jim wasn't both so pig-headed an' set, they might jest ez well o' been married ten year ago ez not," said Mr. Brantley, looking over his spectacles at his wife.

Mrs. Brantley was seeding raisins, and her husband liked to sit and watch the agile movement of her fingers as she deftly extracted the pits from the crinkled skins.

"Yas," she replied, "you better say fifteen year ago, an' I s'pose they'll set up there stiff ez ramrods nex' door to one another for another fifteen year—tell they both dry up of ol' age *an' contrariness*. I dunno which a one I want mos' to whup. Sometimes, when Dr. Jim comes in to 'tend on the children when they're sick, an' I see how kin'-hearted an' good he is, I seem to know it's Lucetty's fault, an' then ag'in, I'll maybe run agin some of her Christian ac's—like her 'doptin' that po' fitty Joe when his ma died, an' takin' keer of 'im clear through his epilepsy tell he passed away—an' then I feel shore it must be Dr. Jim's fault thet they ain't married ; not thet he bein' a good doctor an' she a charitable Christian 'd go to show thet either one was gifted at love-makin',

10

which I reck'n they ain't. It's a mighty strange
case, to my mind. Everybody knows thet neither
one of 'em 'ain't never looked at nobody else sence
they've been two barefeeted children playin' in
the creek together."

"They're jest 'bout of an age, ain't they?
Look out, wife; you dropped one 'thout takin' no
seed out."

"Th' wasn't no seed in that 'n—I jest broke the
skin so's 'twouldn't plump out in the puddin' like
a seedless. I do hate them seedless raisins. They
get in a person's mouth like sort o' roly-polies, an'
give a nervous person the fidgets. Yas, Lucetty
an' Jim 're of an age, lackin' a week—an' she's got
it, too. They'll both be forty 'twix' Christmas
an' New-Year; an' to think o' them a-holdin' off
from one another all these years jest on account o' family nonsense! It's jest simple *re-
dic'lous*!"

"Don't you reck'n ef either one was brought to
death's do', they might give in?"

"Ef they thought they was goin' to die, like ez
not they would. The only reason they don't marry, so the story goes, is thet neither one is willin'
to live in the other one's house. Dr. Jim he says,
't least so they tell me, thet it's a wife's place to
come to her husban's home; an' she 'lows thet
'fore she'd go an' live in ol' Judge Morgan's house,
after all thet's passed between the ol' folks, she'll
live an' die Lucetty Ann Jones."

"I *declare*, wife, you dropped in a seed that

"'THEY DON'T NEITHER ONE KNOW I'VE AST THE OTHER ONE TO DINNER'"

time. *So it is*—caked sugar. Reck'n yore fingers 're better 'n my eyes, anyway. Seem to me *that* 'd be *easy* got over. Why don't he *build* 'er a house ?"

" He's offered to, a thousan' times, but she holds out for 'im to build it on her lan', an' that he won't —'t least that's what they say—an' so there they set. They say the subjec' 'ain't been mentioned between 'em now for mo'n five year. He jest drops in to see 'er, an' talks off-han', reg'lar twice-t a week, less'n she's sick — an' then, of co'se, he stops t' inquire every day; but you know she has Dr. Beasley for her doctor."

" Well, I s'pose that's nachel enough. No girl, ol' or young, wants her beau for her doctor. Somehow pills an' plasters an' love don't seem to go together. A couple has to be spoke over by a minister o' the gospel befo' sech ez that an' love 'll seem to gee."

" Yas, an' even then it's tryin'—at first. It was bad enough for Lucetty to hol' out the way she done while she was well an' had a-plenty o' money —but now, sence that no-'count brother o' hers has done gone an' married an' took the lion sheer of everything, an' she's started to be laid up with first one thing an' then another, it does seem, with a good man within a stone's throw of her, able *an' anxious* to take keer of her, which actions speaks louder than words, an' everybody knows he is, it does seem like a pity. Tell the truth, in these tight days o' men - famine, sence the wah, it's a pity for one good man to go to loss—that's how I look at it."

"An' you think a heap o' both of 'em, I reck'n, wife, don't you ?"

"Well, I should say I do, 'r I wouldn't be sett'n' up here seedin' raisins like I am jest because the Joneses seem to think it 'd be a sacer'lige to eat a Christmas dinner 'thout a plum-puddin'. They don't neither one know I've ast the other one to dinner. I begged 'em sep'rate not to mention to anybody bein' invited — fact, I told 'em both thet they *wasn't* invited—they're jest expected to drop in. I've got a good min' to pleg 'em right out at the dinner-table 'bout the way they're actin' like plumb geese. I've got a roas' goose for dinner, an' I wish 't I could think up some good joke thet 'd sort o' throw them in with *it* in some way—I'd do it in a minute."

"I declare, wife, you're too funny to live. But, shore 'nough, how'd it do to ask 'em, jest off-han', like ez ef you didn't to say mean it, what cotation it 'd be suitable for Miss Lucetty an' the doctor to ask o' the goose ; and when they all git tired guessin'—of co'se nobody wouldn't guess the answer—why, you could jest—well—I reck'n you'd jest have to refuse to tell 'em what."

"I can't jest see where the fun 'd come in, hardly—maybe I'm slow, but—"

"Well, it 'd be *some* fun jest a-mentionin' them in *with* the goose—that 'd sort o' make a laugh, wouldn't it ?"

“But they’d have to be some joke at the end of it, William?”

“So they is; but it’s like the popper at the end of a whup—you have to snap it keerful. I reck’n when they all git up from the table it wouldn’t hurt for you to sort o’ whisper it to ’em *both together*, would it?”

“I declare, William, I don’t know. What is it you’re drivin’ at?”

“Well, how’d it do to sort o’ hint thet they might say to the goose, ‘When will we three meet again?’ jest like they say about donkeys?”

Mrs. Brantley laughed.

“It ’ll jest do ’em up brown—that’s what it ’ll do. An’ ef they act any way stupid about it, I’ll jest pitch into ’em an’ explain the p’int — don’t reck’n they’ll ast many questions, though. I’d o’ argued with Lucetty long ago, but I knew ’twouldn’t be no use. She’d begin to cote Scripture to me. I never could argy with Scripture-cotin’ persons. Somehow I feel like ez ef I was sassin’ the Lord back, an’ I can’t do it.”

“Seem to me you could cote back, wife. You know a-plenty, I’m shore.”

“Yas, I know enough, but I might cote it amiss —like many a well-meanin’ person does. Some o’ the meanest things I’ve ever heerd said has been twisted Scripture-cotin’. Sence the ol’ boy made sech a bad out at it in the Bible, I ’low to ’ply mine to myself, an’ not dole it out to my neighbors—that is, not in jedgment. Of co’se when a person has a chance to speak it for comfort, that's different. But I'd give a heap to see them two married an' settled. What she's to do I *don't* know, an' nobody can't *give* 'er nothin', she's that proud. They say Dr. Jim has dumped wood on the back end of her wood-pile at night tell it's graj'elly moved from close to the kitchen-do' clean down mos' to the cow-lot, an' she don't seem to notice it. Of co'se she always burns it from the front side. An' with it all she's as techy an' independent ez the next one. In askin' 'er to dinner I had to be jest ez keerful to say we wanted 'er for comp'ny. Ef I'd o' once even hinted at her enjoyin' the dinner she never would o' come in the world."

While she was being thus amiably discussed by her prospective host and hostess, Miss Lucetta sat in her little parlor entertaining the gentleman in question. There had been a dearth of conversation between them this evening. Possibly the recurring anniversary brought to both, in a vague, unexplained way, a fresh consciousness of their somewhat strained relations. A long - confessed "understanding " between two persons is apt to feel a sort of stress on occasions which mark the passage of time. During all his visit, to-night Dr. Jim felt the restraint always following upon the imposed avoidance of certain subjects.

"It's always a pleasure to set and watch that chimbly draw," he remarked, late in the evening, after a prolonged pause. "Somehow the blazes seem to roah up it so cheerful."

"'IT'S ALWAYS A PLEASURE TO SET AND WATCH THAT CHIMBLY DRAW'"

“Yas—’tain’t never smoked but once-t—an’ that was fault o’ the wood. Some wood seem to begrudge its own smoke, don’t make no diff’rence what you do with it.”

“It’s mo’ like to be fault o’ the weather when the smoke do that a-way. Take a good chimbly an’ good wood, an’ a ill wind ’ll make ’em quare, spite of everything. My chimbly at home is mighty fastidious an’ notionate. It ’ll draw certain wood-smokes in certain winds, an’ it ’ain’t got no mo’ conscience about switchin’ around an’ vomitin’ smoke it’s done swallered ’n nothin’. I often thought I’d have it fixed, but seem like ef I didn’t have that to bother about I’d have somethin’ else, so I thought I’d let my troubles begin in smoke, anyway. I on’y wish ’t they ended that a-way.”

He sighed.

“I hate to hear you talk so down-hearted, Jim. Reck’n you an’ I ’ve both got a heap to be thankful for, ’f we only thought about it. Any man thet can raise the sick the way you are providentially enabled to do ought to be happy.”

“Well, reck’n I’m ’bout ez happy ez anybody in my conditions could be well. I never worry about that. The thing I do fret over is not bein’ able to make them I’d like *to* make happy *ez* happy ez seem like I *could* make ’em—ef they’d let me.”

Miss Lucetta did not answer. She stirred the fire instead.

“It does me good to see yo’ arm out o’ the sling

ag'in," her guest continued. "Don't reck'n it ever aches any mo', does it?"

"Thet's jest about all it does do out o' the way. It jest sort o' has the dead ache in it half o' the time. Co'se the jumpin' pain is all gone out o' my thumb, an' it's all healed up."

"I'd 'vise you to use it mighty keerful for a while. Treat that hand like company; give it a easy time, an' don't ast no favors of it. I s'pose ol' Aunt Judy waits on you good, don't she? Better let 'er do all the liftin' an' carryin' for you tell that arm forgets all about how it feels. She tends on you good, don't she—Aunt Judy?"

"She does everything I ast her to do—good ez she can."

"That's right. I'm glad to know it. It's bad enough for you to be a-livin' here in this lonesome, crepe-myrtle grove by yoreself, with no comp'ny but a half-blind ol' nigger an' a deef dog, not to mention a lapwing mockin'-bird, an' I'm glad to know the ol' nigger does her part by you. I've missed yore piano-playin' awful sence you've had the felon. Many's the night I've sat in my study there at home an' caught them purty slidin'-down notes of the 'Maiden's Prayer' when the wind come from this way, an' it has eased my mind consider'ble. I know when you play that a-way you ain't frettin'. An' of co'se when *you're* satisfied it 'd—it 'd be mighty ungrateful for *me* not to be," he sighed. "But they's some mysteries in this worl' thet I don't reck'n 'll be made plain this side o' the gulch."

" Yas—that's jest what I often say to myself. Here we see ez men, darkly, but there we shall see face to face."

" But it does seem—don't it never seem to you thet maybe ef some o' the mists was cleared away we might have the pleasure o' seein' mo' clear in this worl'? Now of co'se I'm not a-goin' to tech on fo'bidden things to-night, no mo'n to say thet ef I *was* to express myself ez I've did a many a time, it 'd all be jest ez true ez it ever was. I could shut my eyes an'—not insinuatin' thet I'd like to do it, of co'se—but I *could* shet my eyes an' take a holt of yore han' an' tell you jest them same identical facts thet I related to you a Christmas Eve seventeen year ago, a-walkin' home from Mrs. Gibbs's quiltin' party; an' they'd be jest ez precious to my soul and jest ez true ez they ever was—which I have reminded you, ez delicate ez I could, every Christmas sence—'thout breakin' my promise not to pester you no mo' about it, either."

Miss Lucetta looked steadily into the fire. Presently she said : " Well, Jim, I don't say you've broke your promise; an' ef you *'ain't*, th' ain't nothin' for me to say, ez I can see. Reck'n we both been raised to know our own minds, an' we ain't weather-vanes, neither one of us."

" No, I reck'n we ain't," said he, rising from his chair. " Sometimes I wish-t we was—either one of us, or both. I'm goin' to ride over to ole

Judge Jarvis's, an' see how he is, jest about day-light to-morrer, an' reck'n you won't mind ef I holler 'Merry Christmas' to you, will you? Reck'n *anybody* could say *that* to you, couldn't they?"

"Th' ain't nobody I'd ruther hear sayin' it, Jim, an' you know it," she replied, extending her hand. "An' I say 'God bless you!' to-night, too, an' look down in mercy upon us both. Good-night, Jim."

Dr. Jim did not answer, but, dropping her hand suddenly, turned away. Closing the door, Miss Lucetta stood watching his retreating figure from the window as he crossed the moonlit yard, until he mounted his horse at the gate and disappeared. The wind blew from the direction of the Morgan place, and for a long time she heard the tramp of the horse's feet upon the hard road. When the sound died in the distance she turned and went back to the fire.

"I do wish-t Jim wouldn't fret about me the way he does," she said, presently, with a sigh. It seems to fret him for me to trus' myself right here where I been born an' raised, jest because ol' Aunt Judy is half blind and half foolish an' Rover is deef. That comes o' not havin' proper faith. Ef I didn't have the religious faith I've got, may-be I might be lonesome or skeered. I don't say but I am lonesome sometimes, an', tell the truth, to-night's one o' the times. Seem like sence my bone felon's stopped painin' me I feel mo' lone-some 'n what I did when I walked the flo' all

"'YOU WON'T MIND EF I HOLLER "MERRY CHRISTMAS" TO YOU?'"

night with it. What short-sighted mortals we are, 'anyhow! Many's the lonely hour a good throbbin' pain saves us, ef we only knew it. Still, turn about's fair play, an' I'm jest ez pleased to rest off from my bone felon an' take a turn at lonesomeness for a spell. I'm mighty proud this thumb j'int didn't shed. Somehow nobody don't seem to have proper respec' for their thumbs, nohow, tell somethin' goes wrong with one of 'em, an' they see what a gift for discipline lays in the little things ef they once-t get their backs up. To look at this little underhanded, hump-shouldered stub, a person couldn't believe it could strike the terror it did. They wasn't a atom in me for two solid weeks thet didn't pay its respec's to that thumb. But I'm mighty glad to 've had that bone sound. I'd hate to be in any part mislaid at the resurrection. Seem like it's bad enough for sech ez have been called on to ex-plode, or to be exploded, to lay around in all p'ints o' the compass, much less 'n for a quiet, home-stayin' somebody like me to lose the run o' my bones. They wouldn't be no earthly ex-cuse for it, an' ef I was a bone short, I'd feel that I oughtn't never to let it get away from me, less'n somethin' might happen 'fore I'd get it back. I spent three whole nights tryin' to *devise* a place to keep that thumb bone about me in case it was to shed, an' I never did hit on any place that was cheerful an' safe. Pore doctors! They both think they saved it, but they little know. Dr.

Beasley he lanced it, an' Jim he consulted with him an' poulticed it, an' not a thing eased it mo'n water on a duck's back tell—well, tell I come to my senses. It was mighty hard for me to promise the Lord I wouldn't play dance music for parties any mo', and I wrastled purty severe with the sperit 'fore I give in. An' ez long as I helt out that bone kep' loosened up, ready to drop out, an' the night I give my word it settled back in its socket, an' there it's stayed. That shows the beauty of divine justice. The good Lord lets me have the comfort *an'* the credit of lettin' go of sin, when, to look at it straight, they wasn't nothin' else for me to do. The only question was would I stop playin' party music with or without my thumb bone—couldn't play it 'thout it—an' I had the sense to give in in time. Of co'se, not playin' at parties 'll be a heavy loss to me. Two dollars and a half every time come in mighty handy ; I don't reck'n anybody knew jest how handy it did come in.

"Reck'n ef the worst come to the worst—well, I dunno what I would do. They's jest one person I'd hate worst in the worl' to know I'm pressed, an' that's Dr. Jim. He can fret ez much ez he's a mind to about me livin' by myself, 'cause he knows I've laid off to do it, but I wouldn't have him to s'picion thet I 'ain't tasted wheat bread fo' mo'n a month—not for a purty. It kind o' struck me ez funny for him to fetch me that loaf o' stale bread for my poultice—like ez ef he knew I didn't have any—but of co'se when he said thet it 'd make a better poultice 'n any fresh bread I might have, I couldn't take exceptions. So I jest used 'bout a inch or so off o' the loaf, an' sent the res' back. It's jest ez well to let him see thet in asmuch ez he's a neighbor an' a doctor, an' of co'se a good friend, I'm perfectly willin' he should bread my hand—but he can't han' me bread, leastways not bread leavened iu ol' Dr. John Morgan's kitchen.

"It's a hard thing for folks to have to live out other people's fusses, an' keep on the right side of partitions they never made, but so it is—an' sence they *are* made, an' I know who made 'em an' how —well! Jim an' me 're landed purty high an' dry on each side of a family row, an' pa's grave is on this side—an' here I intend to stay—less'n, of co'se, anything was to happen to Jim, an' they couldn't move 'im—and sometimes—reck'n I'm a awful sinner, but I do wish 't—

"Wonder what that was moved! I don't see why 'tis, but I'm jest ez skeery to-night! Ef that wasn't a step, it sounded mightily like it. I do wish 't Rover wasn't deef ; but of co'se, ef he'd o' had his hearin', Buddy would o' took 'im, an' he's a heap o' comp'ny. Reck'n 'twasn't nothin' but the fire poppin'. Even po' Richard looks sort o' droopy to-night. His lame wing seems to flag mo'n common. I often wish 't he could lif' that wing, but of co'se ef he hadn't o' fell out o' the crepe myrtle-tree an' broke it, I wouldn't have him. The ill wind thet upset his nest has brought me many a sweet song. I wish 't he'd sing to night.

"Funny how I always set up Christmas Eves. Sence I been livin' to myself I can't go to sleep a Christmas Eve, save my life. Th' ain't a stockin' I ever hung up, nor a present I ever got or give, nor one o' the folks thet give 'em or took 'em, but 'd come an' pass befo' my face quick ez I'd shet my eyes to-night. But when twelve o'clock is once-t passed, I can lay down an' sleep jest like a baby. It's mos' twelve now. I'm a-goin' to slip Richard's new drinkin'-cup in his cage, an' put his big egg-ball by him, so's when he wakes up he'll find his Christmas breakfast-table a'ready set— an' b'lieve I'll hang Rover's new collar right by him, too—it's a mighty nice collar, considerin' it's made out o' ol' shoes. Goodness! what is that a-rumblin' on that back gallery? The matter with me to-night is jest thet I've clean neglected my duty. That's what it is, an' I'm a-goin' this min-ute an' get my Bible an' read my chapter, an' maybe my nerves 'll be less nervous. I feel 's ef I could laugh or cry jest ez easy ez not.

Miss Lucetta drew her chair to the table before the fire and opened the Book. While she sat thus seeking tranquillity of mind in her lonely room, her lover, in his study, scarce more than out of sight beyond the grove, was restlessly pacing the floor, his hands nervously clasped behind his back. In the centre of the room, upon the floor, lay a

"'I DON'T SAY BUT I AM LONESOME SOMETIMES'"

huge cotton sack, closely filled with sundry parcels of various sizes and shapes. Ever and anon, as he walked, he stopped before the bag, thinking. He was evidently worried.

"Jest how to get it there I don't know," he said aloud, in one of these pauses, "less'n I jest go an' dump it on the back gallery an' run—'n' then ten to one she'd seek the dog on me, 'n' I'd have to own up or get bit. The idea of her not tellin' me thet she'd let Aunt Judy take holiday ! Never was so 'stonished in my life ez when I sneaked roun' to ast Judy to listen for me an' he'p me out, to find her do' shet an' locked, an' she gone. How to do now I don't know. I got a great mind to rig up like a peddler an' sneak roun' to the back do' with my pack, an' then, ef she hears me an' I'm put to it, I'll jest act it out. Don't reck'n it 'd skeer 'er—I wouldn't frighten 'er for nothin'. That's jest the way I'll work it. Like ez not she won't hear me, an' I'll leave the pack right outside 'er do'—an' ef she does, reck'n I'm that good of a actor to play it out. Do wish 't I knew some special, pertic'lar thing she'd like for Christmas. I daresn't put too many drug-sto' things in, less'n she'd s'pect me. I've done wrapped the flesh-bresh up in the bolt o' caliker, an' put the sweet soap in with the sardines an' buckwheat — heap o' the groceries sells sweet-smellin' soap. An' the pills—I'm most afeerd to put them in at all ; but the whites of her eyes is a mighty yaller color ; reck'n they better go in ;

they're jest dropped in, accidental like, in among
the nutmegs an' things. I'm mighty glad I thought
about this air-pillar. She won't never s'pect this,
cause th' 'ain't never been one sold in this town.
This 'n is jest a sample they sent me for the sto',
an' it 'll be mighty nice for 'er to lay 'er lame arm
on to sort o' rest it an' cool it. Better blow it up,
I reck'n, so she'll know what it is. She *might*
mistake it for a hot-water bag. That's it," he
added, with satisfaction, surveying the inflated
pillow—" that's jest about solid enough to feel
good. It 'll be mighty nice for the hammock,
too. Hope she'll like a red hammock. I could o'
got a blue one, but I thought when she'd lay in it
in the summer under the trees the red would sort
o' match the crepe-myrtle flowers. Th' ain't a
thing mo' I can think of thet I'd like to put in the
bag, less'n it's mo' physic, an' reck'n I don't dare
to. An' now I'm a-goin' to rig out. Pa's ol' wig
an' ol' Uncle Mose's blanket-overcoat, an'—an'—
reck'n I better button a piller in the front o' this
overcoat—'n' *then* it's full loose. I'll put a little
o' this chimbly black on my eyebrows, an'—wonder ef she wouldn't know my walk? She's often
tol' me she did. If I had a crutch—or no, here's
the thing ! Here's the thick-soled shoe I've jest
got made for Jim Toland's short leg — I'll put
that on. That's the ticket ! Anybody thet 'd
know me now 'd be welcome to own me. Jim-
miny ! But it's awkward an' clumsy liftin' that
bundle with this shoe on. Reck'n I better take

off the shoe tell I get the bag 'cross my saddle, less'n I'll break my neck."

It was the work of full half an hour to steady the cumbersome bag across the pommel of his saddle, replace the discarded shoe, and, with many a narrow escape from slipping disastrously, finally poise himself safely behind his burden, the difficulty being considerably aggravated by the fact that the right stirrup refused to accommodate the foot with a four-inch sole, so that to maintain the equilibrium of the structure was no mean test of horsemanship.

"Purty way, this, for a man to take his Christmas gifts to his sweetheart," he said, with a nervous chuckle, as finally he started into the footpath across the narrow wood. "Purty way, creepin' roun' like a thief in the dark; but I reck'n it's jest about in keepin' with the rest o' my co'tin'. For the first time in my life I'm glad that dog's deef," he added, as finally he halted a moment, listening at the back gate.

Dr. Jim Morgan was a dignified figure, of an erect slenderness of person, and an air that only his extreme kindliness of manner redeemed from pomposity. There could have been nothing more out of keeping with his own personality than his present disguise—nothing more characteristic than that in his eagerness to serve another he should have lost all thought of himself. With the utmost caution he deliberately opened the gate and, leading his horse now, stealthily crossed the yard.

11

He had just reached and mounted the steps, when he remembered the chance of having to speak. His voice would surely betray him, unless— He took hastily from his vest-pocket a stick of licorice and bit off a piece. The chewing itself would help the disguise. And now, steadying himself against the horse a moment, he reached over and lifted the sack from the saddle. He would not essay to carry it up to the door. The heavy shoe was as noisy as a crutch. He dare not risk a single step upon the porch, but, turning cautiously, would deposit his burden at the head of the steps, and springing into his saddle, make good his escape. He did turn cautiously, but, alas for a leg suddenly grown long, a bulky weight, a time-worn floor! Suddenly as he turned, never so cautiously, something slipped—then everything! The collapse which shook the house frightened the horse, who wisely took to his heels with a bound into the darkness. Before Dr. Jim could recover himself or gather his scattered senses, not to mention his hat and wig, the key turned in the door. In a moment more Miss Lucetta stood in the opening.

"What 'll you have, sir?" she asked, steadily peering out upon the towering figure that reared itself before her, dimly outlined in the darkness.

If she was frightened she did not show it. The Bible lay open on the table behind her.

Advancing laboriously, in mortal terror of a second tumble, Dr. Jim turned the licorice in his mouth and spat upon the floor. Then he spoke :

“ Would the good people thet lives here let a po’
wayfarin’ man lay his burden down for the night?”

The form of speech was Biblical. Whether
consciously so or not, it was a stroke of genius.

“ My ’umble do’ is always open to shelter a wayfarin’ pilgrim,” she replied, as, stepping back, she
produced a candle.

The wayfarer made a movement as if to deposit
his load outside the door, but with a swift motion
of the hand she invited him in.

“ It might rain du’in’ the night. Better lay it
on the side o’ the hearth,” she said, kindly.

“ Thanky mightily, ma’am,” he responded, send-
ing a licorice-colored spray over the reddened
bricks as he spoke.

His extremity was desperate, and this volley
was wholly defensive. Turning, and hobbling
grotesquely now, he prepared to depart.

“ Ef you’d like to stay yourself, I can let you
have the key of a good yard-room,” she added,
following him to the door.

“ Thanky; no, ’m—no, thanky, ma’am ; I’ve got
cover for myself, thanky. Good-night, ma’am.
I’ll call roun’ in the mornin’, ma’am.”

And before she knew it, her grotesque midnight
visitor had hobbled down the steps and was gone.
In the bestowal of sympathy she had forgotten
all fear now, and, turning back, she closed and
mechanically locked the door. But the incident
had restored her drowsing faculties to full wake-
fulness. It was well past midnight ; but instead

of going to bed, she threw an armful of wood upon the fire and took her seat. No sooner had she sat down, however, than, naturally scanning the bag, she was seized with a sudden fear. It was so much larger than she had realized. It had rolled over heavily. What was it?

In a twinkling it seemed that the clock was running a race with her heart, and the strokes of both were terrific—like those of a blacksmith's anvil. Then she felt her face grow red and pale, as breathlessly she watched the bag. She watched in silence while the clock ticked sixty seconds, a hundred and twenty—she never knew why she counted them, but she did — one hundred and twenty — and then she lost count. She had reached a dècision. And now she rose, and, moving alertly, piled wood upon the fire, as much as the chimney would accommodate, and drawing forward a pot - hook, she suspended upon it the teakettle, ready filled with water for the morning's coffee. Then she sat down again, and the clock hammered forty-seven times while she studied the bag again. Then rising once more, she tried all the windows, secured their bolts, and, lifting the heavy iron hook, rarely used now, she doubly fastened the door. Returning to the kettle, which had by this time begun to sing, she tied a long twine to its handle, and moving backwards, drew it taut, and sat down again and studied the bag. As she watched it she felt sure that she saw it move—just a little, as one cautiously breathing, with occasionally just the suspicion of a quiver. But she was not frightened now. She was only patiently, alertly awaiting developments. The fire was roaring, and the room grew hot. She moved back her chair, retaining the end of the twine, which in its passage from the kettle to her hand extended over the bag. How long she would have sat thus it is impossible to say, had there not occurred a sudden unmistakable movement in the bag. With a swishing sound, distinctly like an unsuppressed sigh, there was a sinking in the outline of the figure before her. For a moment she felt as if she should smother, so fast did her heart flutter; but this soon passed, and before she knew she had spoken, she had said aloud :

"I'm compelled to tell you, sir, thet they's a kittle full o' b'ilin' water right over yore head, an' ef you move I'll be fo'ced to douse you all over with it, so don't stir! An' now good - evenin', sir," she continued, pausing. "Maybe you don't see me, 'cause I can't see jest which way you're a-layin', but don't pretend you don't hear. I say good-evenin', sir !"

Another pause.

"You don't lay off to speak, don't you? Well, I can't say I'm s'prised much, though I *have* heerd thet sech ez you was mighty polite an' mannerly. But ef you ain't settin' out to be civilized, that don't hender me none—an' you're in my house, an' though I've got to say some plain things to you, I lay to say 'em jest ez polite ez ef they wasn't so

plain. Of co'se, I take it you're a man. Th'
ain't no woman got quite so far down ez to be
where you are, ez far ez I've heerd tell; an' ef
they was to do it, they'd take some other night
than Christmas Eve for it. So I nachelly take it
you're a man, though not a very big one, less'n
you're considerable cramped, the way you're doubled up; but you're a male person, of the sex
planned *an' executed*—that is to say, made—for
the special pertection of women-folks an' children,
instead o' which you've deliberately started out
to pester an' rob, ef not to murder, a lone, unper-
tected woman. You 'lowed thet she'd get to bed
purty early, an' you'd get out o' yore sack an'
open the do' for yore crowd. Th' ain't nothin'
very new in yore plan. I've heerd about burglars
brought in by peddlers in packs 'fore to-night, an'
stowed away under oak staircases; but I 'ain't
never heerd of none takin' so much trouble less'n
they was mo' to steal 'n what I've got. I don't
say I 'ain't got nothin', mind you, but what I
have got I don't ca'culate to let you have. I
s'picioned you was in that sack most ez quick ez
yore pardner went out, 'n' I was pretty shore I
seen you trimble long befo' you sighed out aloud.
I don't wonder you're low-sperited, an' I'm glad
to see it. It make me have hopes thet you're not
wholly give over to evil. Ef you'd o' chuckled,
layin' there the way you are, I'd hardly had the
heart to pray for you, much less to reason with
you ez I hope to do. The kittle o' b'ilin' water is

hangin', ez I said, on a pot-hook purty nigh over yore head or yore feet, one, an' I've got a string tied to it, so's a quick jerk 'd give you a mighty fiery baptism; but I don't ca'culate to spring it on you less'n you move. So ef you feel a sneeze or anything sudden comin' on you, I'd advise you to tell me befo'hand, 'cause ef you was to stir sudden I might souse you 'fo' I'd be able to stop myself. When I first seen you trimble I don't deny I was purty tolerable skeered, not havin' no man 'round, but my skeer didn't last long, 'cause I mighty soon reelized thet ef anybody *in* a tight place ever had cause for gratitude, I was that person. I don't reck'n there ever was a lone person that was attackted by a burglar thet wouldn't o' give a heap to 've had 'im tied up in a bag same ez I've got you—even ef you have got the way to get out, you'd have to fumble consider'ble to do it. So, stid o' frettin' over it, I jest reasoned thet you wouldn't nachelly stir tell I was asleep, 'cep'n' I let on I saw you, which of co'se I didn't 'low to do tell I was prepared to entertain you. So now I've piled on a good fire, an' I've hung on two pots o' water besides the kittle, an' I've b'iled a pot o' coffee while I been talkin' to you, so even ef you ain't very sprightly I won't get sleepy. I 'ain't never scalted no live thing 'cep'n' my own foot once-t, an' I know how it feels—an' ef I do have to douse you it 'll pain me mightily.

Now I reck'n we both understand one another,

an' I tell you what I lay off to do. I don't reck'n
you've been to no religious service much lately;
'n' ef you have, you've perverted their teachin'
sinfully, and I reckon I couldn't put in this time
'twixt now an' time yore crowd comes better 'n
by a little Scripture readin' an' prayer. Now I'm
a-holtin' on to the kittle rope while I open the
Bible, an' I needn't to tell you it's a-b'ilin', 'cause
you can hear it, less'n you're deef, even ef yore
head's the other way, which—I—don't—think it
—is, come to look close-t. I reck'n the kittle 'd
upset jest about over yore eyes ef I'd jerk it easy ;
an' ef I'd give it a hard snap yore stummick an'
maybe yore legs 'd get it ; but, howsoever, I trust I
won't be called to give you no sech warm reception,
bein' ez you're my comp'ny. Of co'se, all I'm a-sayin' is said 'thout a bit o' pers'nal feelin's; not even
knowin' who you be, it couldn't well be otherwise.
I don't even know ef you're black or white—that
is, 'cep'n my sense tells me you're white. They's
a plenty of our colored folks thet's up to a heap
o' meanness, but this ain't their sort. No, you
ain't no nigger—an' you ain't a woman. You're
some pore misguided man—or boy. Of co'se, I
hope you ain't none of our county boys. Th'
ain't but two thet you could be—an' on'y one o'
them—because you ain't big enough for Tommy
Towns. But maybe you're Ned Jenkins—not
accusin' you, Ned, ef it shouldn't be you—but ef
it *is* I want to say a few words to call to mind
yore raisin'. I knew yore mother before you was

born, Ned, an' her mother before her, leastways her step-mother, 'n' they wasn't better folks nowhere 'n they was. Yore mother died a Christian death, exultin' in the faith an'—oh, Lordy, ef it *should* be you, Ned, I'd like to know it, so 's I could reason with you ez I should. Ef I knew for shore it was you, I'd be mos' tempted to let go this string an' let you out decenter 'n' how you come in; but even ef you was to confess, I'd have no call to believe you. You might be lyin', so 'twouldn't do no good, cep'n' for the relief of yore own soul. Now, the first thing I'm agoin' to do is to read a po'tion of scripture to you, an' ef you are anybody else, I trust you'll apply it to yoreself jest the same.

"What's that smell?" Starting suddenly, Miss Lucetta nearly upset the kettle in her fright. "You're a-tryin' to chloroform me, are you?"

There was undoubtedly a sudden revelation throughout the room of a strange heavy odor. Miss Lucetta laid down her book, and, going to the window, retaining the string the while, lifted the sash. Then she drew back the table, and set her chair near it.

"I reck'n I can set here an' sniff enough o' the air ez it comes thro' the cracks to spile that game. An' I'll take a good whiff o' coffee, too. They say it 'll outdo chloroform ef it's took in time, so I'll take it right now. I'm a-keepin' the string, mind you, while I po' the coffee. It does seem unmannerly to drink it down 'thout offerin' you none, 'specially after you passin' yo' refreshments roun' the way you're doin'.' "

She drank the coffee.

"Now I'm wide enough awake to sniff a pint of yore stuff 'thout feelin' it, an' I'd advise you, *ez a Christian*, to stop up that bottle. 'Befo' readin', let's both of us spend a moment in silent prayer. Ef you're partly on yore knees already, I reckon that 'll do, an' ef you ain't, I'll promise not to jerk the cord tell you kneel down—ef you can ; an' ef you can't, I reck'n the Lord 'll excuse yore attitude, even ef sin did put you there."

She inclined her head, and her moving lips had begun a silent invocation, when suddenly Rover sprang from his sleep with a bound and a yelp. A coal had popped from the fire upon him. With a terrified ejaculation, Miss Lucetta sprang to her feet, the kettle of boiling water deluging the sack.

For a moment she came near fainting. Then a new terror seized her. There was no response to the fiery bath. Manifestly the occupant of the sack had died some moments before. The sigh she had heard was no doubt a dying gasp. The old man who had deposited him upon her hearth was his murderer. A terrible fear seized her. She sank into her chair, trembling like an aspen leaf, the twine falling from her hand upon the floor. How long she sat thus she never knew. It seemed an age that, never taking her eyes from the uncanny thing that lay before her, she patiently waited for the dawn. Indeed, sitting thus within the closely fastened room, impenetrable by the first weak rays of the morning, she knew not that the end of her weary wake was approaching, until suddenly, just behind her, outside the front window, she heard the welcome and cheery voice of Dr. Jim :

"A merry Christmas to you, dearie !"

Starting, she hardly knew how, she strode to the front door, raised its heavy hook, and turned the key.

It was nearly an hour later when she opened her eyes, to find herself lying upon the parlor sofa. Dr. Jim was kneeling beside her, chafing her hands.

" An' to think of me not knowin' the pore man was dyin' tell it was too late !" She began to cry wildly. " But I did talk to him ez serious ez I could, Jim—but, oh, ef I could just 've converted 'im ! I'd think maybe I had, ef he hadn't o' tried to chloroform me the las' thing he did on earth, so I know he died in sin—right befo' my face, and me threatenin' 'im with hot water."

Poor Dr. Jim thought that some unexplained tragedy had bereft her of her reason. It was only after she had recovered herself sufficiently to rise and speak coherently that the truth began slowly to dawn upon him.

" An' to think of me a-spendin' half o' the night, Jim, a-arguin' with a corpse. I'm 'feerd to see you open the bag, less'n it might be—anybody we know."

" But it ain't, honey, I 'shore you it ain't." He

sat beside her, and his arm, for the first time in thirteen years, supported her shoulders. "Th' ain't nobody in there—I'll wager they ain't," he insisted, soothingly.

"But I saw 'im die, I tell you, Jim. I saw 'im breathe his last, and heerd 'im. I'm not a foolish child, Jim. I tell you they's a terrible deed been did, 'n' the sooner it's found out the better."

The situation was too tragic for laughter.

"They's some mighty foolish things been did, I don't deny, honey, an' I been a-doin' a few myself," he said, tenderly. "But they's some sensible things *goin'* to be did—an' I'm goin' to come in for a sheer o' them, too. Now, Lucetty, honey, you're all overwrought an' worked up, an' I'm goin' to do yore thinkin' for the next hour or two. Go get your hat, honey—or lemme get it."

"What you want with my hat, Jim—an' a dead man lyin' on the flo'—not even laid out decent?"

"Here, now, honey. Here's yore hat, an' I've got my buggy out here, an' *you're comin' with me.*"

She turned and looked at him.

"Come on, now; they ain't no time to lose. Ef the strength of mind the Lord's jest give me ain't used quick, it might forsake me. *Come on, honey!* You don't want another thing but just what you've got on. *That's it.*"

She had obediently risen, and, silently wondering, walked to the buggy with him as one in a dream or hypnotized by sheer force of will.

"Where you goin' now, Jim?" she asked, feebly, when they were safely within and driving down the road.

"I'm a-goin' in here for jest a minute," he said, presently, "an' I want you to hold the reins, please, till I come out."

They were at the judge's gate. Miss Lucetta held the reins. In a few minutes he returned, smilingly folding a slip of paper in his hand.

"An' now we're goin' over to the preacher's," he said, calmly, as he turned the horses the other way.

"What for, Jim?" In her voice was no faint suggestion of protest. She asked it as a child—"What for, Jim?"

"We're goin' over to 'range things so's I can say whether or not strange fool men can dump their dog-gone foolishness into yore bedroom all hours o' the night—that's what we're goin' to do. 'N' 'ef I'd o' had any mo' sperit 'n a baked biscuit-man, it 'd o' been did long ago."

"But, Jim—"

"Th' ain't no 'buts' to it, honey, this time. It's jest come down to good solid horse-sense behavior on my part—the way I ought to 've behaved time out o' mind."

"But, Jim, where 're we goin' to—to stay?"

She was recovering her bearings.

"Stay! Why, honey, we'll stay *wherever we happen*, I reckon. I'll go to stay with you tell you pack up, an' you can stay with me a spell—or we won't stay no place, ef you say you. What's *stayin'* got to do with it? I'll stay with you, an' you'll stay with me—less'n we get divo'ced, which we never will, world without end, amen! That's the way I feel about it. 'N' now, honey, how do you feel?"

For answer she laid her hand in his.

"But s'pose they lay that murder on me, Jim—an' we don't even know who it is? We'd both be in disgrace."

"Never mind about who it is. 'Tain't nobody, I tell you. An' don't you mention a word about it in here—do you hear, honey?"

They had arrived at the minister's door. The marriage ceremony is short—and it even shrinks on occasions such as these. A half-hour in the parlor on Christmas morning, just at the time when the little ones are discovering old Santa's gifts, is a terrible interruption to a family man, such as the Rev. Mr. Franklin ; but so happy was he over this morning's work that he declared it was "worth mo' to him than the whole o' Christmas to see such faithful hearts united at last."

The news was too good to be kept, but bride and groom would not leave until they carried his reluctant promise of secrecy until such time as they should themselves make it known. Not even the terrible secret of her bosom, the conviction that a murdered man lay upon her hearth, could keep the happiness that had come to her from shining in Miss Lucetta's pallid face as they turned towards home.

"I brought the buggy out a-purpose this mornin', honey, to beg you, whether or no, to get in it an' go with me—but I didn't 'low to run off with you 'the way I did ; an' as 'tis, I *didn't* ask you, an' it's did anyhow."

"You wouldn't of *ast* me again, after your promise, would you ? Jim, I don't believe it of you."

"Co'se I'd of did it ! Ef I had to take my choice o' crimes I'd o' did that ruther 'n let you live an' die 'fore my very eyes, 'thout anybody to look after you—co'se I would ! All last night, sence I found out that Aunt Judy wasn't on the lot—"

"An' how did you find it out, I like to know ?"

"I jest found it out, I tell you, 'an' it set me to thinkin' s'pose some dare-devil *was* to come in an' scare the wits out of you—whose fault 'd it be ? An' I said to myself same ez Nathan said to David, 'Thou art the man.' An' with that I commenced to think, an' the mo' I thought the foolisher I 'peared to myself. You an' me 've been settin' up here frettin' ourselves about a lot o' nonsense, honey. We've talked about my pa and yore pa an' their little friendly disputes, an' they bein' on each side o' this blamed fence, an' all sech ez that ; an' when you come to think about it, the fence don't run down mo'n two feet in the groun', an' they're a-layin' side by side away down below it—not frettin' 'bout fences no mo'n they do 'bout the grass that grows over 'em."

There was yet quite a little ordeal to undergo in introducing her to the contents of the fateful bag ; and even when this was done Miss Lucetta

was still mystified at the strange and unexplained
phenomenon of the breathing which, she declared,
she saw and heard. For a time Dr. Jim was inclined to laugh at her fancy, but presently the mystery was cleared. The flabby remains of the air-
pillow with a round hole burned in its side told
the tale. It had breathed its last from a coal of
fire which burned into its very vitals, and had
given up the ghost most becomingly, with a gasp.

"An' who in creation you reckon it was thet
fetched the thing, Jim ; an' what you reckon he'll
say 'bout its bein' half burned up an' wet the way
it is ?" said Miss Lucetta, when finally her wonder
was spent.

"Like ez not he won't never come for it, honey.
Like ez not he's some—"

"But for gracious sakes, Jim, look a-here!"

She had taken from the floor a slip of paper,
upon which was written, in a cramped backhand :
"Miss Lucetty Jones. Merry Christmas — from
Santa Claus !" It had evidently fallen out of the
mouth of the sack. .

"Now, who in kingdom *do* you think, Jim?"

Dr. Jim scratched his head. How had he forgotten the inscription written by his own hand?

"Well, honey, I think *this*, ef you want to
know. I think some dern good-hearted fool, with
mo' good intention than brains, has made a jack
of 'isself—that's what I think. I s'pose he 'lowed
thet you wouldn't min' havin' a few little handy
things roun' the house, an' Christmas was a good

time for 'em to drop in ; an' he knew for certain that the weak-kneed somebody thet wears men's cloes an' perfessed all his blame life to love an' cherish you, wouldn't have the grit to come in the front do', an' claim his own, an' pervide for it; so he snook up the back steps an'. played Santa Claus an' fool at the same time—the weak-minded, chicken-hearted—"

Miss Lucetta had listened attentively all the way through ; but now, going to his side, she laid her hand upon his lips.

"That 'll do now, Jim. Don't call yoreself no mo' names. 'You ain't no mo' fool than the one you've done married; not a bit. I never would o' knowed you in creation, an' I wouldn't 've guessed it now 'f it hadn't o' been for yore strong language. You *never* would abuse another person that-a-way, no matter what he done ; 'n' you haven't washed that enduin' brown stuff off o' yore lips good, Jim."

"'Ain't I, shore enough ?" he replied, as he took her in his arms. "I wouldn't do this," he added in a moment, as he kissed her lips, "but we've swapped liquorish-root too many times in school for me to think you'll mind the teenchy tinechy bit on my lips. So you didn't know me, didn't you ? An' you forgive me for skeerin' you ; an' it's all right ?"

"Yas, Jim, it's all right; an' you forgive me for puttin' you to it the way I did, tell you was obliged to stoop to all sorts o' foolishness to do yore part by me. Reck'n you better put half o'
12

them things back in the drug-sto', though—this flesh-bresh, for instance."

He chuckled.

"Reck'n a flesh-bresh *was* a funny present for a man's sweetheart—but they was some so much mo' outlandish things a-layin' roun' the show-case thet it looked mighty suitable to me."

Neither Dr. Jim nor his wife ever told the true story of their Christmas wedding, nor how Miss Lucetta labored for the conversion of her novel burglar; but the doctor often assures her that her night's devotions were not in vain. "For," he declares, "ef any po' fool sinner ever was suddenly lifted out o' plumb darkness an' his eyes opened unto the light through human agency, I was that person; an' ef you wasn't the agent, I dunno who else it was."

Bride and groom went by mutual agreement separately to the Brantley dinner to avert possible suspicion. The occasion was more than ordinarily brilliant, for, in spite of a weary, sleepless night, the guest of honor was animated beyond her habit; while Dr. Jim, as Mr. Brantley afterwards remarked, was "positively giddy, ef not to say silly."

The goose joke came in, in good time, during the discussion of the lordly bird.

"An' now," said mine host, plunging the fork into the rotund breast, "I want to know ef Miss Lucetty an' Dr. Jim — two intelligent, sensible Christians—was to ask a question o' the goose—

"'I WANT TO KNOW EF MISS LUCETTY AN' DR. JIM WAS TO ASK A QUESTION O' THE GOOSE—'"

or to put a cotation to it—I want to know what
'd be a suitable thing for 'em to say."

There was a full minute's pause, and then, having exchanged glances with his wife and read her
consent in her eyes, Dr. Jim rose to his feet. The
bare mention of a goose is a menace in provincial
repartee, and the objects of the evident threat
were quick to perceive the situation.

" Well, Mr. Brantley, sense you've put the question," said Dr. Jim, "I'll tell you. Seems to me
thet the mos' suitable thing *we could do, under
the circumstances*, might be to fall on the goose's
bosom an' say, 'Farewell, Mr. Goose, we've jest—'
Stand up, honey, an' help me out, won't you?"
Lucetta rose, her face scarlet. " Would be, I say,
to fall on his neck an' say, ' Farewell, Mr. Goose,
we've just married out o' yore family.' Ladies an'
gentlemen, *an' the goose*, let me interduce my wife,
Mis' Dr. Jim Morgan, M.D. An' mo' than that,"
he resumed, as soon as he could recover a hearing
amid the din of congratulations—"an' mo' than
that," he insisted, his face now in a broad grin,
" Mis' Morgan and me we wish right now to present our compliments to the goose, an' to say thet
we're sorry his untimely fate makes it impossible
for us to expect him, but thet *all of his family circle
now present* are corjally invited to partake of New-
Year's dinner with us—one week from to-day !"

An invitation unanimously and uproariously accepted.

CÆSAR

CÆSAR

THE moon made a pretty picture, one summer night, out of a lot of commonplace things: two shabby old men on the bank of the Mississippi River, a jagged dark line where young willows grow close to the water's edge on one side, and beyond; where the stream doubled its width in a sudden turn, a suggestion of almost sea-space, marked by a shimmering line.

A keen adjuster of artistic values, when she wills it, is the moon. She knows just what to hold in safe shadow, where to lend herself in delicate silver edging, where to spend her glory like a prodigal.

One of the men, a portly old gentleman whose flowing hair was gleaming silver to-night, and whose face showed a patrician uplifting even in the half-revelation of the moon, walked slowly up and down at the water's edge, halting occasionally and muttering.

The other man was black. Had the moon been less an artist, she would have ignored his humble personality, blending it with the shadows, and the picture would have lacked its story.

He sat flat upon the levee, beside an empty

rocking-chair, and solicitously watched the walker near the water. Rising presently and seizing a straw hat that lay in the chair, he approached the white man.

"Marse Taylor," he said, presenting the hat with some trepidation, "you thinks a heap o' de Taylor blood, doncher?"

The old gentleman paused.

"Taylor blood?" he repeated, absently. Then, firing suddenly, he added: "Who says anything about the Taylor blood?"

"Me. I seh, Marse Taylor, seem lak you done los' intruss in de Taylor blood, de way you feedin' it out ter fatten 'bout a million o' muskitties a-swarmin' roun' yo' haid. Deze heah gallinippers ain't got no mo' rispec' fur a'stokercy 'n hongry cannibal-eaters; but dey sha'n't start a bobbecue on yo' haid, not whiles Cæsar's heah ter haid 'em orf. Heah, Marse Taylor, four Gord sake, please, sir, put on yo' hat."

Instead of taking the hat, however, the gentleman addressed said:

"Go and get your own hat, you black, baldheaded rascal, you!"

Cæsar laughed.

"Hursh, Marse Taylor, hursh. Any gallinipper dat kin meek a square meal off'n my haid, de way I done swivelled up an' all gone ter dandruff, kin teck it an' welcome. Ef dey'd all come an' breck orf dey punctuatiom-p'ints in my hide 'fo' dey samples de Taylor blood, I wouldn't keer.

Dcy puts in dcy pipes on yo' white skin, an' turn on de suction tell dcy mos' busses open, den come set roun' on my haid an' pick dey toofs an' hiccough. I done watched 'em, an' I des' shoos 'em off fo' dey impidence."

Still the white man did not take the hat, but resumed his promenade, Cæsar following at his side now, and talking incessantly while furtively watching his face.

Finally the old gentleman turned suddenly, and, with a weary sigh, sank into the rocking-chair. As he sat, Cæsar, by a quick movement, dropped the hat upon his head.

"What do you mean, sir, by your impertinence?" he exclaimed. But the negro had already started forward, and was pointing excitedly into the air while he cried:

"Look, four Gord sake, Marse Taylor! Is you see dat great big gallinipper fly off my haid an' knock yo' hat right out'n my hand? Yonder he goes, todes de river! I tell yer, sir, a gallinipper is de meanes' thing on top dis roun' worl' *sence de wah!* 'Fo' de wah, dey was nex' in meanness ter a nigger slave-owner. Dem was *de* meanes'! You ricollec' ole Kinky Jean Baptiste, wha' used ter tie 'is niggers up an' whup 'em wid briars?"

The old man had taken his seat at his master's feet, and, ignoring the hat which still rested forgotten where he had dropped it, continued without a pause:

"Who-ee! Don't talk ter me 'bout no nigger

slave-owners! Dey warn't nothin' but a cross twix' a vampire an'—an' a wil'-cat—dat what dey was! An' now ole Kinky Jean a-settin' up in a jedge's cheer, a-dolin' out jestice lak he knowed it when he seed it! He don't know no mo' 'bout jestice 'n—'n I does 'bout grammar—not a bit. He twis' it ter spress 'is own intruss, des' same as I does speech. Pusson what git in tight passages can't stop to reg'late speech by books, I tell yer! He boun' ter talk 'is way out'n de tunnel, grammar ur no grammar. But eh, Lord! Ef I had 'a' had educatiom, I'd 'a' made things whiz roun' heah sence de wah! Ricollec' how you used ter try ter teach me readin' out'n a Bible-book, Marse Taylor? I d'know huccome I 'come so thick-skulled. Look lak my min' done tooken sich a lodgmint in my *haid*, dat I can't th'ow it out inter a book ter save my good-fur-nothin' black skin! Tell de trufe, I'd a heap ruther wrastle wid a tiger 'n a book any day, 'caze I'd know 'is language an' give 'im good as he sen'—ur miss it, one. But a book! A book's des' de same ter me as Gord. Look lak hit's a-settin' in jedgmint over me, 'caze hit's got a wisdom dat I can't tech. Dat's what meck me git so still-moufed in de evenin's, Marse Taylor, settin' on de hyarth in yo' libr'y. I des' looks roun' dem walls an' views de still knowledge an' keep silence."

The old man was borne onward into unconscious eloquence by an awakening interest in the theme into which he had drifted in his effort to di-

vert the mind of his master, who had not spoken
again. Cæsar was anxious at this long silence.

"Look lak you's low-sperited to-night, marster," he resumed, presently. "Fur Gord sake,
boss, don't let go yo' grip ; 'caze time you give
up Cæsar gwine let down too, an' dat 'll be a
purty howdy-do ! Is you got any news in a letter,
Marse Taylor ?"

"No news, Cæsar. It's only the old story—
hard times—hard times."

Cæsar laughed.

" De idee o' you talkin' 'bout hard times, boss,
settin' up heah wid a whole gol' toof a-shinin' in
yo' mouf dis minute ! Hyah ! Look a' me, wid
nothin' but two ol' snags lef', an' dey nex'-do'
neighbors. I des' gums it fur all I's wuth, an'
bless Gord fur de soup-pot."

Cæsar's heart was relieved. If poverty were
all, there was little to worry about. He had
never been able to understand how genuine quality white-folk could be really poor. There were
plenty of "poor white trash " within his ken who
had been born to poverty and poor ways—who
talked long, dipped snuff, went barefoot, and
who, mannerless and moneyless, were entirely beneath the contempt of a quality negro such as
himself. He could comprehend how such as these
could actually feel hard times and privation, conditions treated only in the abstract by aristo-
crats.

In a certain way, of course, he apprehended

that money difficulties formed an important fac-
tor in the post-bellum situation ; but they were
big difficulties—gentlemen's straits—arising peri-
odically at the annual reckonings, and in no way
affected the ultimate question of wealth, excepting
possibly to enhance its dignity. A financial
strength that, rising superior to high-sounding
debts, could survive year after year was a thing
to respect.

If his old master had grown careless about his
toilet, if the house needed paint and the fences
were tottering, were not these merely the signs
of the passage of time, which had borne them all
into the period of old age ?—old age, that pro-
verbially scorns outwardnesses, concentrating its
last vitalities on inward considerations, spiritual
or otherwise.

Colonel Taylor's time-sharpened proclivities
were not spiritual. They were otherwise. As a
young man he had loved the chase, the oar, a
dozen books, his pretty wife, a good story with
his wine and water and venison steaks. Now all
but the last things had passed away. His wife
had long been but a memory. Horses and boats
were for the young. The *raconteur* is lost without his audience.

But health, appetite, and an environment rich
in material for its gratification were left him, with
Cæsar for gleaner, trapper, hunter, fisher, caterer,
cook — Cæsar, whose culinary fame during four
years of army service had gone abroad through-

out the regiment. The truth was that there were
scarcely now, in all Louisiana, two greater old
epicures than old Colonel Dunbar Taylor, of Ink-
land plantation, and his negro servant, Cæsar.
For ten years they had lived without other com-
panionship in this old plantation-house. For as
many summers Cæsar had carried the rocker out
on the levee outside the gate every evening, and
returned with it upon his head behind his master
when the plantation-bell rang for nine o'clock.

As he did so to-night he noticed for the first
time that peculiar little lurch in the colonel's gait
that suggests mental weakening. Stopping short
in his path to reassure himself, he exclaimed:

"Good Gord!" And again noting the flurried
movement: "Rub yo' eyes, nigger, an' look ag'in!
Yo' ole marster done tooken a new graveyard
step, sho's you born! Hol' on ter 'im tight, ole
man, an' min' 'im good 'fo' he slip away f'om
you. Dey ain' no mo'·Marse Dunbar Taylors in
the Taylor fact'ry. Dis is de las' drap o'· de
Dunbar-Taylor blood a-walkin' down dat levee;
an' ef yer don't nuss it good an' keep it warm,
dey's one ole nigger gwine be settin' on a green
grave, de onies' one lef' ter tell de tale."

With this he hurried forward, and, joining the
old gentleman, touched his elbow gently as if to
steady him.

For some time Cæsar had suffered moments of
anxiety about his master, seeing him preoccupied
and silent, or, as to-night upon the bank, mutter-

ing to himself. The truth was that the white man had a sorrowful secret—the only formulated secret which he held from the black—and it was telling on him. He had, of course, certain reserves, and there were passages in his life—memories now—in which the old negro had no part. But these were matters of course rather than conscious reservations. The agonizing feature of his present secret was that it could no longer be kept. Cæsar must soon know it.

It was this: for several years he had maintained his position on the plantation, after a foreclosed mortgage, only by grace of the new owner, as a salaried overseer. None of the negroes knew this. Cæsar need never have discovered it had the arrangement held. But it was to end: he had been asked to resign. This was his secret.

It was not this specific fact which he so dreaded to confess. It was rather the question that would follow upon its heel which disturbed him: What should he do about Cæsar? For himself, he was strangely devoid of apprehension. He would go to the city, where there was "always room for one more." The world owed him a living, and he would get it.

Comforting himself with such trite philosophies of the unfortunate, he felt no fear. But Cæsar! He could not take him. How could he leave him? The question had preyed upon his mind until, in sheer desperation, he had resolved upon a plan that came as an inspiration. He would run away. Just before the new management should take possession, he would slip out in the night and hail a passing boat. He would leave a note explaining to the old man in terms of affection that business had called him away, and, hating to say good-by, he had not waked him. He would close by wishing him a prosperous connection with the new administration. The note he would enclose with a personal line to the postmistress, begging her to read it to the old man.

We have seen that, on the evening when this story opens, Cæsar had gotten a first inkling that a serious matter was disturbing his master. The suspicion, once lodged within his brain, took unto itself eyes and ears. If real trouble were brewing he would discover what it was.

During the month following this no suspected criminal was ever more closely watched than was the old gentleman who was summoning all his craft—a quality nearly extinct from disuse—to prepare for clandestine flight. Whether he rode into town, remained an hour beyond his habit in field or sugar - house, or repaired at an unusual hour to his library, Cæsar invented some ruse to dog his footsteps.

The old man, despite his own habit of talking to himself, could not prevent a creepy feeling from spreading over him when his master's voice in monologue floated out the library window or announced him even in advance of his attenuated shadow, as he came with irregular step up the western walk in the afternoons. There was in it something uncanny, confirming the impression of an impending crisis.

He was destined soon, however, to discover a clew giving shape and direction to his suspicions. An old sole-leather trunk, unused for a decade, was transferred during his absence from the garret to his master's room, secreted behind his bed, and carefully covered with folds of drapery.

His next discovery was of money in the colonel's purse—great rolls of greenbacks. The first thrill of pleasure at this unprecedented vision was followed by increased apprehension. Money could scarcely be said to be current in these parts in these days, wealth being solely a matter of credit. Pen - scratches on slips of paper floating into the storehouses provided all life's necessaries. Written orders sent to the great city rebounded in supplies by tierce or barrel. The familiar use of money might almost be said to have been in disrepute. It was the only hope of the poor whites or such irresponsible negroes as lived from hand to mouth without contract. Even the blacks whose thrift had lifted them into the outer circle of commercial standing were laboriously inditing certain charmed words on paper bits, keeping their money respectably out of sight.

His discovery of this cash possession disturbed Cæsar more and more as he thought upon it.

His next clew was an important one gleaned

from snatches which he overheard of conversation with a neighbor. They were negotiating for the sale of the colonel's horse.

"He's an old horse, sir, and I'll give you seventy-five dollars for him, and promise you he shall die mine," were the visitor's words.

"He's yours, sir, on that condition," was the reply. "You take him the day I go. I'd rather sell him to you with this assurance than to get double the sum without it. Tell you the truth, sir, there's only one living thing I think more of than my horse, and that's that old black rascal Cæsar. I love that darkey. The day I leave this plantation I sneak away like a runaway nigger because I can't tell him good-bye. And recollect, I trust you to be silent."

Cæsar, eavesdropping, crouched on all-fours behind the honeysuckle vine, rolled over backward, and retreated sobbing at this point. The mystery was solved. From his hiding-place he hastened, sniffling as he went, to the river-bank. It was he now who, walking up and down, talked to himself.

"De idee!" he sobbed. "I knowed it—knowed it des' as well 'fo' I heerd it as I does now. De idee! An' a Taylor, too—an' a Dunbar Taylor at dat—to—to—to ac' des' lak a sneak-thief! Well, Cæsar, my boy, look lak yo' wisdom-toofs ain't come an' gone fur nothin'. You ain't got but des' one ob 'em lef' in yo' jaw; but I reckin, wid hit, Cæsar kin keep up wid Marse Dunbar Taylor, ef he is able ter outdo Gord an' cut gol' toofs in place o' bone ones. So you gwine travellin', is you, Cæsar? Seem lak you is. An' you better hump yo'se'f, nigger, 'caze dat trunk o' yo' marster's is half packed now."

Thus he talked on until the visitor was seen to depart, when he hastened within his master's call. .

That very night it was that, leaving the colonel snoring, he betook himself straightway to the house of Kinky Jean Baptiste, the parish judge. They had been in close converse for an hour when Cæsar said for about the tenth time : "You see, I come ter you, jedge, 'caze you got de papers in de co't-house, an' you knows. I don't owe nobody a cent. An' I'll sell you my mule an' wagon an' plough an' de spotted yearlin' an' de red heifer an' dat brindled steer an'—"

"An' yo' dog?"

"No, sir. I ain't name de dog. I seh I'll sell what I done said an' my crop, which is three acres o' bottom-lan' all in cotton, for three honderd dollars; an' you kin meck out de papers to suit yo'se'f, des' so you pays me de money cash down an' write in de paper dat dis here's a secret sale. An' ef you tell it 'fo' I go, de sale's done broke."

"But what unfroward succumstance has befell you, Cæsar, to predispose you to exchange yo' domicile so suddently?" pompously demanded the lettered administrator of justice.

"Dis is des' a little business 'twix' me an' Marse Taylor, jedge, an' I never tells out de

fam'ly business. An' I wants de money to-morrer
night. You kin 'quire 'bout me at de sto'e in de
mornin', an' see how I stan's all roun'. An' to-
morrer, please Gord, 'bout dis time, I'll be back
heah."

On the second day after this another clandestine trunk-packing was under way. Like his
shadow Cæsar followed his old master. Not
knowing the date of the proposed flight, he was
nervous at the passage of every boat going either
way. To the three hundred dollars realized from
the first sale he had added about fifty more from
minor transactions ; and on the last day—as it
proved—on counting the contents of the colonel's
purse during the old gentleman's sleep, he chuckled to find that his own held just one dollar more.

It was on the evening of this same day that
something occurred which convinced Cæsar that
the departure was near at hand. Following the
colonel at a safe distance through the garden
across a meadow, he saw him approach his wife's
grave, and, laying a flower upon it, turn with
bowed head and slowly retrace his steps.

It was a delicate and dignified act, and Cæsar
was much impressed. Instead of proceeding on
the errand on which he had been sent, he turned
into a path leading through a pine thicket to the
left. Gathering wild roses as he went, which
he mixed, regardless of color antagonisms, with
clumps of golden-rod, he turned towards the
plantation cemetery, a stone's-throw beyond.

"You is a low-down nigger, Cæsar," he said to himself as he walked. "You better bless Gord fur white folks dat kin show you manners. I bet you two bits you can't fin' yo' ole 'oman's grave now, you ornery no-'count nigger, even arter yo' marster done showed you de motions o' manners. I bet you hit's done growed up wid jimsen-weeds an' cockle-burs tell you won't know it. But don't you let on, nigger. Ef you can't fin' it, des' step up manful in de presence o' de dead an' meek per-ten' lak you is foun' it."

Halting presently beside a weed-grown heap, and laying thereon his floral tribute, he continued, with measured formality :

"Heah, Calline, ole 'oman, ef you ain't layin' heah, deze few flowers b'longs whar you is, honey. An' good-by—so long! Praise Gord, I say. An' Lor-rd, I do pray, keep a eye on dis po' skittish no-'count ole nigger ; an' ef he loose hisse'f f'om You, don't You loss Yo'se'f f'om him, I pray, Lord, 'caze he's a-gittin' ready fur a jump in de dark, an' he dunno which way nur whar he gwine!"

Turning slowly, he moved sadly homeward, overtaken with emotions that surprised himself. He felt sure the hour of parting with familiar scenes was at hand. During the approaching night a boat was due, descending the river. When it should whistle at the bend five miles above he would watch the colonel's movements, and he was ready to follow. So absorbed was he in reflection that he had proceeded some distance before he descried in the gathering twilight, just before him against the sky, a dark column of smoke spangled with ascending sparks.

The boat was at the landing. There had been no announcing bell nor even the customary whistle. He was being outwitted by a conspiracy. With a single agonized ejaculation he sprang forward, and, clearing outer fence and wood-pile with running leaps, he bounded towards the house.

"You fool nigger—you fool, you—you blame ole black fool!" he cried, beating his breast as he went and sobbing aloud.

A flying tour through the rooms confirmed the truth. The bird had flown. Even the little trunk was gone.

Out over the gallery, down the steps, across the garden, he ran towards the fiery cloud, screaming aloud as he went.

Five minutes later, as the boat pushed out into the stream, the half-dozen men at the wharf fell back in alarm as the figure of a slim black man, emerging from the wood behind them, dashed madly into their midst, and, before they could interfere, had bounded with a single spring across the widening gap.

A unanimous scream of alarm ashore was echoed by a chorus on board; but, in a breath, a second shout went up—a deafening cheer—as the little old man landed on his feet atop a cotton-bale on the lower deck.

He was a shabby little hero, and, as the crew

gathered about his tattered figure, he felt need of all the dignity he could command. His first movement was to mop his forehead and fan himself with his brimless hat.

"What kind o' tug ur flat-boat ur skift *ur what* is y'all a-runnin', dat you can't 'ford no whistle ter give a gemman time ter dress 'isse'f?" he said, finally, surveying his rags with the air of a gentleman surprised *en déshabillé*.

"Cap'n's orders," was the laconic reply from several voices.

"What kind o' sort o' cap'n is y'all got—so stingy wid 'is steam? If he'd 'a' sont me word, I'd 'a' *gi'n* 'im a load o' pine, des' ter feed dat one whistle. What does I look lak, ter go—ter go—"

"Whar you gwine?" asked several voices at once.

Cæsar suddenly remembered that he did not know.

"Whar I gwine? I gwine trabblin'—dat's whar I gwine. Yer reck'n I'd 'a' stepped 'crost dat gap 'f I was gwine stay home? But I wants ter know buccome dis heah lorg raft ain't blowed no whistle, an' I means business! I got de money fur my passage in my waistcoat pocket; an' I done lef' all my trunks an' ban'-boxes, 'count o' yo' deef-an'-dumb nornsense to-night."

"Look heah, nigger," exclaimed a portly ebony swell standing near: "ef you got any bluffin' an' cussin' ter do, s'pose you step up on deck an' call out de cap'n. We ain't never stopped at yo' little one-mule settlemint befo', nohow. Cap'n des' run in dar to-night 'count o' ole Colonel Dunbar Taylor wantin' ter go down ter Noo 'Leans. Whar is you boun' fur, anyhow?"

"Who—me? I boun' fur Noo 'Leans—dat's whar I boun' fur; an' I wants ter settle my trav'lin' spenses now, too. I'm a cash man, I is! Whar's de conductor what c'lects de small change on dis canoe, anyhow?"

With a deliberate nonchalant movement he drew from his pocket a heavy roll of greenbacks.

A change passed over his audience. The identical man who a moment ago had resented his bravado now exclaimed:

"You fellers standin' roun' heah better stop yo' grinnin'. Some day, when you in swimmin', somebody 'll steal yo' clo'es, an' you'll be wuss off 'n dis gemman is. Jes' walk up wid me, mister, an' I'll conduc' you ter de desk ter 'posit yo' fare."

As the old man proceeded up-stairs beside the dazzling personage, who proved to be the steward, it was hard to decide which was the more pompous of the two; and when, an hour later, Cæsar reappeared with the same escort, it was indeed a question which was the greater swell.

From a wealth of discarded garments of assorted conditions, styles, and sizes — the legitimate perquisites of the steward's office—Cæsar had, through the intervention of a goodly share of his money-roll, become a splendid gentleman of so many toilet suggestions that the effect was bewilderingly non-committal.

If the lavender trousers that adorned and somewhat embarrassed the freedom of his thin legs were coarsened in effect by a gaudy plaid waistcoat, both were duly reproved and subdued by a long black coat of clerical pattern, which in its turn was robbed of any undue austerity by a polka-dotted four-in-hand tie and a Derby hat.

But Cæsar was not altogether happy. After he had carefully wrapped and tied his discarded clothing in his plaid kerchief and deposited it beneath the mattress of his bunk, after he had secretly divided his money into several small rolls which he concealed about his person, after he had sprayed his shirt-front with the magic bulb of the perfume-bottle which his benefactor had thrown in as *lagniappe* at the end of his trade, he began to feel restless for a sight of his master.

His intimate relations with the steward made this a comparatively easy matter. It was embarrassed, however, by Cæsar's fear of recognition—a needless apprehension, as his own mother, meeting him unexpectedly, would not have recognized him.

It was not until late at night that he ventured, standing in the darkness outside the door of the gentlemen's cabin, to peep timorously within. The sight that greeted him here filled his old heart with honest pride. The lordly colonel, a veritable grandee in appearance, was the centre of a listening circle, while an offtold tale was renewing its youth under the combined stimulus of recovered opportunity and the departed contents of sundry conspicuous glasses upon the table round which the company were gathered, whereon also a moving pack of cards and a heap of coins added their suggestions of sport and peril to discerning eyes.

But Cæsar, standing in the shadow, saw only that his master was a happy lordling, unembarrassed by all the gorgeousness of gilding and upholstery that was dazzling his own bewildered eyes.

Drawing the heavy folds of the *portière* about him to conceal himself more fully, he sat down to feast his eyes on the sight.

" Umph !" he exclaimed, mentally. " De Taylors nachelly fits in granjer. Des' look at 'im ! Lis'n, chillen : he tellin' 'bout how he fooled de conscrip' gyards. Wonder ef he tol' 'em yit 'bout de Georgy major. No, heah it come now —wid a new cuss-word ev'y time he tell it."

Cæsar's pleasure in the scene was great, but the folds of the curtain were soft and warm against his back ; it was growing late ; the excitement of the day was telling upon him. Looking in upon them, he beheld the figures with lessening distinctness, until they seemed afar off at the end of a lengthening vista. The voices grew indistinct. His head bobbed. He was asleep— asleep suddenly, profoundly, as only old people and little children drop instantaneously into the downy regions of rest.

For several hours the old man had slept, unobserved, that sweet, deep sleep of the two childhoods, when suddenly he heard in thunder-tones his own name:

"Cæsar!"

He was on his feet in a moment, and the next found him in the centre of the gay saloon, shouting in a high-noted voice of command:

"Teck yo' han's off dat gemman, I say! Leave go, I tell yer! Who say it's yo' money? How dast you lay yo' good-fur-nothin' pink fingers on dis gemman? Han's off, I tell you, 'fo' I fo'gits myse'f! You heah me talkin'? Hol' up, Marse Taylor! Stiddy yo'se'f on me! Gimme de money!"

At this the intoxicated old colonel, holding the disputed possession aloft in his clinched hands, turned upon the negro.

"Who are you, you impertinent black peacock?" he cried, livid with rage. "One of the gang, in your checkered livery—one of their blasted confederates! Out with him! Hold! Help!"

Overpowered at last by two agile little men, who, scaling his tall figure as a ladder, seized the treasure, he fell to the floor with a despairing cry:

"Murder! Thieves! My God! Where's—where's Cæs-ur-a? Cæsar!"

Cæsar was, for the moment, *non est,* but now returning, breathless, he cried :

"Heah me, marster! I done flung dat bluebreeches one over de banisters. Whar's de yethers? Gorn, is dey? But I'll ketch up wid 'em yit. Open yo' mouf, Marse Taylor, an' drink dis."

The old gentleman opened his eyes for a second only, and, shrinking visibly, cried in terror :

"Hands off, you rascally black confederate—you black—

Cæsar began to cry.

"Yas, I is Confedrit, marster. We all is. You know we is. Ain't I fit wid you all indu'in' de wah? Open yo' eyes, marster, an' look ag'in !"

But he did not look again. His tongue was heavy as he said :

"Here, sir! I hear him. Come here, Cæsar, you old fel–fl–fellow, and take off this rasc'ly—"

He began to snore.

Seeing him sleeping, Cæsar seized a pillow from the divan, and, slipping it under his head, peered cautiously about the apartment. The gentlemen of the game were nowhere visible, but in the doorway, his face in a broad grin, stood his friend the steward.

"Seem lak de ole sport got de wust of it, ain't he ?" was his ill-timed and irreverent greeting.

"Ole what ?" Cæsar moved towards him with clinched fist.

"I say, seem lak de ole gemman got de wust o' de game," he repeated.

"Look heah, nigger! I'll have you know dis here game ain't but des' started. De colonel's des' teckin' a res', an' I'm gwine leave 'im fur a minute whils' I tends ter a little business."

"Yas, you better go an' let gemmen's fusses alone. Dat's my legal advice ter you. Dey was a yo'ng man th'owed over the gyards des' now, on dis boat; an' ef dey ketch you meddlin' up heah, dey li'ble ter treat you lakwise."

"Dey is, is dey? Mh - hm! You see, I happens ter know de gemman what th'owed dat yo'ng man over de railin'. He's des' teckin' a nap yonder on de flo'—res'in' 'isse'f; an' ef you'll des' set down an' bresh de muskitties off'n 'im tell I come back, hit'll be wuth a couple o' dimes ter you."

If the steward took his pay in the dollars which he found scattered around the floor, instead of in dimes as agreed, Cæsar was none the wiser.

When presently the little old man returned, he was clad again in all his plantation rags, even to the faded kerchief about his neck. Forgetful of the steward, he knelt at his master's side.

"Heah's Cæsar, Marse Taylor," he said, touching his shoulder. "Weck up, marster, an' look. Come, let Cæsar he'p you ter bed."

Cæsar could not rouse him, however; and it was only when, with the steward's aid, he had lifted him up, that he opened his heavy eyes, and, with quivering lips, cried:

"Wh—why, Cæsar! Why didn't you come

before ? I needed—needed you, you black—black rascal, you—"

Cæsar had no voice left ; but by prompt action, now no longer resisted, the two men had soon gotten the old gentleman on his feet and virtually carried him to his state-room.

The colonel had lost nothing of his prestige in the steward's regard because of the present incident. Such were the ways of many popular "big men"—such the ups and downs of many gentlemen of his ken who travelled the river. Nor had Cæsar lost, but rather gained in importance by establishing his connection with Colonel Dunbar Taylor, even though he had donned his honors on his knees in a livery of rags.

On the day ensuing, when by his negative consent and feeble recognition Cæsar was duly installed as the colonel's body-servant with upper-cabin privileges, an improved toilet became obviously imperative. Although unwitnessed, it was a pathetic spectacle when he proceeded by slow stages, watching the effect of each garment in turn, to rearray himself.

The old gentleman kept his berth during the rest of the trip ; and when Cæsar felt the shiver of the boat, as she seemed to steady herself preparatory to landing, he was seized with an internal panic. Bills had come in for the colonel's passage and for wine and cigars on that fateful night—bills which by a little strategy he had settled in his master's name, with fabricated messages of regret at the delay; and the finances of the firm were very low.

The silent partner in the firm — the unrecognized contributor of both the money and the experience — as he trod the gang-plank with his master's arm, beset by doubt, ignorance, fear, not knowing which way to turn, walked yet with the resolute step of one with a fixed resolve. This resolve was, in the unexpressed phraseology of his heart, to "keep his eyes skinned an' look out four ole marster."

His only hope lay in following the crowd. As they threaded their way through the throng upon the levee, the old man, with more fervor than was his wont, muttered a prayer like unto this:

"O Lor-rd, four Gord sake, lead deze two po' ole pilgums an' show 'em whar ter go—"

"What do you say, Cæsar?" asked his companion.

"Who—me? I des' hummin' a chune, Marse Taylor."

"And you are going to the St. Charles Hotel, as I ordered?"

"Yassir, co'se I is. Hit's down dis way a little piece." Then mentally, "An' oh, my Gord, forgive me four lyin,' 'caze you know my money wouldn't hol' out a week at no S'in' Charles Hotel. You know it wouldn't, Gord, Yo'se'f — an' ole marster callin' fur champagne all de time. You know his haid ain't nuver come straight fur two days, an' I bleeged ter lie to-night, Gord, an' don't You charge me wid it."

In this fashion, formulating every thought as a prayer, he stumbled blindly on. It was dark, and the city lights were lit. They had proceeded a half-dozen squares, perhaps, when something happened. A man walking ahead stopped and read a sign upon a door.

"Furnished rooms to rent," were the charmed words Cæsar heard.

Without a moment's hesitation, he mounted the narrow steps jutting out over the banquette and raised the iron knocker. The colonel's protest was disregarded.

"Set down on de step a minute, marster, tell I go in an' 'quire de way," he said, with a finality of tone not to be opposed.

A moment's conference with the copper-colored landlady within—long enough, nevertheless, for the prepayment of a week's rent—resulted in her returning with Cæsar to assure monsieur :

"Oh yas, 'tis de Sen' Charle' Hotel, yas, of co'se—de side do'. De gentleman's room is all prepare. Egscuse me, monsieur, if I assis' you. Doze step is so very much slippy."

And so, before he could frame a protest, the old colonel felt himself lifted firmly and gently up and assisted into the "side door of the St. Charles Hotel."

If the low portal of this modest house of *Chambres Garnies* fell short of his memory-picture of the brilliant rotunda of the St. Charles Hotel, where in years past he had always been greeted by a convivial welcoming crowd, the discrepancy was soon forgotten in the presence of immediate comfort.

Though among the less prosperous of her class, Ma'm Zulime was an artist to a degree, and she knew her people. The gentleman with a body-servant, able to prepay, was instantly recognized and taken in.

From its interior, the apartment in which our friends found themselves might have been a modest chamber in any fairly appointed provincial hotel. Here were velvet carpets and upholstery —faded, it is true—gas-lights, a pitcher of ice-water presented with a tap at the door—yes, surely, after all, it was the St. Charles Hotel.

This thought one minute, forgetfulness the next, now realization of a want — a toddy, less light or more, a cigar, a third pillow, another blanket over his feet—a dim sense of confusion, then a snore.

Cæsar, sitting alone beside the bed, breathed a sigh, half relief, half of apprehension, at the sound. The snoring, mingled with the roar of the city without, seemed a resumption of the stentorian breathing of the boat.

He knew intuitively that his master's condition was serious. He had seen him prostrate from over-much wine, at rare intervals, in years past ; but the symptoms were more fleeting and differ-cnt. He felt very lonely, and his little lavender-clad legs ached. The situation was really too tragic to contemplate seriously.

Rising from his seat, he crossed the room, and, approaching an old mirror opposite, regarded himself, chuckling :

"Well, Cæsar, ole gemman, look lak you in a tight place, ef you is got on good clo'es. You better be dressed up, you ole plantation moke, you, ter match dat roa'in' granjer outside. Des' lis'n ! Z-z-z-z ! R-r-r-r ! Gol' granjer rollin' on silver wheels ! Silks a-swishin' ! Corks a-poppin' ! Bells an' toot-horns an' whistles all th'owed in together ! Des' lis'n at de city ! Lis'n what it say, ole man ! 'Z-z-z ! I know you ! You's a country nigger ! Can't fool me, if you is got on secon'-han' finery ! Z-z-z ! Ef yer want ter keep up wid me, yer better walk fas', ole man !' Dat what it say, an' you better read yo' lesson right ter-night, Cæsar ! Tune yo'se'f up ter de city music, an' don't forgit you's a Taylor nigger, an' a Dunbar-Taylor nigger at dat. How much money you got lef', anyhow, Cæsar ?"

Sitting flat upon the floor before the glass, he soon produced from various hiding places about his person a half-dozen rolls of bills, which he proceeded to count.

"Well," he exclaimed, finally, "hit mought be better ; an' den ag'in, it mought be wus."

Soliloquizing in this fashion, he sat here until finally, growing drowsy, he threw himself back-

14

ward upon the cot provided for him, and fell asleep.

His first days in the strange city were times of sore trial. The old colonel grew mentally worse rather than better; but it was not until a week had passed that Cæsar made the startling discovery that his feet were dead to sensation and · he could not stand.

Though choking with emotion, the old man's exclamation was one of thanksgiving at the revelation.

"Praise Gord, I say, fur turnin' de key on 'is foots tell He onlock 'is haid. Praise Gord, I say!" were his words, uttered with a sob.

The old man's constant dread had been lest his charge, difficult and unreasonable enough as things were, should some day sally forth on a tour of investigation. It was enough that he daily swore against the new management of the St. Charles Hotel, and demanded delicacies difficult and often impossible to procure.

Cæsar had soon won his way into the modest kitchen of Ma'm Zulime, who was pleased to yield a corner of her stove to the artist who could fabricate so many epicurean delicacies. And Cæsar was so funny, so droll, so entertaining! In the evenings, when the colonel went to sleep early, he would sit on the floor beside her and relate most marvellous stories of the magnificence of his plantation home. His tales were like those of the "Arabian Nights," not only in gorgeousness of coloring, but in each night's recital excelling the preceding in grandeur.

It was needful that he should have some relief for the panic that raged within him; and since he could not vent it in kind, he continued consistently to translate it into a note of bravado. The lower the market-money dwindled, the funnier grew his jokes, the more extravagant his stories.

The day he changed his last twenty-dollar bill at a game-stall, he was so facetious over the transaction that the market-folk were in a roar of laughter when he left them; and as he crossed the street he stepped rhythmically into a dancing measure while he sang the plantation medley beginning:

"My white folks is rich as a cup o' cream.
    Come along, Miss Nancy!
Dey money flows out in a silver stream.
    Come along, Miss Nancy!
Dey'll give us all a dance ev'y Sa'ddy night,
An' a boat on the river when de moon is bright,
An' you won't know de diffunce but what you's white.
    Come along, Miss Nancy!

This was followed by a shout of applause, amid which a man from the saloon at the corner threw the performer a nickel.

Quick as a flash he picked it up and dropped it into his hat, which forthwith he proceeded to pass round, singing as he went:

"Oh, Nancy Ann is hard to beat.
    Come along, Miss Nancy!

Shuffle right along an' twis' yo' feet.
  Come along, Miss Nancy!
She wears number 'leven, but it fits her neat,
An' her mouf is a rose, an' her lips is sweet
As de sugar - cane juice when it turns to cuite.
  Come along, Miss Nancy!"

The chorus which follows, rendered in a voice altered to suit the changed jig movement and ending with a high kick, was no mean performance.

  "Oh, Miss Nancy,
    You's my fancy.
    You is de neates'
      An' de fleetes'
        An' de sweetes'
          Gal in town."

At its close several volunteered coins were thrown towards him; and when the old man finally clapped the hat, contents and all, upon his head, and with a bow turned homeward, there was a new idea within his woolly pate that sent a fresh spring into his gait—a bona-fide impulse of hope untainted by bravado.

The five coins earned in as many minutes by drawing upon an inexhaustible fund of plantation-lore were answering the momentous question of the immediate future. If city white folk would pay for such as this, they should have all they wanted.

His eagerness for the experiment could not possess itself in patience till the morrow; and on this same evening, as soon as his charge was asleep, he slipped noiselessly away and was soon prancing up and down, singing at the top of his voice before a gay saloon, now coquétting in interpretation of a love-ditty, now grotesquely hopping up and down as he sang:

"Ole Mister Frog ain't much ter sing,
But he cl'ars a log wid a single spring."

The morning's earnings were soon more than doubled, and when Cæsar crept on tiptoe into the room that night he was so exhilarated that sleep was impossible. No prospective millionaire after an initial success in Wall Street was ever more inflated than he.

The old colonel was sleeping heavily when he entered. Turning up the gas, the negro stood beside him a moment, studying his face.

"I got good news fur we all, marster," he said, audibly, yet secure in the knowledge that no ordinary voice would penetrate that heavy slumber. "Yo' ole nigger done struck riches. Look heah!" He took from his hat a handful of nickels. "Deze heah same ole songs I used ter sing fur you on de levee done reached Heaven an' pierced de golden streets ter let down de golden showers. I ain't gwine fool you no mo' now, marster, wid no cheap cat-fish fur red-snapper—no, I ain't; an' dat ole bare porter-house steak bone what I done cooked up wid roun' cuts so long ter lay on yo' plate, I gwine th'ow it away now, yer heah?

Gwine see ef we can't work up de style o' dis here S'in' Charles Hotel table—dat I is! Po' ole marster! Des' look at 'im. Ev'ything 'bout 'im layin' dar des' as nachel *but 'cep' 'isse'f.* Look lak whiles Gord was a-teckin', he mought des' as well 'a' tooken his appertite. 'Tis a hard case, Lord, ter teck a man's sense an' jedgmint an' money, an' leave 'im a wide-awake appertite. But nemmine; I'm glad I-done moved 'im back heah in dis cheap room, anyhow. Hit's des' as good an' two bottles o' champagne a month better. Dem's des de figgers. Po' ole marster! Doctor seh he ain't gwine come ter 'isse'f no mo', an' I's glad of it. Hisse'f done got too fur down ter come back ter, dat's a fac'. An' ef he was ter come ter 'isse'f, de fus' thing he'd do 'd be ter discharge me fur lyin'—an' I'd deserve it, too; but how'd he git along? I *could* loosen up 'is laigs wid mullein leaves b'iled down in lard an' rubbed in onder 'is knees good. I could do it, don't keer what de doctor say; but I ain't gwine do it, less'n 'is haid come straight. Gord knowed His business when He turned de lock on bofe de same day. Yas, You is, Lord.

Ter-morrer I gwine put on my ole plantation clo'es an' go out an' dance a break-down fur 'em. Deze heah blue breeches, I'm tired of 'em, anyway. Dey bags at de knees tur'ble. I'd a heap ruther have pants bag all over 'n bag at de knees. Hit gives a pusson a ongodly figgur—dat it do. Well, Cæsar, you's done good work to-day, an' I pats you on de haid ; but you better hush talkin' now, ole man, an' go ter baid— dat what you better, so good-night."

Parting with himself thus, he lowered the gas, and, with slight preparation, was soon asleep.

If in the portrayal of Cæsar's character that of old Colonel Dunbar seems but a misty outline, it is only because his erst active and interesting personality was already passing into the shadows which yet envelop him when first we beheld him in the dim moonlight by the river. It would be an unfriendly hand that, pursuing him through all the abnormal developments of gathering adversities, would vividly portray him in the depths of his humiliation. For every encounter with his present unreasonableness, irritability, or selfishness, Cæsar cherished a hundred tender memories of the past.

With varying success the old negro pursued his new calling, and in the course of several months had become quite a local celebrity as street-singer about the French market; and it is freely said since, by those who knew the circumstances, that more than one tempting offer came to him during this period to appear before the foot-lights ; but he always declined, saying his master was rich— he didn't need money.

"I des' tecks de small change dee gimme," he would add, "'caze I so 'stravagant. I laks ciggars an' champagne. Boss won't gimme much champagne ; 'feerd I'll git de gout, lak he got. An' I laks fine onderclo'es, too — des' look;" and, rolling up his sleeve, he would display a silken under-. sleeve, old finery of the colonel's, protesting: "I des' wears deze outside plantation-cloe's fur style, dat's all. Dat's de *style o' gemman I is—planta-tion-riz f'om de groun' up!*"

During this period, the life-long attachment between these two old men, intensified on one side by utter dependence, and on the other by the very nature and constancy of his ministrations, was strengthening, insensibly to both, into a tie that can be likened unto nothing less than the love between mother and child.

Cæsar did not even realize that he had grown to address his old master in "baby-talk" nowadays, nor that, when he would approach his bedside, tray in hand, the eager eyes of his charge would fill with tears as he laughed nervously, even as a babe with tear-brimmed eyes crows aloud as his mother approaches the cradle.

"Deze heah mush-a-roons is solid money," he would say. "You chew 'em good wid yo' gol' toof, honey," and, turning away, he would add: "I wouldn't sell out dat gol' toof fur nothin'. Hit has ter stan' fur all de 'fo'-de-wah granjer, dat gol' toof do."

So their lives drifted for a brief period only.

One day, when Cæsar approached the bed with steaming tray, the shining tooth of gold between the parted lips was his only greeting. A second stroke, noiseless and mysterious as the first that had clipped life's cord to the point of unravelling, had now cut it in twain.

An accidental intrusion at the moment of the discovery moved even Ma'm Zulime to close the door softly and go away sobbing ; and that night, as she stood at the fence, talking to her neighbor, she declared :

" Me, I never see somet'ing lique dat. For two hours dat ole nigger ees cryne sem lique a mudder loss a chile. An' de breakfas' he ees prepare, he ces just set it outside, so ; an' me, I haf to eat it myself—fine chevrette all pack in mash ice, an' poach egg on toas', an' chop an' coffee—haf to eat it all myself or give it to de flies. So now I haf to change tenant again. Well, 'tis a hard worl'. Was a good tenant, an' I'm goin' charge for de full munt' ; biccause a de't', dat injure yo' house, yas. Well, hany'ow, de ole nigger, he's got 'im lay out nice. He's lay out Protes'ant, dough— no candle, no nutting, po' man. Well, God is good ; maybe He take 'im so. He is nutting to me, but God forgive me if I done wrong—I christen 'im las' week, w'ile 'e was sleepin'. I seen de't' on 'im. Well, I ain't got much, but t'ank God I know my rilligion ; an' if I didn', I blief some good Cat'lic 'll do dat much for me w'en I was dyin'. De ole man, he's gone out now. Blief maybe ees gone for license for buryin'. Well, Ma'm Jacques, w'en you know somebody need a room, I put dat one down cheap de first munt', till I run de ghos' out."

While M'm Zulime gossipped with her neighbor, Cæsar, in his shabby plantation-rags, was making his way towards the saloon near the market. After first outburst of grief, during which, sobbing aloud, he had fallen upon his knees, lain upon the floor, hugged his master's feet, and cried to Heaven for mercy, the old man had wiped his face and proceeded to perform the last sad duties to the dead.

When he had lovingly arranged the body for burial he covered the face with a square of mosquito-netting purloined from the back of the bed-drapery, and, locking the door, started out to make arrangements for the home journey; for he would lay his master among his kindred in the old Taylor graveyard.

He had tried to anticipate this crisis, but somehow he had failed. Even after depositing the colonel's watch at a certain *mont de piété* at the corner, in exchange for sixty dollars and a redemption-ticket, the augmented sum in hand proved inadequate to death's demands.

He had easily arranged to work his own passage up the river, but a coffined passenger must pay full fare. The second-hand furniture-dealer would carry the casket to the boat for half the cost of an undertaker's wagon, but since they were going home where familiar friends would meet them, a handsome burial-case was imperative. He would gladly have borne it on his shoulder to the boat, among strangers in New Orleans, had it been possible thereby to add a bit of tinsel to its decoration.

For a month past two rival saloon-keepers had been offering Cæsar tempting sums to sing exclusively at their doors, but he had preferred the fun of carrying the crowd with him.

But to-night he would capitulate. Wiping his eyes and tipping back his hat as he stepped into its blaze of light, he entered the first saloon. A welcoming exclamation greeted him; but stepping up to the bar and displaying a roll of money, he quietly called for a schooner of beer.

He had counted on the crowd that soon surrounded him, and, as he calmly emptied his glass, he remarked:

"Well, it's Sunday, an' I ain't nuver is dánced on Sunday yit; but I got sech a dancin'-fit on me ter-night, I gwine ter Tony's coffee-house, whar de nickels is thick, an' I'm gwine dance dis fit off, ef it tecks me all night."

Kicking his feet impatiently as he went, he started out, when, as he intended he should do, the proprietor called him back. In a few moments he had been persuaded to accept prepayment in cash, to sing every evening of a week following exclusively at this corner—the arrangement not to interfere with the usual collections, and the performance to begin to-night.

As he folded the few bills in with the others and involuntarily measured the roll against the home needs, he began to feel that singing would come hard to-night. Still, he did not hesitate beyond a lordly demand for another drink, when, with a bow, he faced the company.

It was only when some one said, "Sing 'All alone on the shore to-night,'" one of his most popular performances, that for a moment he felt in danger of utter failure. A sudden convulsive sob surprised him before he could master himself; but, quickly pulling his hat down over his eyes and reaching in his pocket for his "bones," he struck out into a dance, saying to himself as he went: "Hush, you ole fool, you—dance! Dance, I say, Cæsar, dance! Up wid yo' foots! Kick de air!"

He never did the corn-shucking break-down better; and when it was finished he volunteered and with a steady voice sang "I'm all alone on the shore to-night" with such tenderness that several old men, listening, wiped their eyes and turned away.

Having fulfilled his engagement here with unusual profit, Cæsar turned ostensibly homeward, only to proceed by a circuitous route to the rival saloon, where he unblushingly entered into a similar contract, to take effect on the morrow.

It may seem strange that these two men should have trusted him to this extent; but the manifest advantage of commanding him, should he come into the neighborhood, made it worth the risk, which indeed seemed small, in face of the well-feigned reluctance with which the money was accepted.

It was late now, but yet Cæsar made another detour to-night, a journey involving no little perplexity.

The deaths in the Taylor family had, time immemorial, been matters of honorable announcement in the local papers ; and the family record in the old Bible in the colonel's trunk held printed tributes opposite each sad entry during a period of more than half a century. When Cæsar should carry the old Book to the minister at home, to have the last name registered upon its tablet, he would not be without the printed accompaniment to paste against it.

At no point were his ignorance and sagacity, his loyalty and unscrupulousness, his pride and poverty, more pathetically displayed than in this visit to the newspaper office. After much parleying, however, he declared himself satisfied with the notice, which should pay a concise tribute to the families of Taylor and Dunbar, flatteringly note the colonel's rank as a Confederate officer, and close by cordially inviting friends to the funeral, from the family city residence, on the morrow at five o'clock.

True, by this hour Cæsar would be steaming up the river, with a copy of the paper folded in his pocket ; but so much the better. When the implied funeral cortege should fail to materialize, even though there should be no interested witnesses, he would be glad to be out of the way. He would prefer, too, to be unembarrassed by any facts in the account he should give at home of the funeral procession.

After breakfast the next morning, Ma'm Zulime donned her best black gown, in simple respect to the presence of death beneath her roof ; and though its dread embodiment lay in a back upper chamber, she walked softly about the house, and started at every sudden noise. So, when upon the abrupt stopping of wheels before her door there followed the clang of its iron knocker, she called the names of a half-dozen attributes of divinity in a breath, and with consciously beating heart opened the door.

Somehow, although 'her mysterious tenant had never had a visitor, she was not surprised when the foremost of the three well-dressed men who stood without pronounced the name of Colonel Dunbar Taylor.

It was nearly dark in the evening when Ma'm Zulime stood again talking with Ma'm Jacques at the back fence.

"Tell de troot, Ma'm Jacques," she was saying, "'twas jes' good-luck dey di'n 'ketched me wid nutting but my camisole. 'Twas hot to-day, yas, fo' dat alapaca dress ; but I say to myself, 'Po' man, I'll do dat much fo' heem, hany'ow— put a black dress till dey carry eem out—I do dat fo' whatever rillation he ain't got ; he had, any- 'ow, once, a mudder—so, w'en fo' nobody else, I do it fo' her.' So, like I tell you, I hadn' no mo'n jes' hook de las' heye on my belt, w'en I lis'n de w'eel stop, an' I look hout an' see t'ree fine gen'lemans read somet'ing in de paper an' look de nombre to my 'ouse. Who you t'ink ees put dat de't'-notice in de paper, Ma'm Jacques? I ax de ol' nigger, an' he tell he know nutting 'bout it— he say some o' doze gen'ral an' capt'in wa't fight in de war wid eem, maybe dey hear it an' pay it in. Well, maybe 'tis true, biccause doze was sure fo' fine carri'geful o' gen'lemans wa't come at de funeral.

"Well, w'en doze t'ree gen'lemans ees come in an' set down, an' I tole dat de ol' colonel an' de nigger is live in my back yard since six munt', dey was 'stonish, yas, an' dey question me close till I tell all since de *beginnin'*. W'ile we talk so, de ol' nigger he's come in, an' maybe you t'ink it's a lie I'm tellin' you, Ma'm Jacques, but God can strike me dead if two o' doze fash'nible mans, w'en dey see de ol' nigger, dey *begin* to cry an' talk nutting but war-time. So much was true, hany'ow, dat de ol' nigger always tell me—'ow he was fight in de war. Well, m'am, terreckly all de four ees gone up-stairs an' talk, talk, talk wid de ol' man ; an' w'en dey go hout, de ol' nigger ees gone too, an' bimeby he ees come back, dressed everyt'ing new—hat, shoes, all—an' ees got a gol' watch, too ; an' me, I blief—mais, I am not sure, but I blief—'twas de watch of de colonel.

"Well, Ma'm Jacques, since doze strange mans

ees come, everyt'ing ees change ; even de coffin w'ere ee was layin' ees sen' back, an' dey put eem again in wan fine wan wid all silver handle, an' yo'self ees see de fine corbillard wid doze high pompon w'at ees come carry eem at de boat. W'en I was so big, dey had halways doze big pompon on all de fine *char funêtre.* Now dey come back again. Well, dey got fashion fo' every-t'ing. I blief, w'en I get to heaven—if I'm dat lucky — I'll fin' some fashion, too, honly every-body can follow : not like here — some got no chance.

"Well, I'll miss dat ol' nigger, yas. Since de t'ird day he come I ain't never make no fire, needer bring a bucket o' water. Dat ol' man, he's got a black skin, 'tis true ; but his insides ees w'ite, you take my word. Well, you see me so, Ma'm Jacques, I hate to go in de 'ouse to-night. Fo' w'at you can't come an' set down wid me till ees time fo' make de gas ? Come, an' hany'ow I'll ope a couple o' ginger-pop. 'Tis warm, yas ; I blief it make rain to-morrow."

Ma'm Zulime had spoken the truth when she said that since the arrival of the three gentlemen everything had been changed.

When they had met the old negro beside his master's body in the upper gallery chamber of death there had been little left for him to tell ; for if M'am Zulime had told half the pitiful story, the other half was written all about the cheap appointments of the mean little apartment above.

To "change everything," to send an old comrade honorably and decently home to his last rest, and his faithful friend and servant proud and rejoicing on his melancholy journey, was the easy result of a moment's whispered conference.

The home funeral, prearranged by telegraph, was all that Cæsar's fondest ambition could have desired; and as his withered little figure turned away from the covered grave, lonely and heart-sore though he was, he trod the earth with head erect, in full consciousness of the dignity that had descended to him as "de las' one o' de Dunbar-Taylor a'stokercy lef' ter tell de tale."

Such, indeed, were his exact words, as, surrounded by a gaping circle of his plantation comrades, he told over and over again the marvellous tale of his master's social triumphs in the great city.

"Why, sir," he would say, "you - all on dis plantation ain't nuver rightly knowed who Marse Dunbar Taylor was. Why, I kin go myself down yonder ter Noo 'Leans to-morrer, an' kin draw my five dollars a day—dey lookin' fur me now ter fill a ingagement in two big houses—"

"Five dollars a day ter do what sort o' work?" asks an old man near, with doubtful credulity.

"Work! Who you talkin' ter, nigger? I ain't done a stroke o' work sence I struck de city. Look at my han's—sof' as a baby's. Wages ter walk up an' down an' talk an' sing an' spit, ef I feel lak it—dat what dey'd pay me wages fur. I

seen de day I been doin' dat-a-way, walkin' up an'
down, singin', wid my han's in my pockets, an'
dey'd th'ow money at me in de streets—"

"Umh! Shet yo' mouf, Cæsar. What 'd dey
th'ow money at you fur?"

"Caze dey knowed I b'longed ter ol' Colonel
Dunbar Taylor, an' live wid him in de big stone
house whar de two big iron dogs stan' fo' de do',
an' de fountains play in de gyard'n — an' dey
knowed I useter wait on de table when all de
guvners an' mayors useter teck champagne 'dinner wid we-all, while de brass ban' played 'fo' de
do'; dat what dey th'owed money at me fur—
fur cormplimint ter Colonel Dunbar Taylor! Yer
don't reck'n dey th'owed it at me 'count o' my ole
swivelled-up black face, is yer? Ef any o' y'-all
is ca'culatin' ter teck yo' black faces ter de city
fur targets fur 'em ter th'ow money at, I 'vize you
ter stay home—dat I does."

AUNT DELPHI'S DILEMMA

AUNT DELPHI'S DILEMMA

AUNT DELPHI'S DILEMMA

A Plantation Incident

OLD "Aunt Delphi," a superannuated crone of two hundred avoirdupois or thereabouts, was a privileged character on Honeyfield plantation.

A pensioner upon the bounty of her former owners, she had not an earthly responsibility excepting the self-assumed care of a thriving vegetable garden and poultry - yard, the proceeds of which, sold to her benefactors, supplied her with pocket-money.

Aunt Delphi had been a belle in colored society in her day and generation, and, if the whole truth must be told, the history of her matrimonial alliances is rather a tangled skein.

She was now a widow as truly as she had ever been a wife, excepting on a first occasion, when the legal bond had proven all too brittle for her playful handling. Since old age with its withering processes had overtaken her, Aunt Delphi had surrendered all her waning vitalities to religion, thus springing at a single bound from the position of a warning to that of a Christian example on the plantation. So, again, is the angle of reflection equal to the angle of incidence. The woman so recently notorious as a fisher of men for the mere sport of the angling had become a quoter of Scripture, a spiritual exhorter, even a visitor among the sick and the dying, a closer of the eyes of the dead.

Since her conversion, her new peace had, as was befitting it should, seemed to permeate all her human relations, and she regarded the whole world benignly, both upward and downward. She carried counsel and delicacies to the humble cabins of the distressed or ailing with the same serene, beaming face that she bore when she wended her way to the great house with a nest of empty tin cans upon her arm, ostensibly to seek the advice of "Ole miss" upon some trivial subject.

The advice was given or withheld according to the indications, but the cans were always taken from her to the pantry, filled, and returned.

These visits were generally paid just before dinner, and after her conference with "the white folks" the old woman would repair to the kitchen "to he'p thoo de dish-washin'," though she always consented with becoming hesitation to remain for a social meal with her chum, the cook.

As the usual interval between these social overtures was a week or ten days, Mrs. Stanley was somewhat surprised one summer morning to see Delphi trudging up the front walk three days after a former visit; and as she approached, a most mournful expression of face declared that she was in great distress of mind. Her ample lips were puckered into a royal purple flower set upon the most doleful of faces. She carried no petition in the shape of can or basket, and as she laboriously seated herself on the inverted top of the sewing-machine beside her mistress, the purple blossom declared her to be in great tribulation.

"Look lak I can't see my way straight dis mornin', mistus. Won't you please, ma'am, gimme a little drap o' some'h'n' 'nother ter raise my cour'ge tell I talks ter yer?"

The servant was called to bring some water, whereupon, with an indescribable play of features that resembled nothing so much as summer lightning, Aunt Delphi turned upon her mistress a look half reproach, half protest.

"What I wants wid water, mistus?" she pleaded. "You knows yo'se'f, ef you po's water in anything hit weakens it down. I's weakened down too much now. My *cour'ge* needs strenkenin', mistus, an' you knows dey ain't no cour'ge in water."

The "courage" being duly supplied from a bottle labelled "Blackberry Cordial," Aunt Delphi proceeded with her story. "You knows jestice an' 'ligion, ole miss," she resumed, "an' I wants ter insult you 'bout how I gwine ac' in dis heah trouble what's come ter me. How far down do a step-mammy's juties corndescend?"

The young ladies of the family had by this time drawn their chairs near, and the old woman had looked from one face to another as she put her

question. As no one in the least understood her
meaning, she proceeded to explain.

"Well, yer see, babies, I got a letter f'om the
pos'-orfice las' night, an' Yaller Steve he read it
out ter me, an' hit's f'om my step-son, Wash. I
ain't heerd tell o' Wash sence 'fo' de wah; but he
done written ter tell me dat he done got married,
an' he got two sets o' twin babies, an' now he's
wife she up an' dies, an' he got de unmotherless
twins on 'is han's. An' Wash he say, bein' as I
allus tole 'im I'd be a good mother ter 'im ef he'd
commit me—he say he gwine trus' me ter raise
dem sets o' twins."

Fumbling in her pocket, she presently produced
a yellow envelope.

"You say there are four children?" said her
mistress, by way of filling a pause.

"Yas, mistus, two full sets o' twins, 'cordin' ter
what he say. Wash allus was a double-dealin' boy."

It was hard to repress a rising smile, but the
old woman's disturbance of soul was so genuine
that her mistress remarked, sympathetically,

"But Wash is only your step-son, if I remember rightly, Delphi?"

"Oh, yas, 'm. He's my fus' husban's boy. He's
pa's a-livin' down in de Ozan bottom now. He
an' me we been parted too long ter talk about,
an' you know, mistus, I been married an' unmar-
ried, off 'n' on, sence den. But, in co'se, all deze
circumstancial go-betweens dey don't meck Wash
ain't my step-son. Yer see, mistus, *I stood up in*

de chu'ch wid his daddy, an' I wants ter do my juty by Wash, mo' inspecial caze I done put 'im out'n de house on de 'count o' 'im a-raisin' his han' ter me, an 'I 'ain't nuver is laid eyes on 'im sence. An' sence I foun' peace in 'ligion I 'ain't done nothin' but pray Gord ter lemme meck up wid Wash, an' now seem lak de answer done come ; but hit's come loaded up purty heavy." She sighed, even wiped her eyes, as she continued : "I 'ain't see de way I kin raise dem fo' twins— no, I 'ain't."

"How old are they ?" asked several at once.

"He 'ain't sign dey ages down by no special figgur, but, de way de letter run, I knows dey's des 'bout runnin' roun' an' cryin' size. Dat's des whar de trouble come in. Yer see I got nigh onter two honderd fryin'-size chickens in my little yard, an' ef I has ter turn fo' cryin'-size chillen in 'mongst 'em, hit 'll be tur'ble. 'Caze I 'ain't nuver is seed a cryin'-size yit wha' 'ain't love ter chase de fryin'-size. Tell me, chillen, an' ole miss —you knows 'ligion an' jestice—how fur down do de step-mammy's juties corndescend ?"

The question seemed so absurd that it was with difficulty that Mrs. Stanley, by assuming her look of greatest severity, forbade even an exchange of glances between her daughters. The old woman, in the meantime, had presented the letter to one of the young ladies to read. It proved to be in substance as she had quoted, and was signed "Yore Truely Son, Gorge Washington Brown."

"Dat soun' mighty sweet—'your truly son,'"
said the old woman, as she heard the words read
—"dat soun' mighty sweet—an' yit—an' yit I
'sputes de jestice. I wants ter be cancelized wid
Wash, an' yit when he come ter me, fo'-in-han' like,
an' offer me de whole load—tell de trufe, I don'
know. Seem like we mought 'vide up de 'sporn-
serbility some way, an' I'd even gin 'im he's ch'ice
o' sets. Den agin, look lak dat ain't riverind jestice nuther, bein' as I ain't nothin' but he's step-
mammy, an' ain't in no way 'spornserble fo' dem
twins. Ef I was h'es reel nachel mammy, in co'se
I'd be, as yer mought say, backhandedly 'spornserble fur 'em. But as I is, I don't see it—no, I
don't—less'n me a puttin' 'im out'n de house in
a manner aggervated 'im ter it. I 'ain't done nothin' but walk de flo' all de endurin' night an'
pray, an' I 'ain't see no light yit."

"I'll attend to this whole matter for you, Delphi," says her old mistress, taking advantage of a
first real pause. "Let me write to Wash for you,
telling him that you will take one of the older
children, but that as you are getting old, you
cannot do more."

The smile of relief and gratitude that spread
over the old woman's face was really touching as
she answered : "Thank Gord, ole Miss! I b'lieve
myse'f dat's de full jestice. I sho' do. I tries ter
squander my shubshance on righteous livin', good
as I kin, des lak de preacher say. An' you write
de letter, mistus, an' tell 'im I say seek de Lord

while it's day." And with profuse expression of gratitude, Aunt Delphi proceeded homeward with a lighter step and a cleared brow.

"This arrangement will be just the thing," said her·mistress, as she moved away. "I have been trying to secure a child to live with the old woman and wait on her, but the mothers on the place scorn to have their children serve one of their own color. If old Delphi is at once appeasing her conscience and securing needed service, I shall congratulate myself upon helping her in the matter."

The letter was duly written.

It was about two weeks later when one morning after breakfast Aunt Delphi presented herself again at the front steps of the great house.

Hesitating here and casting upward to the group of ladies who sat within the hall door the most woe-begone of faces, she groaned aloud. Then, in a voice actually sepulchral in its deep intensity, she exclaimed:

"Why'n't yer ax me some'h'n', chillen? Quizzify me. Put de questioms. Ax me whar is I trapped deze heah black rabbits."

With this she lifted into view four little black children, starting them up the steps before her, while she followed, actually groaning aloud.

"Why'n't yer talk, chillen?" she continued, addressing the ladies, still keeping the children ahead of her. "Why'n't yer ax me is I see double, ur is you see double, ur is Wash behave

’isse’f double?” And throwing herself into a chair, Aunt Delphi fell to actual weeping.

The little girls, absurdly alike even as to size, though their ages were about four and five years respectively, stood in a row, each sucking her thumb, and in no wise embarrassed by the presence of strangers ; and yet when in a moment one of them began slowly to back from the company, they all followed, until, touching the wall, they sat down in a row.

“Are these Wash’s children?” asked her mistress, as soon as she could command her voice.

“Yas, Lord,” she moaned, swaying her body to and fro.

“And so he brought them all. Where is he? When did they come?”

“Hol’ on, mistus,” she exclaimed, waving her hand to command silence. “Hol’ on an’ lemme start straight. In de searchin’ hour o’ midnight las’ night, when eve’y hones’ pusson was buried in Christian sleep, heah come ‘a-rap-a-tap-tap !’ on my kyabin do’, des easy lak an’ sof’, lak some h’n’ sperityal ; an’ I retched up an’ stricken a match, an’ open de do’ an’ listen, an’ I ’ain’t heerd no soun’ but ’cep’ one o’ deze heah onsleepless morkin’-birds chantin’ out secon’-han’ music, an’ I commenced ter wonder is a pecker-wood done riz me out’n my baid ter listen to free music ; an’ all de time my eyes was turned high, an’ I nuver ’spicioned nothin’, tell right onder my foots deze heah fo’ p’intedly matched babies come a-walkin’ in, des lak you see 'em now, ev'y one a-suckin' 'er fis'."

"But where did they come from? Did Wash bring them?"

"What ails you, chillen, dat you don't heah me what I say. I don't know no mo'n dey say, an' dey 'ain't showed speech yit."

"And you haven't seen Wash?"

"Ain't I talkin' straight, baby? I say I 'ain't seed nothin', neither heerd nothin'. Tell de trufe, 'cep'n' fur de co'n-brade dey done et, I'd look fur dem babies ter vanige out'n my sight des lak dey come. Co'se I done set 'em down ter Wash, bein' as he done 'nounced 'isse'f in de twins trade. But eh Lord! What I gwine do wid 'em? An' de las' one o' 'em cryin'-sizes!"

The ladies call the children to them, and by dint of coaxing learn that they "comed wid daddy—to find mammy," and that they answer to the endearing names of Shug, Pud, Hun, and Babe. The conventional list of names had apparently not been taxed for their designation.

It is evidently a deeply laid scheme. Wash's letter was only a ruse to ascertain whether the old woman Delphi still lived or not, and he had cast his children upon her.

Poor old Delphi, chafing under the imposition, and overcome with the weight of so heavy a responsibility, sat softly weeping, while the ladies assured her that she should be relieved.

Wash, the poltroon, had covered his tracks

well. No one on the place had seen or heard him, and the wheels whose tracks approached the fence had soon returned to the old ruts, and left no trace of their course.

Delphi's cabin was the same in which Wash had lived as a child. This fact Mrs. Stanley had unwittingly betrayed in her letter, in which she pleaded its single room as added excuse for her not taking more than one child.

During the two weeks following this, letters of inquiry concerning his lordship, the delectable sire George Washington Brown, were sent to leading persons in the town from whence his letter had been posted; but though several citizens of color bore this identical distinguished if not distinguishing name, no trace of the father of the twins was found.

A party of negroes en route for Kansas had recently passed within five miles of Honeyfield plantation. Presumably Wash had been of this number. Starting out to begin life afresh, he had no doubt made good his proposal to his step-mother to "let by-gones be by-gones."

A month passed, and no news had come of the recreant father, neither had the sensation caused by Aunt Delphi's sudden acquisition of family begun to abate. The children, through whom she had been an object of interest far and near, and whose presence had brought generous gifts from all directions to the little cabin, were still there awaiting developments, and pending a decision as to the best disposition to be made of them.

Feeling that the matter had better be arranged and the old woman relieved, Mrs. Stanley decided one morning to call at the little cabin herself to talk the matter over. She had found good homes ready to welcome two of the children, and would take a third herself until she could be permanently provided for.

She found Aunt Delphi sitting on the door-step, holding one of the four on either knee, while the other two sat on the ground at her feet. All were munching huge chunks of corn-bread and chattering like magpies. At sight of her mistress the old woman slipped the children to the ground, and, with elaborate apologies for the state of her cabin, which was indeed strewn with trash, improvised rag babies, and pallets, she proceeded to wipe off a chair with her apron before presenting it.

"Have you decided which one of the little girls you are going to keep?" Mrs. Stanley asked, after the usual interchange of civilities.

The old woman had seated herself opposite her mistress, and at the question she rolled her eyes mysteriously a moment before answering. Finally she said: "I b'lieve you's a min'-reader, mistus, I sho does, caze you done read out de subjec' dat's been on my min' all day; but yer 'ain't read it straight, ole miss—no, yer 'ain't." Turning, she looked fondly upon the children and chuckled. "Des look how happy dey is!" she said. "Dey des as happy as a nes' o' kittens, dat dey is! Why, mistus, I been overrun wid cats all my life, des caze I couldn't say de drowndin' ur pizenin' word ter air kitten what look ter me in weakness. I done let a chicken-devourin' rat out'n a trap des caze I ketched a prayer in 'is eye. De way a cock-roach run fur 'is life meek me draw back my bro-gan an' let 'im go. How is I gwine part wid any o' dem human babies?"

"What do you mean, Delphi? You surely can-not wish to keep four children to bring up at your time of life. It would be absurd."

"Hol' on, mistus, hol' on—don't go so fas'! Dem chillen done preached a heap o' sermons ter me, an' dey all got de same tex'; an' dat tex' hit splains out a new set o' argimints ev'y time. How yer reckon I feels, mistus, when I looks at dem babies an' see how p'intedly dey favors dey gramper? Lookin' at 'em ev'y day tecks my min' way back ter my co'tin' days, when love soun' in my ears lak a music chune picked on a banjer. An' when I looks back on my life I see how I loved de endurin' soun' so much I ain't keer who play de music. So de by-gone pictur's come back ter me one by one; but de one dat stay wid me is de one wha' show me my fus' hus-ban', Dan; an' I see how I done trifled wid 'im, an' de quar'l we had, when I sassed back an' go one better'n him ev'y time ('caze we was bofe high-temprate). An' den I 'member de fight he fit wid Abum Saunders, 'caze Abum's love chune please my hearin'. Den come back a yether pictur — *ole Dan* de way my min' see 'im now, 'cripit an' gray, maybe, an' lonesome an' failin', an' me his lawful wedded wife, an' all o' deze heah peart little gran'babies o' his'n right heah— next do' ter 'im, de way Gord reckon space. Dat's de way de sermon read, an' deze onconscious infams dey preaches it at me, unbeknowinst, ter meek up wid dey gramper, *an' I ain't gwine zist de sperit no mo'*. I gwine meek de movemint ter be cancelized wid Dan; an' ef he's sick, I gwine nuss 'im; an' ef he's cranky an' fussy, I gwine shet my mouf an' say nothin ; *but I gwine back ter' im —dat is, ef he'll teck me!* An' ef you got a argimint agin it, mistus, don't spressify it in my hearin', please, ma'am, 'caze *my min' made up*."

Mrs. Stanley realized that it would be somewhat inconsistent with her own professions to oppose a reconciliation between husband and wife, and as soon as she could recover from her surprise at the unexpected turn the affair was taking she wished the old woman all possible success and happiness in the step she had resolved to take. Indeed, before she had left the cabin she had herself written at her dictation the letter the old wife sent the next day to the husband from whom she had been estranged for thirty years or more.

A few days afterward there was an important arrival at Delphi's cabin. The letter had brought the old husband back to the feet of his early love.

A week later the departure took place. A capacious plantation wagon was piled high with bedding, boxes, and sundry household belongings, laid upon a foundation of chicken-coops, out of which curious feathered heads gazed in alternate-eyed wonder at the unusual proceeding. On the summit of the edifice sat the old couple in a veritable rose garden of little bobbing pink sun-bonnets.

They were going to the old man's home. Delphi had made her formal adieux at the house, and wept her parting tears, but through them the sun of a new happiness was shining.

As the wagon moved out the gate the ladies waved good-bye from the gallery of the great house, and the old man, perceiving them, lifted his hat, bowing his body in a manner that was distinctly courtly.

Aunt Delphi up to this moment had been absorbed in her maternal task of safely seating the children, but now realizing that the supreme moment of last leave-taking was come, she threw one arm around her old husband, waving the other high in air as she began to sing. The wagon moved slowly down the road, and as the early sun coming through the pines covered it at intervals, it gleamed in the light, a bright bouquet of color. An occasional gust of wind brought snatches of her song even while the wagon was but a speck of color in the vista, and the effect was much heightened by the sound of a second voice, a wiry high tenor, playing all around the wind-wafted words—

"... to part no mo'—no mo'."

DUKE'S CHRISTMAS

"You des gimme de white folks's Christmus-dinner plates, time dey git thoo eatin', an' lemme scrape 'em in a pan an' set dat pan in my lap an' blow out de light an' *go it bline!* Hush, honey, hush, while I shet my eyes now an' tas'e all de samples what 'd come out'n dat pan—cramberries, an' tukkey-stuffin' wid *puck*ons in it, an' ham an' fried oyscher an'—an' minch-meat, an' chow-chow pickle an'—an' jelly! Umh! Don' keer which-a-one I strack fust—dey all got de Christmus seasonin!"

Old Uncle Mose closed his eyes and smiled, even smacked his lips in contemplation of the imaginary feast which he summoned at will from his early memories. Little Duke, his grandchild, sitting beside him on the floor, rolled his big eyes and looked troubled. Black as a raven, nine years old and small of his age, but agile and shrewd as a little fox, he was at present the practical head of this family of two.

This state of affairs had existed for more than two months, ever since a last attack of rheumatism had lifted his grandfather's leg upon the chair before him and held it there.

Duke's success as a provider was somewhat phenomenal, considering his size, color, and limited education.

True, he had no rent to pay, for their one-roomed cabin, standing on uncertain stilts outside the old levee, had been deserted during the last high-water, when Uncle Mose had "tooken de chances" and moved in. But then Mose had been able to earn his seventy-five cents a day at wood-sawing; and besides, by keeping his fishing-lines baited and set out the back and front doors — there were no windows — he had often drawn in a catfish, or his shrimp-bag had yielded breakfast for two.

Duke's responsibilities had come with the winter and its greater needs, when the receding waters had withdrawn even the small chance of landing a dinner with hook and line. True, it had been done on several occasions, when Duke had come home to find fricasseed chickens for dinner; but somehow the neighbors' chickens had grown wary, and refused to be enticed by the corn that lay under Mose's cabin.

The few occasions when one of their number, swallowing an innocent - looking grain, had been suddenly lifted up into space, disappearing through the floor above, seemed to have impressed the survivors.

Mose was a church - member, and would have scorned to rob a hen-roost, but he declared "when strange chickens come a-foolin' roun' bitin' on my fish-lines, I des twisses dey necks ter put 'em out'n dey misery."

It had been a long time since he had met with any success at this poultry-fishing, and yet he always kept a few lines out.

He *professed* to be fishing for crayfish—as if crayfish ever bit on a hook or ate corn! Still, it eased his conscience, for he did try to set his grandson a Christian example consistent with his precepts.

It was Christmas Eve, and the boy felt a sort of moral responsibility in the matter of providing a suitable Christmas dinner for the morrow. His question as to what the old man would like to have had elicited the enthusiastic bit of reminiscence with which this story opens. Here was a poser! His grandfather had described just the identical kind of dinner which he felt powerless to procure. If he had said oysters, or chicken, or even turkey, Duke thought he could have managed it; but a pan of rich fragments was simply out of the question.

" Wouldn't you des as lief have a pone o' hot aig-bread, gran'dad, an'—an'—an' maybe a nice baked chicken—ur—ur a—"

" Ur a nothin', boy! Don't talk to me! I'd a heap 'd ruther have a secon'-han' white Christmus dinner 'n de bes' fus'-han' nigger one you ever seed, an' I ain't no spring-chicken, nuther. I done had 'spe'unce o' Christmus dinners. An' what you talkin' 'bout, anyhow? Whar you gwine git roas' chicken, nigger?"

"I don' know, less'n I'd meck a heap o' money to-day; but I could sho' git a whole chicken ter roas' easier'n I could git dat pan full o' goodies *you's* a-talkin' 'bout.

"Is you gwine crawfishin' to-day, gran'daddy?" he continued, cautiously, rolling his eyes. "Caze when I cross de road, terreckly, I gwine shoo off some o' dem big fat hens dat scratches up so much dus'. Dey des a puffec' nuisance, scratchin' dus' clean inter my eyes ev'y time I go down de road."

"Dey is, is dey? De nasty, impident things! You better not shoo' none of 'em over heah, less'n you want me ter wring dey necks—which I boun' ter do ef dey pester my crawfish-lines."

"Well, I'm gwine now, gran'dad. Ev'ything is done did an' set whar you kin reach—I gwine down de road an' shoo dem sassy chickens away. Dis here 'bucket o' brick-dus' sho' is heavy," he added, as he lifted to his head a huge pail.

Starting out, he gathered up a few grains of corn, dropping them along in his wake until he reached the open where the chickens were; when, making a circuit round them, he drove them slowly until he saw them begin to pick up the corn. Then he turned, whistling as he went, into a side street, and proceeded on his way.

Old Mose chuckled audibly as Duke passed out, and baiting his lines with corn and scraps of meat, he lifted the bit of broken plank from the floor, and set about his day's sport.

"Now, Mr. Chicken, I'm settin' deze heah lines

fur crawfish, an' ef you smarties come a-foolin' roun' 'em, I gwine punish you 'cordin' ter de law. You heah me!" He chuckled as he thus presented his defence anew before the bar of his own conscience.

But the chickens did not bite to-day — not a mother's son or daughter of them—though they ventured cautiously to the very edge of the cabin.

It was a discouraging business, and the day seemed very long. It was nearly nightfall when Mose recognized Duke's familiar whistle from the levee. And when he heard the little bare feet pattering on the single plank that led from the brow of the bank to the cabin door, he coughed and chuckled as if to disguise a certain eager agitation that always seized him when the little boy came home at night.

"Here me," Duke called, still outside the door; adding as he entered, while he set his pail beside the old man, "How you is to-night, gran'-dad?"

"Des po'ly, thank Gord. How you yo'se'f, my man?" There was a note of affection in the old man's voice as he addressed the little pickaninny, who seemed in the twilight a mere midget.

"An' what you got dyah?" he continued, turning to the pail, beside which Duke knelt, lighting a candle.

"*Picayune* o' light-brade, an' *lagnappe** o' salt," Duke began, lifting out the parcels, "an' *picayune* o' molasses an' *lagnappe* of coal ile—ter rub yo' laig wid—heah hit in de tin can; an' *picayune*

* Pronounced lan-yap.

o' coffee an' *lagnappe* o' matches—heah dey is, fo'teen an' a half, but de half ain't got no fizz on it. An' deze heah in de bottom, dey des chips I picked up 'long de road."

"An' you ain't axed fur no *lagnappe* fo' yo'-self, Juke. Whyn't you ax fur des one *lagnappe* o' sugar-plums, baby, bein's it's Christmus? Yo' ole gran'dad ain't got nothin' fur you, an' you know to-morrer is sho' 'nough Christmus, boy. I ain't got even ter say a crawfish bite on my lines to-day, much less'n some'h'n' fittin' fur a Christmus gif'. I did set heah an' whittle you a little whistle, but some'h'n' went wrong wid it. Hit won't blow. But tell me, how's business ter-day, boy? I see you done sol' yo' brick-dus'?"

"Yas sir, but I toted it purty nigh all day fo' I *is* sol' it. De folks wharever I went, dey say no-body don't want to scour on Christmus Eve. An' one time I set it down an' made three nickels cut-tin' grass an' holdin' a white man's horse, an' dat gimme a res'. An' I started out ag'in, an' I walked inter a big house an' ax de lady ain't she want ter buy some pounded brick. An', gran'dad, you know what meck she buy it? Caze she seh my bucket is mos' as big as I is, an' ef I had de grit ter tote it clean ter her house on Christmus Eve, she seh I sha'n't pack it back—an' she gimme a dime fur it, too, stid a nickel. An' she gimme two hole-in-de-middle cakes, wid sugar on 'em. Heah dey is." Duke took two sorry-looking rings from his hat and presented them to the old man. "I done et

de sugar off 'em," he continued. "Caze I knowed
it 'd give you de toofache in yo' gums. An' I
tol' 'er what you say, gran'dad !"

Mose turned quickly.

"What you tol' dat white lady I say, nigger ?"

"I des tol' 'er what you say 'bout scrapin' de
plates inter a pan."

Mose grinned broadly. "Is you had de face
ter tell dat strange white 'oman sech talk as dat?
An' what she say ?"

"She des looked at me up an' down fur a minute, an' den she broke out in a laugh, an' she seh :
' You sho' is de littles' coon I ever seed out fora-
gin' !' An' wid dat she seh : 'Ef you'll come
roun' to-morrer night, 'bout dark, I'll give you as
big a pan o' scraps as you kin tote.' "

There were tears in the old man's eyes, and he
actually giggled.

"Is she ? Well done ! But ain't you feerd
you'll los' yo'self, gwine way down town at night?"

"Los' who, gran'dad ? You can't los' me in dis
city, so long as de red-light Pertania cars is runnin'.
I kin ketch on berhine tell dey fling me off, den
teck de nex' one tell dey fling me off ag'in—an'
hit ain't so fur dat-a-way."

"Does dey fling yer off rough, boy ? Look out
dey don't bre'k yo' bones !"

"Dey ain't gwine crack none o' my bones.
Sometimes de drivers kicks me off, an' sometimes
dey cusses me off, tell I lets go des ter save Gord's
name—dat's a fac'."

"Dat's right. Save it when you kin, boy. So she gwine scrape de Christmus plates fur me, is she? I wonder what sort o' white folks dis here tar-baby o' mine done strucken in wid, anyhow? You sho' dey reel quality white folks, is yer, Juke? Caze I ain't gwine sile my mouf on no po' white-trash scraps."

"I ain't no sho'er 'n des what I tell yer, gran'-dad. Ef dey ain't quality, I don' know northin' 't all 'bout it. I tell yer when I walked roun' dat yard clean ter de kitchen on dem flag-stones wid dat bucket o' brick on my hade, I had ter stop an' ketch my bref fo' I could talk, an' de cook, a sassy, fat, black lady, she would o' sont me out, but de madam, she seed me 'erse'f, an' she tooken took notice ter me, an' tell me set my bucket down, an' de yo'ng ladies, beatin' aigs in de kitchen, dey was makin' spote o' me, too—ax' me is I weaned yit, an' one ob 'em ax me is my nuss los' me! Den dey gimme deze heah hole-in-de-middle cakes, an' some reesons. I des fotched you a few reesons, but I done et de mos' ob 'em —I ain't gwine tell you no lie 'bout it."

"Dat's right, baby. I'm glad you is et 'em—des so dey don't cramp yer up—an' come 'long now an' eat yo' dinner. I saved you a good pan o' greens an' meat. What else is you et ter-day, boy?"

"De ladies in de kitchen dey gimme two burnt cakes, an' I swapped half o' my reesons wid a white boy fur a biscuit—but I sho' is hongry."

"Yas, an' you sleepy, too—I know you is."

"But I gwine git up soon, gran'dad. One market-lady she sch ef I come early in de mornin' an' tote baskits home, she gwine gimme some'h'n' good ; an' I'm gwine ketch all dem butchers an' fish-ladies in dat Mag'zine markit 'Christmus gif'!' An' I bet yer dey'll gimme some'h'n' ter fetch home. Las' Christmus I got seven nickels an' a whole passel o' marketin' des a-ketchin' 'em Christmus-gif'. Deze heah black molasses I brung yer home to-night—how yer like 'em, gran'dad ?"

"Fust-rate, boy. Don't yer see me eatin' 'em? Say yo' pra'rs now, Juke, an' lay down, caze I gwine weck you up by sun-up."

It was not long before little Duke was snoring on his pallet, when old Mose, reaching behind the mantel, produced a finely-braided leather whip, which he laid beside the sleeping boy.

"Wush't I had a apple ur orwange ur stick o' candy ur some'h'n' sweet ter lay by 'im fur Christmus," he said, fondly, as he looked upon the little sleeping figure. "Reck'n I mought bile dem molasses down inter a little candy—seem lak hit's de onlies' chance dey is."

And turning back to the low fire, Mose stirred the coals a little, poured the remains of Duke's "*picayune* o' molasses" into a tomato-can, and began his labor of love.

Like much of such service, it was for a long time simply a question of waiting ; and Mose found it no simple task, even when it had reached the desired point, to pull the hot candy to a fairness of complexion approaching whiteness. When, however, he was able at last to lay a heavy, copper-colored twist with the whip beside the sleeping boy, he counted the trouble as nothing ; and hobbling over to his own cot, he was soon also sleeping.

.   .   .   .   .   .

The sun was showing in a gleam on the river next morning, when Mose called, lustily, "Week up, Juke, week up ! Christmus gif', boy, Christmus gif' !"

Duke turned heavily once ; then, catching the words, he sprang up with a bound.

"Christmus gif', gran'dad !" he returned, rubbing his eyes ; then fully waking, he cried, "Look onder de chips in de bucket, gran'dad."

And the old man choked up again as he produced the bag of tobacco over which he had actually cried a little last night, when he had found it hidden beneath the chips with which he had cooked Duke's candy.

"I 'clare, Juke, I 'clare you is a caution," was all he could say.

"An' who gimme all deze ?" Duke exclaimed, suddenly seeing his own gifts.

"I don' know nothin' 't all 'bout it, less'n ole Santa Claus mought o' tooken a rest in our mud chimbley las' night," said the old man, between laughter and tears.

And Duke, the knowing little scamp, cracking

his whip, munching his candy and grinning, replied :

"I s'pec' he is, gran'dad ; an' I s'pec' he come
down an' b'iled up yo' nickel o' molasses, too, ter
meek me dis candy. Tell·yer, dis whup, she's
got a daisy snapper on 'er, gran'dad ! She's wuth
a dozen o' deze heah white-boy *w'ips*, she is !"

The last thing Mose heard, as Duke descended
the levee that morning, was the crack of the new
whip; and he said, as he filled his pipe, " De idee
o' dat little tar-baby o' mine fetchin' me a Christmus gif' !"

It was past noon when Duke got home again,
bearing upon his shoulder, like a veritable little
Santa Claus himself, a half-filled coffee-sack, the
joint results of his service in the market and of
the munificence of its autocrats.

The latter had apparently measured their gra-
tuities by the size of their beneficiary, as their
gifts were very small. Still, as the little fellow
emptied the sack upon the floor, they made quite
a tempting display. There were oranges, apples,
bananas, several of each ; a bunch of soup-greens,
scraps of fresh meat—evidently butcher's "trim-
mings"—odds and ends of vegetables ; while in
the midst of the mêlée three live crabs struck out
in as many directions for freedom.

They were soon landed in a pot ; while Mose,
who was really no mean cook, was preparing what
seemed a sumptuous mid-day meal.

Late in the afternoon, while Mose nodded in

his chair, Duke sat in the open doorway, stuffing the last banana into his little stomach, which was already as tight as a kettle-drum. He had cracked his whip until he was tired, but he still kept cracking it. He cracked it at every fly that lit on the floor, at the motes that floated into the shaft of sunlight before him, at special knots in the door-sill, or at nothing, as the spirit moved him. A sort of holiday feeling, such as he felt on Sundays, had kept him at home this afternoon. If he had known that to be a little too full of good things, and a little tired of cracking whips or tooting horns or drumming was the happy condition of most of the rich boys of the land at that identical moment, he could not have been more content than he was. If his stomach ached just a little, he thought of all the good things in it, and was rather pleased to have it ache—just this little. It accentuated his realization of Christmas.

As the evening wore on, and the crabs and bananas and molasses-candy stopped arguing with one another down in his little stomach, he found himself thinking, with some pleasure, of the pan of scraps he was to get for his grandfather, and he wished for the hour when he should go. He was glad when at last the old man waked with a start and began talking to him.

"I been wushin' you'd weck up an' talk, gran'-dad," he said, "'caze I wants ter ax yer what's all dishere dey say 'bout Christmus? When I wus comin' 'long ter-day I stopped in a big chu'ch, an' dey was a preacher-man standin' up wid a white night-gown on, an' he seh dishere's our Lord's birf-day. I heerd 'im seh it myse'f. Is dat so?"

"Cose it is, Juke. Huccome you ax me seeh ignunt questioms? Gimme dat Bible, boy, an' lemme read you some 'ligion."

Mose had been a sort of lay-preacher in his day, and really could read a little, spelling or stumbling over the long words. Taking the book reverently, he leaned forward until the shaft of sunlight fell upon the open page; when with halting speech he read to the little boy, who listened with open-mouthed attention, the story of the birth at Bethlehem.

"An' look heah, Juke, my boy," he said, finally, closing the book, "hit's been on my min' all day ter tell yer I ain't gwine fishin' no mo' tell de high-water come back—you heah? 'Caze yer know somebody's chickens *mought* come an' pick up de bait, an' I'd be 'bleeged ter kill 'em ter save 'em, an' we ain' gwine do dat no mo', me an' you. You heah, Juke?" Duke rolled his eyes around and looked pretty serious.

"Yas, sir, I heah," he said.

"An' me an' you, we done made dis bargain on de Lord's birf-day—yer heah, boy?—wid Gord's sunshine kiverin' us all over, an' my han' layin' on de page. Heah, lay yo' little han' on top o' mine, Juke, an' promise me you gwine be a *square man*, so he'p yer. Dat's it. Say it out loud, an' yo' ole gran'dad he done said it, too. Wrop up

17

dem fishin'-lines, now, an' th'ow 'em up on de rafters. Now come set down heah, an' lemme tell
yer 'bout Christmus on de ole plantation. Look
out how you pop dat whup 'crost my laig ! Dat's
a reg'lar horse-fly killer, wid a coal o' fire on 'er
tip." Duke laughed.

"Now han' me a live coal fur my pipe. Dishere
terbacca you brung me, hit smokes sweet as sugar,
boy. Set down, now, close by me—so.'ᴬ

Duke never tired of his grandfather's reminis-
cences, and he crept up close to the old man's knee
as the story began.

"When de big plantation-bell used ter ring on
Christmus mornin', all de darkies had to march
up ter de gre't house fur dey Christmus gif's ; an'
us what wucked *at* de house, we had ter stan' in
front o' de fiel'-han's. An' atter ole marster axed
a blessin', an' de string-ban' play, an' we all sing
a song—air one we choose—boss, he'd call out de
names, an' we'd step up, one by one, ter git our
presents ; an' ef we'd walk too shamefaced ur too
'boveish, he'd pass a joke on us, ter set ev'ybody
laughin'.

"I ricollec' one Christmus-time I was co'tin'
yo' gran'ma. I done had been co'tin' 'er two
years, an' she helt 'er head so high I was 'feerd ter
speak. An' when Christmus come an' I marched
up ter git my present, ole marster gimme my bundle an' I started back, grinnin' lak a chessy-cat,
an' he calt me back an' he say : ' Hol' on, Moses,'
he say, ' I got 'nother present fur you ter-day.

Heah's a finger-ring I got fur you, an' ef it don't
fit you, I reckon hit'll fit Zephyr—you know yo'
gran'ma, she was name Zephyr. An' wid dat he
run his thumb in 'is pocket an' fotch me out a
little gal's ring—"

"A gol' ring, gran'dad ?"

"No, boy, but a silver ring—ginniwine German silver. Well, I wush't you could o' heerd
dem darkies holler an' laugh ! An' Zephyr, ef
she hadn't o' been so yaller, she'd o' been red as
dat sky yonder, de way she did blush buff."

"An' what did you do, gran'dad ?"

"Who, me ? Dey warn't but des one thing *fur*
me to do. I des gi'n Zephyr de ring, an' she ax
me is I mean it, an'—an' I ax her is *she* mean it,
an'—an' we bofe say—none o' yo' business what
we say ! What you lookin' at me so quizzical fur,
Juke ? Ef yer wants ter know, we des had a weddin' dat Christmus night—dat what we done—
an' dat's huccome you got yo' gran'ma.

"But I'm talkin' 'bout Christmus now. When
we'd all go home, we'd open our bundles, an' of
all de purty things, *an'* funny things, *an'* jokes
you ever heerd of, dey'd be in dem Christmus
bundles—some'h'n' ter suit ev'y one, and hit 'im
square on his funny-bone ev'y time. An' all de
little bundles o' buckwheat ur flour 'd have *pica-
yunes* an' dimes in 'em ! We used ter reg'lar sif'
'em out wid a sifter. Dat was des *our* white
folks's way. None o' de yether fam'lies 'long de
coas' done it. You see all the diffe'nt fam'lies had

diffe'nt ways. But ole marster an' ole miss dey'd think up some new foolishness ev'y year. We nuver knowed what was gwine to be did nex'— on'y one thing. *Dey allus put money in de buck-wheat-bag*—an' you know we nuver tas'e no buckwheat 'cep'n on'y Christmus. Oh, boy, ef we could des meet up wid some o' we's white folks ag'in !"

"How is we got los' f'om 'em, gran'dad ?" said Duke, inviting a hundredth repetition of the story he knew so well.

"How did we git los' f'om we's white folks ? Dats a sad story fur Christmus, Juke, but ef you sesso—

"Hit all happened in one night, time o' de big break in de levee, seven years gone by. We was lookin' fur de bank ter crack crost de river f'om us, an' so boss done had tooken all han's over, cep'n us ole folks an' chillen, ter he'p work an' watch de yether side. 'Bout midnight, whiles we was all sleepin', come a roa'in' soun', an' fus' thing we knowed, all in de pitchy darkness, we was floatin' away—nobody cep'n des you an' me an' yo' mammy in de cabin—floatin' an' bumpin' an' rockin' *an' all de time dark as pitch*. So we kep' on—one minute stiddy, nex' minute *cher-plunk* gins' a tree ur some'h'n' nother—*all in de dark*— an' one minute you'd cry—you was des a weanin' baby den—an' nex' minute I'd heah de bed you an' yo' ma was in bump gins' de wall, an' you'd laugh out loud an' yo' mammy she'd holler—*all in de dark*. An' so we travelled, up an' down, bunkety-bunk, seem lak a honderd hours; tell treckly a *termenjus* wave come an' I had sca'cely felt it boomin' onder me when I pitched, an' ev'ything went travellin'. An' when I put out my han', I felt you by me—but yo' mammy, she warn't nowhar.

"Hol' up yo' face an' don't cry, boy. I been a mighty poor mammy ter yer, but I blesses Gord to-night fur savin' dat little black baby ter me—*all in de win' an' de storm an' de dark dat night.*

"You see, yo' daddy, he was out wid de gang wuckin' de levee crost de river—an' dats huccome yo' ma was 'feerd ter stay by 'erse'f an' sont fur me.

"Well, baby, when I knowed yo' mammy was gone, I helt you tight an' prayed. An' atter a while—seem lak a million hours—come a pale streak o' day, an' fo' de sun was up, heah come a steamboat puffin' down de river, an' treckly hit blowed a whistle an' ringed a bell an' stop an took us on boa'd, an' brung us on down heah ter de city."

"An' you never seed my mammy no mo', gran'dad?" Little Duke's lips quivered just a little.

"Yo' mammy was safe at Home in de Golden City, Juke, long 'fore we teched even de low lan' o' dis yearth.

"An' dats how we got los' f'om we's white folks.

"An' time we struck de city I was so twis' up wid rheumatiz I lay fur six munts in de Cha'ity

Hospit'l ; an' you bein' so puny, cuttin' yo' toofs, dey kep' you right along in de baby-ward tell I was able to start out. An' sence I stepped out o' dat hospit'l do' wid yo' little bow-legs trottin' by me, so I been goin' ever sence. Days I'd go out sawin' wood, I'd set you on de wood-pile by me ; an' when de cook 'd slip me out a plate o' soup, I'd ax fur two spoons. An' so you an' me, we been pardners right along, an' *I wouldn't swap pardners wid nobody*—you heah, Juke? Dis-here's Christmus, an' I'm talkin' ter yer."

Duke looked so serious that a feather's weight would have tipped the balance and made him cry ; but he only blinked.

"An' it's gittin' latè, now, pardner," the old man continued, "an' you better be gwine—less'n you feerd? Ef you is, des sesso now, an' we'll meck out wid de col' victuals in de press."

"Who's afeerd, gran'dad ?" Juke's face had broken into a broad grin now, and he was cracking his whip again.

"Don't eat no supper, tell I come," he added, as he started out into the night. But as he turned down the street, he muttered to himself :

"I wouldn't keer, ef all dem sassy boys didn't pleg me—say I ain't got no mammy—ur daddy— ur nothin'. But dey won't say it ter me ag'in, not whiles I got dis whup in my han' ! She sting lak a rattlesnake, she do ! She's a daisy an' a half ! Cher-whack ! You gwine sass me any mo', you grea' big over-my-size coward, you? Take dat !

An' dat ! *An' dat!* Now run ! Whoop ! Heah come de red light !"

So, in fancy avenging his little wrongs, Duke recovered his spirits and proceeded to catch on behind the Prytania car, that was to help him on his way to get his second-hand Christmas dinner.

His benefactress had not forgotten her promise ; and in addition to a heavy pan of scraps, Duke took home, almost staggering beneath its weight, a huge, compact bundle.

Old Mose was snoring vociferously when he reached the cabin. Depositing his parcel, the little fellow lit a candle which he placed beside the sleeper ; then, uncovering the pan, he laid it gently upon his lap. And now, seizing a spoon and tin cup, he banged it with all his might.

"Heah de plantation-bell ! Come git yo' Christmus gif's !"

And when his grandfather sprang up, nearly upsetting the pan in his fright, Duke rolled backward on the floor, screaming with laughter.

" I 'clare, Juke, boy," said Mose, when he found voice, " I wouldn't o' jumped so, but yo' foolishness des fitted inter my dream. I was dreamin' o' ole times, an' des when I come ter de ringin' o' de plantation-bell, I heerd *cher-plang!* An' it nachelly riz me off'n my foots. What's dis heah? Did you git de dinner sho' 'nough ?"

The pan of scraps quite equalled that of the old man's memory, every familiar fragment evoking a reminiscence.

"You is sho' struck quality white folks dis time, Juke," he said, finally, as he pushed back the pan—Duke had long ago finished—"but di-; here tukkey-stuffin'—I don't say 'tain' good, but *hit don't quite come up ter de mark o' ole miss's puckon stuffin'!*"

Duke was nodding in his chair, when finally the old man, turning to go to bed, spied the un-opened parcel, which, in his excitement, Duke had forgotten. Placing it upon the table before him, Mose began to open it. It was a package worth getting—just such a generous Christmas bundle as he had described to Duke this after-noon. Perhaps it was some vague impression of this sort that made his old fingers tremble as he untied the strings, peeping or sniffing into the little parcels of tea and coffee and flour. Sud-denly something happened. Out of a little sack of buckwheat, accidentally upset, rolled a ten-cent piece. The old man threw up his arms, fell forward over the table, and in a moment was sob-bing aloud.

It was some time before he could make Duke comprehend the situation, but finally, pointing to the coin lying before him, he cried: "Look, boy, look! Wharbouts is you got dat bundle? Open yo' mouf, boy! Look at de money in de buck-wheat-bag! Oh, my ole mistuss! Nobody but you is tied up dat bundle! Praise Gord, I say!"

There was no sleep for either Mose or Duke now; and, late as it was, they soon started out, the old man steadying himself on Duke's shoulder, to find their people.

.   .   .   .   .   .

It was hard for little Duke to believe, even after they had hugged all 'round and laughed and cried, that the stylish black gentleman who answered the door-bell, silver tray in hand, was his own father! He had often longed for a regular blue-shirted plantation " daddy," but never, in his most ambitious moments, had he aspired to filial relations with so august a personage as this !

But while Duke was swelling up, rolling his eyes, and wondering, Mose stood in the centre of a crowd of his white people, while a gray-haired old lady, holding his trembling hand in both of hers, was saying, as the tears trickled down her cheeks :

" But why didn't you get some one to write to us for you, Moses ?"

Then Mose, sniffling still, told of his long illness in the hospital, and of his having afterwards met a man from the coast who told the story of the sale of the plantation, but did not know where the family had gone.

" When I fixed up that bundle," the old lady resumed, " I was thinking of you, Moses. Every year we have sent out such little packages to any needy colored people of whom we knew, as a sort of memorial to our lost ones, always half-hoping that they might actually reach some of them. And I thought of you 'specially, Moses," she continued, mischievously, " when I put in all that turkey-stuffing. Do you remember how greedy you always were about pecan-stuffing? It wasn't quite as good as usual this year."

" No'm ; dat what I say," said Mose. " I tol' Juke dat stuffin' warn't quite up ter de mark— ain't I, Juke? Fur gracious sake, look at Juke, settin' on his daddy's shoulder, with a face on 'im ole as a man! Put dat boy down, Pete! Dat's a business-man you foolin' wid !"

Whereupon little Duke—man of affairs, forager, financier—overcome at last with the fulness of the situation, made a really babyish square mouth, and threw himself sobbing upon his father's bosom.

POEMS

ROSE

Oh, my Rose ain't white,
   An' my Rose ain't red,
An' my Rose don't grow
   On de vine on de shed,

But she lives in de cabin
   Whar de roses twines,
An' she rings out 'er clo'es
   In de shade o' de vines.

An' de red leaves fall,
   An' de white rose sheds,
Tell dey kiver all de groun'
   Whar my brown Rose treads.

An' de butterfly comes,
   An' de bumble-bee, too,
An' de hummin'-bird hums
   All de long day thoo.

An' dey sip at de white,
   An' dey tas'e at de red,

An' dey fly in an' out
  O' de vines roun' de shed,

While I comes along
  An' I gethers some buds,
An' I meeks some remarks
  About renchin' or suds.

But de birds an' de bees
  An' de rest of us knows
Dat we all hangin' roun'
  Des ter look at my Rose.

WINNIE

A ROMANCE IN VERSE

When Winnie steps out ter de stable
   You nuver would know—*'less you knowed,*
Dat she had been, sence she was able
Ter reach on tiptoe at the table,
   De biggest humbugger dat growed.

'Caze me, I ben *riz up* wid Winnie—
   I'm talkin' 'bout dat what *I know.*
I'd have ter be wuss 'n a ninny
Ef I could forgit all de shinny
   An' chinies* we played long ago.

When she warn't no bigger 'n a minute
   I follered 'er roun' like a pup ;
We'd sneak ter de creek and wade in it—
She'd tuck up 'er frock, an' I'd pin it,
   An' dat's des de way we growed up.

Why, once-t, when she tromped on a briar,
   'Way down by de gin-wagon track,
I stepped in de bramble right by 'er,
Wid my foots a-stingin' like fire,
   An' toted 'er home on my back.

* Marbles.

Of co'se I was des like 'er brother
  (I'm fetchin' dis up des fur proofs).
We could o' sot down close-t together,
An' pulled out de thorns fur each other,
  Excep'n' nair one had front toofs.

An' so she helt on ter my shoulder,
  An' talked 'er sweet talk in my ear:
Let on dat she liked me ter hold 'er,
An' all sech as dat, tell I told 'er—
  Well, 'tain't no use tellin' it here;

But when we got down ter de open,
  Instid o' me cross-cuttin' short,
I tuck de long road, an' it slopin',
An' limped all de way, des a-hopin'
  She'd 'preshuate me like she ought.

But after me packin' 'er keerful,
  An' settin' 'er down at 'er do',
Instid o' her thankin' me cheerful,
De way she cut up was des fearful.—
  She slid f'om my back to de flo',

An' 'fo' I could gether my senses
  Dat gal, she was dancin' a jig;
She des had been makin' pertences!
An' here I had clumb over fences
  Wid her—*an' she weighed like a pig.*

Of co'se dis was whiles we was chillen,
  But when we growed up it was wuss;

De way she'd pervoke me was *killin'*,
Tell sometimes I'd feel like a villain,
    An', Lord, but I'd in'ardly cuss!

She'd ax me ter tote 'er pail for 'er,
    An' walk by my side, an' she'd laugh,
An' tell me some joy or some sorrer
Dat fretted 'er min'. Den to-morrer
    She'd git me ter hol' off de calf

While Pete, a big boy dat I hated,
    Would come an' stan' close-t by 'er side,
An' stiddy de cow, while I waited
'Way off 'cross de yard, so frustrated
    Dat some days I purty nigh cried.

Dey wasn't no principle in 'er,
    Come down ter sech doin's as dat,
'Caze Pete was a miser'ble sinner,
An' 'cep' I was littler an' thinner,
    Some days I'd o' laid 'im out flat!

Well, sir, dat's de way Winnie acted—
    She fooled me straight thoo all my life;
An' when she had got me *clair 'stracted,*
Tell *I run at Pete,* an' *got whackted,*
    She turned roun', an'—well, she's my wife.

My 'spe'unce wid Peter was bitter,
    But sometimes it pays ter git hit;
18

’Caze Winnie’s a curious critter,
An’ ’cep’ I had resked all ter git ’er,
    I’d be holdin’ off de calf yit.

VOICES

I reckon I is, like you say, sir,
   Pa'lized an' half-'stracted an' blin',
An' maybe de voice dat I hear *is*
   De win' when it comes thoo de pine.

I can't 'spute no white pusson's knowledge,
   I don't know de *hows* nur de *whys*,
An' when I hears heavenly voices
   Dat *seem* like dey come f'om de skies,

I don't fret myse'f wid book-questioms,
   But listens ter ketch eve'y note,
An' when a bird sings me harp-music,
   Don't s'picion de shape of 'is th'oat.

De katydid close-t to my shoulder,
   I knows he des saws wid 'is wings,
But when de Lord sends 'im to cheer me,
   He sets in de vines an' *he sings*.

He sings songs I half disremember,
   An' all o' my mammy's ole hymns
She used to sing while she was washin'
   Right under dese same ole tree limbs.

An' even de brook dat's all dried up,
   Dat used to run down f'om de springs,

De katydid mixes its tricklin'
  Right in wid de songs mammy sings.

An' often she'll stop in a measure,
  An' I'll hear 'er dip down 'er clo'es,
An' wring 'em, an' bat 'em, an' rench 'em—
  All keepin' good time as she goes.

Yas, I knows de katydids' music
  Ain't no mo' 'n shufflin' o' feet,
But dat nuver hindered 'em learnin'
  To sing other folks's song sweet.

Dis ole pine-tree over my cabin,
  Dat's growed thoo a hole in de shed,
I knows it's all blighted and knotted,
  An' half of its needles is dead.

I know whar de thunder-bolt struck it,
  Its heart is split open an' bare,
An' folks say de spiders is tuck it,
  An' swung dey gray webs ever'where.

But when de night win' passes thoo it,
  An' all de plantation's asleep,
It sings me some heavenly prormise
  Dat 'minds me I'm in de Lord's keep.

Dey ain't a dry twig ur a needle
  But sings its purticilar note,

An' even de holler dat's blasted
  Seem like it turns inter a th'oat.

Yas, I knows I's pa'lized an' blinded
  An' half-'stracted, des like you say,
An' co'se I ain't got educatiom
  To 'splain all my comforts away.

So, when a ole bumble-bee fetches
  Some story 'bout when I was young,
Dat I done forgot, 'cep' in snatches,
  I don't make 'im show me 'is tongue.

I don't ax no impident questioms,
  But listens to ketch eve'y note;
An' when a bird plays me harp-music,
  Don't s'picion de shape of 'is th'oat.

THE END

By MARY E. WILKINS

MADELON. A Novel. 16mo, Cloth, Ornamental, $1 25.

PEMBROKE. A Novel. Illustrated. 16mo, Cloth, Ornamental, $1 50.

JANE FIELD. A Novel. Illustrated. 16mo, Cloth, Ornamental, $1 25. '

A NEW ENGLAND NUN, and Other Stories. 16mo, Cloth, Ornamental, $1 25.

A HUMBLE ROMANCE, and Other Stories. 16mo, Cloth, Ornamental, $1 25.

YOUNG LUCRETIA, and Other Stories. Illustrated. Post 8vo. Cloth, Ornamental, $1 52.

GILES COREY, YEOMAN. A Play. Illustrated. 32mo, Cloth, Ornamental, 50 cents.

Mary E. Wilkins writes of New England country life, analyzes New England country character, with the skill and deftness of one who knows it through and through, and yet never forgets that, while realistic, she is first and last an artist.—*Boston Advertiser.*

Miss Wilkins has attained an eminent position among her literary contemporaries as one of the most careful, natural, and effective writers of brief dramatic incident. Few surpass her in expressing the homely pathos of the poor and ignorant, while the humor of her stories is quiet, pervasive, and suggestive.—*Philadelphia Press.*

It takes just such distinguished literary art as Mary E. Wilkins possesses to give an episode of New England its soul, pathos, and poetry.—*N. Y. Times.*

The charm of Miss Wilkins's stories is in her intimate acquaintance and comprehension of humble life, and the sweet human interest she feels and makes her readers partake of, in the simple, common, homely people she draws.— *Springfield Republican.*